BEYOND SILENCE

OTHER LOTUS TITLES

Ajit Bhattacharjea	*Sheikh Mohammad Abdullah: Tragic Hero of Kashmir*
Amarinder Singh	*The Last Sunset: The Rise and Fall of Lahore Durbar*
Aitzaz Ahsan	*The Indus Saga: The Making of Pakistan*
Alam Srinivas & TR Vivek	*IPL: The Inside Story*
Amir Mir	*The True Face of Jehadis: Inside Pakistan's Terror Networks*
Ashok Mitra	*The Starkness of It*
H.L.O. Garrett	*The Trial of Bahadur Shah Zafar*
L.S. Rathore	*The Regal Patriot: The Maharaja Ganga Singh of Bikaner*
M.B. Naqvi	*Pakistan at Knife's Edge*
M.J. Akbar	*India: The Siege Within*
M.J. Akbar	*Kashmir: Behind the Vale*
M.J. Akbar	*The Shade of Swords*
M.J. Akbar	*Blood Brothers: A Family Saga*
Maj. Gen. Ian Cardozo	*Param Vir: Our Heroes in Battle*
Maj. Gen. Ian Cardozo	*The Sinking of INS Khukri: What Happened in 1971*
Madhu Trehan	*Tehelka as Metaphor*
Mushirul Hasan	*India Partitioned. 2 Vols*
Mushirul Hasan	*John Company to the Republic*
Mushirul Hasan	*Knowledge, Power and Politics*
Nayantara Sahgal (ed.)	*Before Freedom: Nehru's Letters to His Sister*
Peter Church	*Added Value: The Life Stories of Indian Business Leaders*
Robert Hutchison	*The Raja of Harsil: The Legend of Frederick 'Pahari' Wilson*
Sharmishta Gooptu and Boria Majumdar (eds)	*Revisiting 1857: Myth, Memory, History*
Shashi Joshi	*The Last Durbar*
Shashi Tharoor & Shaharyar M. Khan	*Shadows Across the Playing Field*
Shrabani Basu	*Spy Princess: The Life of Noor Inayat Khan*
Shyam Bhatia	*Goodbye Shahzadi: A Political Biography*
Sunil Gupta	*Living on the Adge at JhandeWalan Thompson*
Susan Visvanathan	*The Children of Nature: The Life and Legacy of Ramana Maharshi*
V. Srinivasan	*New Age Management Philosophy from Ancient Indian Wisdom*
Zubin Mehta	*The Score of My Life*

FORTHCOMING TITLES

M.J. Akbar	*Have Pen, Will Travel*
Michel De Grece	*The Bourbon Rajah*
S.B. Misra as told to Neelash Misra	*Dreamchasing: The Story of an Ordinary Indian*

BEYOND SILENCE

KUSUM ANSAL

SHOWCASE
Roli Books

Showcase, Roli Books

First published in 2010
Showcase
An imprint of
Roli Books Pvt Ltd
M-75, Greater Kailash II Market
New Delhi 110 048
Phone: ++91 (011) 4068 2000
Fax: ++91 (011) 2921 7185
E-mail: info@rolibooks.com; Website: www.rolibooks.com

Also at
Bangalore, Chennai, Jaipur, Kolkata & Mumbai

Front Cover Photograph: Immigration records originally used in a propagand
the Indian in South Africa (State Information Office)

Cover Design: Divya Saxena

ISBN: 978-81-7436-812-6

Typeset in Adobe Garamond Pro by Roli Books Pvt Ltd
and printed at Rakmo Press, New Delhi.

This is an effort to reach out to the Indians who live in South Africa

I like the dreams of the future better
than the history of the past.

– Thomas Jefferson

PREFACE

At the 'Know the Author' session at the Indian Council Building in Durban, South Africa, where I was the key speaker, I came face to face with some Indians amongst the blacks and whites. All those writers were inquisitive about the current trends in Indian writing and contemporary literature. I asked a salwar-kameez clad lady, who had grilled me with many questions, 'Since when have you been living in South Africa?'

'Four generations of my family have born, bred and died on this soil.' As she swirled towards the window a strange shadow of different hues of light covered her face. Her smile, her words stirred my imagination with irresistible inquisitiveness.

Beyond the blinds of the window, there were corridors that echoed with history, with racial bigotry and oppression, with a world of ties and knots, with light and darkness, fear and hope, friends and foes but something still remained unearthed, something unsaid. I stumbled, as I felt the atmosphere was heavy with some kind of mystery, something I wanted to discover and unravel.

During my stay in South Africa, specially in Durban, I heard and experienced strange and touching incidents about the lives and values of the Indians who lived there. Though Johannesburg was different with its Soweto and Cape Town with Robben Island, in spite of their beautifully manicured European appearance, they breathed a different 'lifestyle', which I felt has conditioned the life and ideas of the inhabitants of that continent.

I remained in an energized trance for many days, which compelled me to go back to South Africa (2007) to discover the truth. The unknown truth of their intended laugh, which whispered volumes of truth that echoes under the invisible sheet of their silence.

Augusr 2010
New Delhi

Kusum Ansal
kusumansal@vsnl.net

ONE

1

It was about 5 o'clock when our flight landed at Johannesburg airport. Clearing immigration and other formalities, we came out pulling our luggage. The oppressive feeling of anxiety and of an unknown fear that had been building up within me, for days or even weeks, now hit me. I felt drained. Jivesh turned and smiled at me. 'So, Anvita, here we are … welcome to my country … or should I say your new home.' He looked at me with loving eyes, trying to comfort me. I held his hand and walked with him, lost in my own silence amidst unknown voices, towards an unexpected door.

Then I saw him – he was not very tall and was dressed rather simply. I could not have guessed that he was Jivesh's father, my father in-law, Mr Pratap Singh. He hugged Jivesh with eager fondness and then turning towards me, touched me lightly on my shoulders.

'God bless you … Anvita,' he murmured in a low voice. 'Welcome to our family.' I could see his moist eyes which made my spirit flicker. 'Yes!' I thought and tried to analyze … have I taken my destiny in my hands by mistake … or was it for a purpose? The path was infinite … and unknown. But darkness by default leads to light. Caught up in a train of thought I stood perplexed. Should I touch his feet in the traditional Indian way or …? The only gesture I could muster up was 'namaste' – folding my hands and bowing slightly before his fatherly affection.

Jivesh sat next to his father in his white car. I pushed myself into the backseat along with a pile of books and important papers that I had carried with me from India. We were now heading towards the city. The roads were empty. It was so unlike India where every inch is taken up by cars, rickshaws, street hawkers, beggars and streams of people hurrying to their destinations. I gathered myself – every particle, molecule and atom in me to adjust to this new world. Yet there was something nostalgic about this city that touched my soul.

Everything had happened so fast in the last two months – Jo Jo Uncle and Bua's unexpected death ... meeting Jivesh – Sanju's friend from South Africa ... my marriage, giving up my job, getting a passport. I did not even have time to think about myself, let alone South Africa. The only memory evoked by the name South Africa was a painful one of reading Aldous Huxley's *Roots* and the abolition of slavery; that cruel but exaggerated realism had made a deep impact on my conscience – I could never forget it.

I looked out from the car window. The sun was setting on the left and the contours of a very modern, clean city were taking shape. It will be my future – my destiny – a turning point in my life. Will it be an adventure or the fulfillment of my dreams? Or will I plunge straight into an abyss of darkness? How will I identify myself with unknown people in an unfamiliar land?

I had picked up a few pamphlets and still clutched them tightly in my hand. They described Johannesburg as 'founded in 1886 when gold was discovered. Johannesburg is only 118 years old and one of the youngest cities in the world. Forty per cent of the world's gold is mined here ... hence the name Egoli, signifying the city of gold in the Isixhosa language – one of the eleven official languages of the country.' It was described as a cosmopolitan city, with high levels of energy and activity. Johannesburg had evolved from a tainted mining settlement into one of South Africa's 'most frequented destinations' visited by businessmen and tourists alike. 'It is the business capital for local and foreign entrepreneurs', the pamphlet said.

I was preoccupied with observing the city as diverse but concurrent thoughts kept circling in my mind. Enveloped in curiosity about my future, my future as an architect, when I looked out I saw a profusion of simple red-tiled roofs with British colonial architecture. I imagined how it would be if I created something different – something very Indian – replete with jharokhas and verandahs. Yes, I had to prove my mettle.

The car stopped. Jivesh opened the door and I got down, a bundle of complex emotions. We were standing near a very beautiful Swami Narayan temple. As I stood confused outside this temple in an alien land, my father-in-law came to my rescue. 'Before you enter your new life, we will seek god's blessings ...!' He held my hand as we climbed the stairs. 'Temple, here?' I wondered about the presence of an Indian god in this part of the world.

'Yes! there are many temples here. We have Ramakrishna Mission, Chinmaya Mission, a Krishna Consciousness temple, even an Arya Samaj along with the masjids and other religious abodes,' Jivesh informed me.

This temple was a pink sandstone structure – typically Rajasthani in style. Two intricately-carved stone elephants greeted us at the entrance. We dutifully took off our shoes outside the temple and crossed a large courtyard to reach the sanctum sanctoram where the Radha-Krishna-Balarama deities stood – beautiful marble statues in all their glory adorned with fine clothes and accessories. Their beatific smiles touched me deeply.

There were three or four women in pale-yellow saris preparing for the evening bhajan sandhya. One of them was making garlands of roses of a very unusual hue. They were all submerged in a spiritual aura that transforms the human soul. Their faces wore a childlike innocence.

Jivesh and my father-in-law performed dandawat pranam – prostrated themselves on the temple floor – as Bua did whenever we visited the Sheetla Mandir. I thought of my mother who spent almost her entire life not only praying but sharing everything with God. Jivesh gave me some money to put in the donation box. A pujari promptly appeared from the back of the heavy wooden door with a prayer bowl.

'Swamiji,' said my father-in-law, 'please bless Anvita ... my daughter-in- law ... She has come from India ...'

'Oh, my child ... you have crossed a thousand paths of shadow and light .... Is it a search for light or for life? There is only one Truth ... Tad Ekam!'

I was taken aback. I raised my eyes. He was a middle-aged man with a serene face and a glorious smile. His eyes were powerfully luminescent – it was difficult to look into them. I could feel his fire-like gaze on my face. I could not believe myself as I said, 'Yes, Swamiji, after a long chaotic journey I have come here in search of happiness – or the goal of my life!'

'May God fulfill your desires …' he applied sandalwood paste on my forehead and gave me 'charanamrita'.

We both were very tired after the long journey from Delhi to Johannesburg. We decided to spend the night at a small hotel, which Pratapji had booked in advance and drive to Durban the next day. After setting down the luggage we had our dinner. It was my first experience of staying in a hotel, just as everything around me was happening for the first time, marriage, passport, visa, air travel, father-in-law and being a daughter-in-law.

After a quick bath when I reached the bed, I found Jivesh eagerly waiting for me. He took me in his arms. His passionate kisses were warm and soothing. When his fingers touched my body, fire went raging deep down my veins, every drop of my blood was ablaze. It was an extraordinary feeling. When he entered me I felt as if my whole being was covered with fragrant blossoms. I felt an unfamiliar awakening of sensuousness. It was an unusual feeling, as if I was walking in a dream world. Our love-making was intense.

Next morning after breakfast, Pratapji and Jivesh went out for some work leaving me alone to rest. I found some time to introspect. I sat near the window overlooking a small garden. The picturesque scene forced me back to my consciousness. I found myself overwhelmed with a variety of emotions like fear, pleasure, despair, anxiety and attachment along with adventure and hope. I wondered if it was turmoil or was I undergoing a tremendous transformation? Why had Jivesh suddenly become the nucleus of my world?

A flashback brought alive those three days Jivesh spent with me in my apartment in Chandigarh. I was in a state of depression at that time. I had lost my near and dear relatives, and then there was the ugly rejection by my cousins which haunted me constantly. Jivesh being a stranger, an outsider, he was the only one who understood my situation and provided much needed solace. In school and college, being an introvert, I had no friends. But with Jivesh I felt my senses coming alive and his presence gave me a sense of direction. His love imparted a certain kind of awareness, not only of my own sensitivity but of other people around me, intimate or otherwise. I felt drawn to nature. I noticed all the trees, even the foliage and the clusters of flowers that adorned the garden. All the hues added colour to my feelings and my black-and-white life had transformed now. At first unaware of my own feelings, I was in a dilemma regarding Jivesh's proposal. But soon I felt the accumulated burden of my sorrow and loneliness disappearing. Gently, almost imperceptibly, his opinions and judgements became a part of my consciousness.

When we stayed with Vati Aunty in Delhi she helped with the marriage. She was the one who guided me through and explained to me that, 'If you have found your soulmate then build a relationship based on the foundation of love, trust, faith and hope.' And then she, like a mother, formalized our wedding, complete with all the rituals and ceremonies and created the base of an everlasting bond between me and Jivesh.

2

The next day when we reached Jivesh's house in Durban, we were received by Leelaji, Jivesh's mother. She was dark with imposing features, her short hair dyed jet black. She had an overpowering personality. She wore a long, faded denim skirt and a full-sleeved blouse with a colourful shawl covering her shoulders.

'Hello dear!' She extended her hand first and clutched mine strongly before hugging me and Jivesh together. 'Welcome to our home!' She handed me a bouquet as I embraced her. I was unable to decide the appropriate form of greeting and without much thought I bent to touch her feet. She withdrew, not used to this kind of a greeting.

I entered my new home without the customary rituals or what we have come to know as tradition in serials on television in India. Well, I was not decked up like the traditional Indian bride. I wore a simple salwar kurta. I was in love. In love, you cannot ask questions, in love there is no space for reasoning. Love has brought me here – miles and miles away from home to an entirely different world.

The living room was ordinary with a few sofas and wooden armchairs with a slightly worn-out upholstery. There stood a small dining table in the same room, with cupboards showcasing glasses and crockery. As we sat, Jivesh brought some juice from the kitchen.

'Come sit down, my dear … you are so pretty. I'm proud of Jivesh's choice. Oh! What white skin you have!' She stared at me constantly. And I noticed an unseemly stress on 'white'.

A dark lady entered carrying a plate of sweets and broke the spell. Pratapji, introduced us, 'Laura has been with us for many years. … Laura, meet Jivesh's wife Anvita.'

Laura was a local black. She had well-defined features and curly hair – her skin was glistening. She was well-built with enormous breasts. She was wearing a spaghetti strapped blouse over a black skirt. She smiled at me, 'Come, come dear … Have some sweets.' She bent forward as she lowered the plate.

Food was served on the table. We all sat facing each other. Everyone including Jivesh prayed before eating. The food was Indian – lentils, mixed vegetables, rice and uneven puris. As we ate, the formal introductions took place about who were in my family and in theirs.

Leelaji was the emotional anchor of the family – soft and compassionate when the family argued, but tough when necessary. After lunch, Jivesh and Pratapji went out and Leelaji retired to her room. Laura brought my luggage into Jivesh's room. She wanted to help me unpack, but I wanted to be alone in order to consolidate my thoughts and ponder on the many unanswered questions that intrigued me. The unfamiliarity of the room made me uneasy. Slowly, I unpacked my large suitcases.

It contained so much – all my memories, my books, my certificates and a bundle of Jo Jo Uncle's letters wrapped in a red velvet cloth … letters which he had written to Vati Aunty and her replies. Among my possessions were gifts for my new family. Vati Aunty had made me buy a beautiful sari for Jivesh's mother and a kurta set for his father. And the boxes of sweets would suffice for the other relatives.

As she entered our room, I gave my mother-in-law her gifts. I showed her my mother's jewellery – an antique necklace of gold, kangans and a pair of gold earrings which I had worn on my wedding, paired with a red sari. She was happy when I showed her everything. She loved the sari I had brought for her. 'Thank you, Anvita – What a nice name you have! We will wear all these at your reception party that we are planning to organize … but after that, you must keep everything in the locker. Anvita, my dear, this country is not safe … you will not be able to wear bright clothes or anything too flashy or any jewellery that can be noticed, all that is to be avoided.'

'Oh … In any case, I'm also not used to wearing all this. Vati Aunty had forced me to wear these and the jewellery belongs to my mother. Like a mother she did my kanyadaan – and gave me all these gifts.'

As we settled down with our mugs of coffee, I knew she wanted to know about me. I was equally curious to know about Jivesh's family. I narrated my past – my mother being killed in communal riots, my loveless childhood, Bua – my only support and Jo Jo Uncle and also about my cousins who hated me. Perhaps, that's why I grew up to be a loner, an introvert, communicating only with my books. I had worked hard to finish my architecture degree through scholarships; and taking tuitions; wrestling with difficulties had become a way of life for me.

She kept listening, absorbed in my narrative. She had tears in her eyes by the time I finished. 'I like your straightforwardness, the courage and the way you have shaped your life, she said overwhelmed.'

'Yes!' I said, 'I wanted to be honest and transparent with you and the family. I cannot shy away from my past, whatever its nature may have been. This is a new life, my rebirth in a new country.'

Tears trickled down my cheeks. She got up from the chair and hugged me. 'Oh! Don't cry please,' she consoled me. I could sense a warm and motherly fragrance as she came closer.

Suddenly, I felt all the feelings of neglect and emptiness were evaporating. I realized I had never given a thought to my emotional self. As a result of my complicated past and emotional poverty I had never understood the difference between love and attachment. I wanted to get rid of my painful past. I desperately wanted the void in me to evaporate, dissolve, disappear and thus start afresh.

My past was dead, buried and gone …

Pratapji, Mom, Jivesh and I stood at the entrance of the hall. All of us wore traditional Indian clothes. I wore my wedding sari and my mother's old jewellery. A riotous mix of colours shone under the bright lights of the hall. The melodious music created a festive backdrop. There were flowers and gifts galore. I felt as if God himself had descended to sanctify my marriage with an abundance of blessings of love and happiness. My marriage was not a fairy tale, it was far from one. It was more of an agreement I made with myself to be able to acquire a new life or for an intimacy where the body and soul is dedicated to your partner. I was sure Jivesh was as lost as I was.

'Hey, you beautiful! You remind me of a temple where a flame flickers all the time.'

'Oh!' I turned to look at him. I saw a tall dark man stood towering over me. Jivesh quickly came to my rescue. 'Anvita, meet my friend Kisna – and Kisna this is my wife Anvita. She is an architect ... and Kisna is a famous writer in South Africa.'

'Oh, nice to know that you are so well qualified. I'm sure in India women are doing better than men, acquiring more respectable and powerful jobs.'

Kisna's eyes gleamed with unspoken grace and sophistication.

The lady entered with a bouquet of flowers. She was wearing an ill-fitting green salwar kameez with golden embroidery. She was tall and had a perfect figure and face but there was something strange about her appearance. She smiled at me, 'In India, people marry to go to America or London. How come you married Jivesh and came to our country – long forgotten for its human suffering?'

'Maybe because for love, Jivesh as a person mattered more than anything. Or it may be that we are all seeking the meaning of life and existence regardless of the country.' Until now, Jivesh's body language revealed enormous confidence in me. I was slowly overcoming the risk of rejection and embarrassment I'd suffered in the past. There was a new-found confidence in me. I could be myself and yet be at ease.

'There are billions of men on this planet, yet you chose Jivesh?' This was Julia, another friend.

'It's a matter of the heart,' Jivesh came very close to me and hugged me. 'Love, my dear love. It was love at first sight – love is not like arithmetic – it just happens and as in our case before we could calculate its pro and cons, we were married.'

'Sometimes, it takes decades to come to the right decision, doesn't it, Jivesh?' Julia appeared to be hurt – her face flushed with disappointment.

'How did it happen, Jivesh, where did you meet this beautiful goddess of love?' one of Jivesh's friends asked.

'Was it here or in India?' another one wanted to know.

'Oh, it happened in Agra, on a trip to see the Taj Mahal.'

'Hey, tell us more about it. When did you go there?' said Bano.

'When I was studying in America, I shared a room with Sanju, a friend from India, who had to go back home when his father died. He decided to return to India after receiving the sad news of his father's death. I had already planned to visit India with Sanju, before coming to Durban. So he invited me to be his guest. I met Anvita at his house. She is Sanju's cousin.

'How long was the courtship?'

'There was hardly a courtship because of the death. The family was busy with the rituals of his father's death, and it was in those unusual circumstances, I noticed how very human and sensible a person could be. Anvita was the pillar of strength for everyone.'

'Oh really? You never told me this, Jivesh,' I said, a little surprised.

'Yeah, Anvita, that is why I followed you to Chandigarh. I wanted to know you more because I was very impressed with the way you conducted yourself in that situation and the way you handled the family with poise and courage through the period of their mourning.'

'But we want to know about the romance.'

'Have patience. I am coming to it, Bano, I am sure we both felt some mystical attraction towards each other, during our stay in Delhi with Anvita's aunt. She suggested we visit Agra. When we reached the Taj Mahal, we were awestruck with the beauty and splendour of that magnificent monument of love.'

'Oh *kuch kuch hua na* – something happened, isn't it?'

'Yes, kuch hua, something did, we felt a strong infatuation towards one another. The monsoon and backdrop intensified the feelings that were brewing.' Jivesh held my fingers tightly.

'And when he proposed to me in that magical ambience, I was in a trance. I wondered whether it was real, or a dream led by the symbol of love, the Taj Mahal. The feeling was inexplicable, it was beautiful, I realized I was in love. Yes, it happened to me, finally … for the first time I experienced what I had only heard of or watched in movies.'

'But she is so simple Kisna, not at all romantic. When I said, "Will you marry me Anvita, I think I love you," she started crying. I wanted the scene to look dramatic and to propose to her by going down on one knee, but she cried and cried.'

'Oh, why did you cry so much, that too at such a beautiful moment of your life?' Bano was perplexed.

'I could not help it, as this simple four-letter word "love" never existed in my life. But the intoxicating feeling of the three words, "I love you" was enough for me to skip a heartbeat.'

‘Why Anvita?’ This time Jivesh’s mother came closer to me and took my hands and pressed them between her moist palms. ‘Why dear?’ She seemed curious to know.

‘Because I lost my mother at very young age and in the vacuum of my heart, where a shadow of neglect overpowered my being, a small little flame of hope to love and to be loved flickered.’

Right at that moment I heard the chirping of the birds outside the window. But Jivesh’s mother wanted to convey her feelings too.

‘Anvita my dear,’ she clasped my fingers in both her palms, ‘I am sure there were family vibrations in the moist air of Agra, which inspired Jivesh to propose to you, as it is the city of my forefathers. But a few years back when I visited India, I tried to look for my relatives. As I had no address, I scanned every human face but could not relate to anyone. It was a sinking feeling of rootlessness, which even today leaves me numb.’ The pressure of her hands on my palms tightened and then relaxed.

Jivesh came to my rescue and hugged me very passionately in front of everybody, kissing me on my forehead as tears rolled down my cheeks, saying, ‘There is nobody like you in this whole world.’ I was touched by his gesture, ‘Cheer up darling and don’t cling to the past, learn to live every moment of your life, especially today. It is a very special day of our married life.’

He pulled me away from his friends and took me towards the table where our wedding cake was placed. I could hear someone saying, ‘Women marry for economic stability in India. As we heard, she is an orphan, her parents were killed in some communal riots … in Punjab.’

‘Else, he was on the verge of marrying that white girl Julia.’

I tried to maintain my balance – my nerves were getting entangled as though in a spidery web. Jivesh took me into his arms and said, ‘Come Anvita, enjoy this joyful moment of our lives … don’t worry about the people. Come. Mom is calling us, let’s cut the cake.’

We cut the cake amidst the ceremonial music … It helped me to remain calm and in good spirits. I was vibrant with vitality and joy. There was an unusual melody in my heart which I was unaware of earlier.

3

Here in Durban the geographical journey was as symbolic and meaningful for me as the internal journey of my married life. I was to remember my new address, 'Hertfield Road, Kwazulu, Natal,' which was not only difficult but sounded so surreal. Jivesh proudly told me it was a 'white area' and they had acquired it only after the 'Anglo-Boer or the Zulu-wars' were over. It was all beyond me, but still I was trying to cope up and adjust in my new life. I did not ask many questions, but I was curious to know the name of the fabulous tree with an extraordinarily huge trunk which stood at the entrance of our house covering it with lush green foliage and shade. But Jivesh was not aware of it. He knew the name of the orange flowers which grew in a thick cluster in one corner of the garden, reflecting the golden rays under the setting sun. They were popularly called the 'Bird of Paradise', which to me sounded very romantic. I enjoyed sitting on the rusted, antique iron bench which stood near the bed of flowers, whenever I felt confused or missed Bua's house in India.

There were two large bedrooms, a drawing and dining area and the kitchen on the ground floor. Our bedroom was on the first floor, with lovely bay windows and an open terrace. The house was symbolic of typical British architecture, very different from our old 'haveli' in Punjab. I was still trying to get accustomed to the middle-class norms of Jivesh's family, and was meticulously working towards making the necessary adjustments in order to become an inseparable part of it.

One day I noticed Pratapji walking through a staircase near the guest bedroom which led to the basement. When he noticed me watching him with curiosity, he asked me to follow him. On entering, I saw before me a small room laden with shelves on its walls, stacked with old books and an old study table with a broken chair. There were a few more items of furniture which were covered with plastic sheets. 'Come Anvita,' Pratapji called me, 'this is a room of memories as I call it. When I was working I used it as my private office. Let me tell you, Anvita, sitting on this chair I faced constant disappointment, constant hope, and persistent desire to be more and more successful.'

Before getting enchanted by all his memories, which I was eager to know about, I said, 'If you don't mind can I open the ventilators and clean the room because it is a bit suffocating in here.'

'Yes, Anvita please do that … It's been months since I entered this room.' When I started the cleaning process he also lent me a hand. He uncovered the furniture. When he unveiled the rocking wooden horse, he got excited, 'See Anvita we bought this for Jivesh when he was almost a year old, from a gora sahib's shop. Leela loved it when she saw it, so did Jivesh. He enjoyed rocking on it and sometimes he would fall asleep while doing so.'

At that moment, Leelaji entered the room walking on her wobbly feet, 'Yes Anvita, this was Jivesh's favourite amongst the toys he played with and now I have a dream to see my grandchildren rocking it. She looked at me with meaningful eyes, 'Listen Anvita, I want at least three, if not four grandchildren playing around me.'

'Oh, it's too early to think of children, let me first settle down with Jivesh. At the moment to find a job is my topmost priority. I have to establish myself as an architect, for which I am qualified.'

'Oh yes, we do understand Anvita, it is really important for everyone to work and to reach a goal. I was also a teacher all my life in a British School till I retired, otherwise it would have been difficult to send Jivesh to America for higher education,' she clarified.

'Don't worry. Take your time Anvita, but start moving in the right direction with patience and grace.'

'Yes, I will.'

In the meantime, Pratapji got hold of a box full of photographs and old envelopes. He kept them on the study table, and said, 'This is a reservoir of all the memories of our past, with the snapshots of our failures and achievements. When we purchased this house and started our life with Jivesh, I bought myself this cloth-covered notebook.' He held one notebook in his hand. 'Then I decided to spend ten minutes everyday to record all the happenings. As we tend to forget the good and remember the bad, I thought, I would write everything down, including historical and political events. This I did, now whenever I read it, it lifts my spirits and helps me re-establish my self-esteem.'

When I opened his diary I found that on the first page he had written in bold letters: 'A book of my life', from the second page the story began 'Oh a historic day, 16 November 1860, my ancestors set foot on the alien soil of South Africa. The name of the ship was *Truro* which carried almost 140,000 Indians like caged animals to this continent. Majority of them were Hindus, from Madras, Orissa and Bengal, but our family came from Benaras. All those Indians were called "coolies"; devoid of an identity, they were given numbers for identification. These coolies were made to work not only on sugar-cane plantations but in the railways, dockyards, municipal services or in the coal mines situated in northern Natal and Transval.'

'See this,' Pratapji was holding a very old faded photograph of a ship, 'this is the ship *Truro*, which brought my ancestors to this soil.'

'Oh, its huge!' I could not figure out its shape or dimensions, as I had never seen a ship before. There were many more photographs. Many family portraits were hung on the pale walls of the room. Pratapji took me closer to them explaining who they were. But I could notice the dramatic change in their living standards through all the black and white portraits of men and women. Earlier photographs showed women wearing plain saris carelessly tied in an old style and men wearing badly stitched kurtas and dhotis but, with time, prosperity was reflected in their silk saris with borders tied in a modern style along with jewellery to adorn their beauty. The men wore well-stitched three piece suits with ties and exemplified self-confidence. The sartorial changes faithfully told the tale of their saga through change – from coolies to respected citizens in their respective fields.

Pratapji insisted that I should go through a booklet called *The Settlers*. It was a special millennium edition of the Indian Annual and carried the stories of a few Indian families who were successful in South Africa between 1960 and 2000. The booklet was put together by the grandchildren and dedicated to their 'indentured grandparents'. He opened the page that detailed the travails of his own Singh family. He wanted to acquaint me with how his ancestors had suffered and how they had later sailed out of their ocean of pain and disorientation. How their ruptured souls by dint of their inner courage and determination to prove themselves had led them through the difficulties. 'Read from here, Anvita as I feel you should know about the paradoxical existence of our ancestors.'

The details were indeed heart-rending. For an emigrant, it was a traumatic snap from home and family. When an Indian left his village, they sighed, 'Oh! We will never see him again!' And more often than not, the prophecies turned out to be true. Later statistics from Natal reveal that they did send money back to relatives in India. A few emigrants even corresponded. But that was all.

'The emigrants were provided with soap and encouraged to bathe regularly. When they arrived at the depots or at the ports for embarking, they had already walked for 20-30 days and were in such a poor physical condition that they could hardly stand up. To their amazement, there were hundreds, perhaps thousands, of other prospective emigrants waiting to be shipped. Once they entered the barracks, many developed cold feet and disappeared. Some depots were surrounded with walls to prevent such an eventuality. Conditions in the depot were far from ideal. Use of contaminated water from pools or tanks often led to outbreaks of diseases like cholera and depots were aptly described as places of sickness and death.

'Before stepping onto the ship, each prospective immigrant received a pass and a 'tin ticket' – an identification disc hung around the neck or strapped to the arm. Over decades, bigger and better ships began to be used for transporting them. If it was 800-tonne ships in the 1850s, 3000 tonner-steamers took over to transport the emigrants soon enough.'

Unfortunately, the emigrants had to discover the horror of crossing the 'big black water', or the dreaded Kala Pani, themselves. Most did not have any idea about how long the journey would last or where it would take them ...

4

'Whose photograph is this?' It looks like a tea estate. I can see some women clad in saris, with baskets on their backs plucking tea leaves?' I looked enquiringly at Leelaji. 'You know Anvita there are three kinds of emotions that govern our lives – fear, pleasure and suffering … this is a picture of suffering.'

'What do you mean? The surroundings appear beautiful, however, all of them are expressionless.'

'All of them are labourers. Our ancestors' lives and that of these labourers is a long tale of suffering. All of them worked from sunrise to sunset. When they returned to their humble dwellings in the tea estates or sugar-cane fields, they were exhausted. They prepared their meals from their daily ration of rice and mealie. It was not enough to last till lunch or till the following day. After supper, they fell into a deep sleep only to be woken up by the ringing of the bells and the shouting of the sirdars. Toilets and other facilities hardly existed. They also had to work in rough fields where they had to prepare the grounds, dig pits in even rows and drop equal portions of manure with little tin cans that were dirty, and momentarily blinded them with the reflected sun. They planted in these pits the seed canes that the women had cut up into equal parts of eighteen inches – carefully preserving the "eyes" of the seed cane.

'When the canes matured and stood high, the harvesting began. They became oblivious to everything except the cane. They had to bundle the cane and carry it on their shoulders. The cane never seemed to lose its fragility despite all the work the labourers did on it. When the mill appeared at a distance, they offloaded it on the ox or the mule-drawn carts. The sirdar stood over them to urge them to go faster as the cane would rot otherwise.'

Jivesh also came into the room and joined in our conversation. 'You cannot wipe off the miseries, confusion, hunger and pain from these photographs. Pratapji's diary was a testimony to the acute suffering of our ancestors.'

'All the members of the Indian community you meet here have lived long with it – centuries after centuries of oppression – living in fear, escaping from it, rationalizing it, trying to forget it or completely identifying with something which is not fearful. Even our family has tried all these methods.'

'How about complaints ... the workers did have a right to raise their voices against the system!'

'You know what? All the field workers knew they had to work with the sirdars. The sirdars knew some English men and thereby became an indispensable channel of communication between the masters and the servants. They were also a part of the system abounding in selfishness and self interest – they shielded the masters from the workers' hostility and protected them. To remain in their positions, they had to be their master's men – suppressing every sign of the revolt and setting them right with a lash or two of their whip or docking of the pay. In their terrible frustration and despair, the labourers – at times – hopelessly clutched on to the myth that their white masters were somehow also their distant benefactors.'

'I'm sorry to go into such a dark subject, Jivesh.' This time, I hugged him and Leelaji – who was still lost in the misery of her ancestors. I listened to her as she recovered herself.

'If the sahib was good, Anvita, the hours of work would be according to rules and regulations. There would even be time to cultivate a little patch of land around their hut and plant some vegetables – mostly gourd and lentil they had brought from India, which they introduced to their colony. Dry fish was a luxury for them and they used their half a pound of weekly ration sparingly to flavour the vegetables. When they were served onions and tomato, they braised it in quarter pound of butter or oil they received as a weekly ration and made it into a chutney. This was their feast. At times, they kneaded the mealie into dough and rolled it into flat rounds and baked these rotis on an iron pan on a fire pit dug into the floors of their huts. But opportunities for even such frugal fare were also very rare.

'The standard practice was to make them work from dawn to dusk, Sundays obviously included. The plantation owners were sanguine after providing the rations and securing their labour. Nothing else mattered to them. Their main concern was to economize on the labour. They saved on rations by reducing them to half on the slightest pretext. They had other tricks up their sleeves like replacing a portion of the stipulated rice with a mealie meal and justifying it by saying that it was better for them. They also refused rations to non-working women and children, though they were entitled to these by law. Ultimately, they saw the workers as crucial but vexatious in this deal. They were chagrined at giving unnecessary concessions at their own expense. They refused the workers permission to leave the estates, grudged them their wages and devised ingenious means to deprive them with a "justice" dispensed through fines.'

'How about a revolt, a revolt against the brutal system? Everyone has a right to live ... live the way one wants to!'

'What revolt? It was a struggle for survival – all that they hoped was to keep their body and soul together in those terrible times!'

'What happened during illness or childbirths? Were there crèches or at least some place to keep small children? Or even a school?'

'There was no place to leave the children. Mothers used to tie them to a peg in the hut for their safety and leave them with whatever food they could manage. You can imagine the babies' plight. The newborns mostly died of hunger and neglect. Those workers who became very sick or lost their limbs were sent back to India as cripples – many hanged themselves to escape annoying their sirdars who bullied them to work while they were sick and used to beat them up.

'I want to relate one more incident which I'm sure you won't find in any book of history. One morning, at about 6.30 a.m., some labourers complained about there being less salt in their breakfast – a meal of sour mealie porridge served with dried vinegar chillies. A white farmer overheard it. He not only abused the labourers but urinated in their bowls and terrorized them to drink it. That evening, five Indian laborers hanged themselves ... humiliation is an emotion that can make you choose death ...'

'Oh! Please! Mom ... stop it now!' Jivesh, who had entered the room unnoticed, pulled out Leelaji from her reverie. 'We cannot hear any more ...'

'Can we ever be free from the memories of suffering, Jivesh?'

'No. We can't ... even after so many years, we feel it is lying somewhere deep in our consciousness ...'

'Look Jivesh ... have you read this? You talk of farmers hanging themselves because of the torture by their white masters and sirdars. But, this is the Indian newspaper, the *Times of India* with this headline: "Farmer suicides in prosperous Western UP". It goes on to say, 'Kedar Singh, a Jatav, was a victim of debt and crop failure.'

'And see, he too was from Agra.'

Leelaji came closer as soon as she heard Agra and took the crumpled newspaper from my hand. 'How did you get it here, Anvita?'

'My dry-cleaned clothes were wrapped in this.'

Jivesh read aloud the news item. 'Bhilavati. Agra. Kedar Singh was not a marginal cotton cultivator in the fields of Vidarbha. But like many of them, he was debt ridden. Threatened by the moneylender, distressed by his crop failure and swindled by the man to whom he had sold off his land, the Dalit farmer living in western Uttar Pradesh ended his life last week. "He ate just one roti and went off to sleep on the neighbour's terrace," said his wife, Rajan Devi. They found him hanging from the hook the next morning. The ration card said that he was 40 years old though his relatives insist he was just 26. And looking at Kedar's photograph on the ration card, it's impossible to believe them.

'According to official statistics, 8,263 farmers have committed suicide in seven states – Maharashtra, Karnataka, Kerala, Andhra Pradesh, Tamil Nadu, Punjab and Gujarat. Bountiful western UPites appeared to have bucked the trend. The newspaper also said that his house was located about 25 kilometres from the Taj Mahal city. One gathers that both the grinding poverty as well as the oppressive social structures combined to kill the Jatav farmer.'

'You talk of sufferings and neurotic things happening in South Africa. But is it really any different from India? Even today we come across such incidents. Why does the reality never change anywhere?'

'Unless we bring order in the whole world, the reality will not change. We live in a chaotic world and it is disorderly at all levels – social, moral and even ethical.'

'But Jivesh, we can all observe this disorder in which we live – the conflict, contradictions, paradoxes, pain, suffering, fear, pleasure – everything. The whole structure of disorder is mind-boggling. Who will change the system – the disorder?'

'God will ...,' Leelaji folded her hands and pointed them towards heaven.

'Come Anvita ...get dressed! We will go for a dance recital,' said Jivesh.

'Yes. I think we need to get away from our depressing past.'

Back in our room, Jivesh said, 'I'm sorry Anvita. I hope we have not shaken the dreams that you had about your future?'

'No. Instead I want you to steer away from this lake of tears and fire of hell that you and your family have gone through. But Jivesh, don't you think every country has a bloody past? Even my mother died in the communal riots of Punjab. Exploiters are everywhere – in different colours, shapes and creeds. But dreams do not die, they give us not only the strength but also the purpose to live. They will help us travel from darkness to light.'

Jivesh kissed me hard on my lips, my eyes, my arms ... how different it felt ... like a flame of passion or an elixir of life. At that moment, we both needed it.

In return, I could only offer him some comforting words – my only possessions. Or indeed my being – my honest commitment towards his wishes and his body.

We reached the theatre where many posters adorned the wall near the entrance. We entered a dimly-lit hall that was fairly large. A few people were already seated and whispering among themselves. We sat on our numbered seats – strangely quiet in our stillness, feeling the flow of those hushed noises under our skins. A tall dark figure with typical South Indian features and covered with glittering jewellery, she began her performance after joining her palms while Sanskrit shlokas were being chanted in the background. Her first act was 'Krishna-Leela'. As a gopi, she moved gracefully to plead with the mischievous Lord Krishna to return her clothes she had left on the banks of the river Yamuna while she had gone in to bathe.

Krishna sat nonchalantly on the branch of the imaginary Kadamba tree, playing his flute. The flute's music in the background was shrill and sharp but she made up for it with her subtle movements. With immense grace, she twisted her thumb backwards to say 'No' and the unusual flexibility of her pose through the changing highlights of the scene was engrossing. The 'padas' of Geet Govinda were melodious. She expressed her key points delicately, which were that one should ignite the flame of intuition and that God is an embodiment of human love.

As we came out of the theatre, we saw Kisna walking out with a very pretty girl. She was neither black nor white.

'Hello! Jivesh,' said Kisna walking towards us.

'Hi Kisna. Meet Anvita.'

'Yes! I know your lovely wife. Meet Pereeie, my student. I'm assisting her in her research.'

'Aangename kennis! Pleased to meet you!' Jivesh greeted her in Zulu.

'Oh! I can speak English … and Hindi bhi … thora, thora – a little bit.' She smiled and shook hands with us. I liked her soft features and style. She conducted herself very gracefully.

'How did you like the performance?'

'An accomplished coolie,' Kisna smiled, 'trying to evoke Indian mythology in utter confusion.'

'She wasn't bad.' I found the use of the word 'coolie' very jarring.

'Yeah. I agree. That is why so many of us are here to promote her instead of watching Shakespeare or Beethoven. But I do understand that this kind of show provides us with an awareness of our culture which we have left behind in India.'

'Yes. What we owe to Hinduism is the original landscape of our religious imagination – it gives us the river Yamuna, the Kadamba tree, the holy mountain of … I don't remember the name.'

'Govardhan. A hillock in Brindavan that Lord Krishna lifted on his little finger when it rained heavily for seven days. He wanted to give refuge to his people.'

'Good. Anvita, do come with Jivesh to one of our get togethers whenever you can. Maybe we can learn more about Hinduism from you!'

'Yes … Thank you.' We sat in the car.

'Let's go for dinner!'

'We can't! Anyway, that was Victoria Street where the theatre is located and now we are on Grey Street. Earlier, the Indians were not even allowed on these streets, let alone in the restaurants. Those were always marked 'White Hotel'. Indians could only use places like the Kathiawar Club in their own area. You know what Albert John Luthuli – our Noble Peace Prize winner once said?'

'What?'

'"The Road to Freedom is via the cross." Anyway, we will reach home after 8 o'clock, it is not safe to be out at this time.'

'But Jivesh ...'

'Life is real, life is earnest, And the grave is not its goal.'

'Did Luthuli say this too?'

5

I read her nameplate just next to our main gate – 'Phelela Casu, Interior Decorator'. Being an architect, it seemed like a good idea to meet and talk to her. I was looking for a chance to talk to her when I saw her going out somewhere. But I had to wait for over a month before I finally met her.

That evening, while I stood near the Bird of Paradise grove in our garden, I saw her walking in.

'Hello!'

'Oh! Hello …' She stopped. 'New tenant?'

'No … I'm married to Jivesh …'

'Oh … the young professor?'

'Yes. Can I meet you sometime?' I asked shyly.

'Why not? But I'll call you when I'm free.' There was no overt expression of friendship on her face. Her dark features were broad and she was quite fat. I could not guess her age.

Phelela Casu's office was located in an old building that had previously been occupied by British families, mostly from the admiralty. The building had the charm of that era. It was an original heritage-designated building, built in 1905. Phelela had maintained the old colonial stained-glass arches above the windows but had added some ornamental jaalis which looked very Islamic. But the interiors were very contemporary, with a matching false ceiling. The flourishing potted plants near the staircase were welcoming. For me, visiting such a posh office was an experience in itself. I was impressed. I don't know how much credit she gave to my qualifications but somehow I liked it when she said, 'I hear people saying that in the new South Africa money is the power. But no Anvita, knowledge is and has always been the power. I'm sure you will succeed. You are very qualified.'

I came to know that a series on the 'Great South Africans' was filmed by the local TV channel in her office. Her eyes flashed with sudden tension as she said, 'In South Africa, economy is a problem, and that is because not enough people aspire to be entrepreneurs. Too many people want everything to be given to them. They are afraid of trying ... afraid of failure. But you cannot learn without failing ... so don't worry about the ups and downs, they are a part of one's life.'

This woman had a lot of confidence. It seemed she had never failed in life. It's true that the country now opens more doors to the blacks, than it closes. But it takes drive and determination to walk through these doors. As she herself defined, 'Being an entrepreneur is a gift like music. It's something you are born with. Pre and post-transformation comes to you automatically once you enter the door to plunge into your profession.'

'We in India believe in willpower,' I told her. 'Our biological being consists of two parts – one works according to our desires and the other works independently. When one increases willpower, the other also becomes part of it. I also have faith in my willpower.'

'I wish you all the best. Don't hesitate to come and meet me, whenever you need!'

'Thank you.'

I came out empty handed. She did not give me the addresses of architectural firms. Nor did she pass on any of the contacts I was looking for.

When I related this meeting to Leelaji, she said, 'Oh, Anvita! In this country, nobody helps anyone. Besides, she is very proud of herself and her fame. I believe one of her aunts or some relatives told her that she'd be naming her child after her, Phelela. She responded by renting the use of her name to her friends and relatives for a monthly fee!'

'Really?!' I was shocked.

Laura heard our conversation and added, 'Her mother was a nurse and they sold stolen hospital linen and clothes for extra money.

Maybe it was for her daughter's education. Phelela used to go from door-to-door selling things. This gave her an opportunity to look into big houses. It added to her critical skills and her ability to relate to different kinds of people.'

I marvelled at her ability. She appeared a strong and intelligent woman to me. I was impressed with the way she had dealt with a real challenge of architectural design for her office: to make a connection between what was already there and what was yet to be achieved. I feel that in today's world, the challenge lies in achieving.

It was a strange world I was entering. Everything was in extremes – racism laid its heavy burden on the past while the future was unknown.

6

Soon we reached the hotel. The seashore had come alive, bathed in the orange hues of the setting sun. Unlike the Marine Drive in Bombay, where hundreds of people walk on the narrow lane near the Gateway of India, there were very few people on the beach.

I'm sure fresh air dissolves human tiredness and infuses it with an energy and a sense of happiness. A happiness that helps us to walk wakefully in a dream world. Living in the bland reality of the 'real' world only brings on fatigue and fills you with illusions and ennui. Life after all, is the same everywhere – in any continent or even in any universe.

Shabbir Banoo Bhai's book *If I Could Write* was being released and the launch was organized near the pool. People sitting on the chairs appeared very mature and intellectual. There were clearly more Muslims – the women with their heads covered and the men with flowing beards. They were all immersed in a strange silence. I could see Fatima Meer sitting in her wheelchair in the front row with her nurse. Her presence gave the gathering an air of sophistication.

I picked up the book. It was small with a black cover and looked more like a prayer book than a literary work. The blurb on the cover read, 'Ramadan Letters that can be read on Christmas or any other day'. On the dais, the organizers were describing the writer. One of them began her speech with the Gayatri Mantra – surprising for a book written by a Muslim writer. And then, there was the chanting of a powerful Hindu Vedic mantra by another speaker. Is it that when the doors of the outside were closed in the past, the coolies left their doors open – allowing free passage of ideas to and from each other? Suffering has its own language.

The book discussion was on Sufism. From what I remember, Sufism is a synthesis of Islam and Vedanta. In Sufism, there is no duality between Atma and Paramatma – they see and experience the world as one. For the Sufis, it was one desire, one existence without dichotomy between the human and God – a beautiful synthesis of the two ways of life – Islam and Vedanta. They both want to know and pray to one and only One.

While people talked amongst themselves, I opened a chapter of the book, 'Knowing Pain'. It said, 'A self in pain … is in need of pain.' But we can also take it to mean: a self is in need of love. If we are loved, our psychological pain will nearly always diminish. Why does this happen? I think that a person in pain lacks some knowledge that can help him or her overcome some problem and this lacking gives rise to the pain. Love heals the pain because love is the highest form of healing – someone who is loved knows love and is healed by this essential inner knowledge.'

I could relate easily to one of the new, upcoming writers who got up from the crowd of listeners to speak. He spoke about the Sufism depicted in Banoo Bhai's book. I almost shivered when he spoke. He was young and very articulate. ' ….in a mystical world, but as often it is rooted in the social and political struggles of the world' he was saying. On *If I Could Write* he declared, 'The publication brings to a conclusion an important phase in my life … Whatever happens from now on is an open-ended challenge I intend to treasure. What better way to begin a new life going forward than to be aware that one has persevered in something as important as publishing one's most precious thoughts.'

I could feel that Shabbir Banoo Bhai's main themes were simplicity, humility and selflessness that lead the way to tolerance, compassion, mercy, love and affection for humanity. I sensed that it inspired us to liquidate the ego as a method to attain God. One of the speakers said. 'The sign of a genuine Sufi is that he becomes poor after being rich, he becomes humble after being mighty and he is unknown after being famous … the Sufi must realize the reality of the letter Sufi, "suad" is for purity, "waw" is faithfulness, "fe" is annihilation and "ya" is certainty. The "fakir" must realize the reality of the letter fakir – "fa" is annihilation, "qaf" is nearness, "ye" is certainty and "re" is mercy and affection.'

Kisna asked me why I was there – as an architect attending a Sufi book launch. I was there, I reasoned, as I was in love – in love with a man who belongs to this country … this country that was a complete mystery before I arrived here. Now I want to know everything – including its cruelty and its kindness. Everything lives here for me only because I'm in love with Jivesh and love unites everything – love and pain – as love is God.

7

Pereeie was missing for more than three months. Kisna and I went to search for her.

'Do you know where she was all this while? How did she disappear? As far as I know, she was supposed to finish her research this year,' I asked Kisna.

'Yeah ... I was also worried. I called her on her parent's phone several times but there was no response. Then I came to know of the horrible news,' Kisna told me

'What?'

'Anvita ... she was raped in a train, in front of all the passengers. Then her parents abandoned her!'

'What! Oh! What a shame! She is such a pretty girl. She doesn't even appear like an African to me. I'm sure she is a descendant of white ancestors. Don't you think so, Kisna?'

'She has an Indian father and a Dutch mother – that is why she is Pereeie, an anglicized version of "Pari". Here, in South Africa, every Indian name is Anglicized because of the British rule. And she was researching on Hinduism because of her father.'

'What a horrible thing to happen!'

'It is very common in this country. These incidents happen every day. Haven't you read today's newspaper? The paper says that a teenage girl was tied up, raped and beaten to death before her naked body was dumped next to the Highway No. R554. And if she isn't identified within the next five days, police say the chances of finding her killer and being brought to justice are 'less than zero'. She will become just a statistic – one among some 40,000 women and children killed – the vast majority just remain unidentified. All these bodies are buried in Gauntang's pauper's graveyards. As many as five of these unidentified bodies are buried together in one grave everyday in the remote Elandsfontein cemetery located in the south of Johannesburg. That place is uhh … famous for violent crimes.'

'Why does evil never die?'

'Evil is immortal.'

We remained silent for a while.

'It really breaks one's heart to know that your own parents and relatives are not interested in finding out where you are. They are not even interested in identifying your dead body. I never had parents – so I don't know. But I thought parents are always loving and caring!'

'Yeah, I remember police telling me once that whenever someone comes to identify a body, it becomes a cause for celebration. But it really breaks one's hearts that so many people die in horrible circumstances and are buried in mass graves without a relative by their side to shed tears.'

'Last year our neighbour's teenager daughter went missing for a few days. Though the Indians are very careful, still it happened. When the body was finally recovered by the police, the state of the body suggested that she was held captive before being killed. The nails had begun to chip and her hair was matted at the back of her neck. Her hands and feet had been bound with cable wires – her eyes were bruised and swollen shut. It appeared that clumps of hair were pulled out brutally. Also organs like kidneys, were found missing.'

We walked in the wilderness of a strange silence and reached an old building – shabby and unkempt. A small board outside a gate announced. 'Archer Tailoring House'. Kisna checked the address from a piece of paper.

'Yes,' he said. 'Pereeie works here …'

I was perplexed when Kisna rang the doorbell of that house.

A middle-aged black lady allowed us in very reluctantly. It was a dimly-lit room and there were a few girls sitting on the floor. They were sewing shiny brass buttons on the shirts. Pereeie was surprised to see us.

As she saw Kisna, she almost trembled. But she did not say anything. It was as if her lips were also stitched with the thread she was working with. The only thing that glittered in the room were those brass buttons which lay on the floor.

'Have you come to meet Baba?' the lady asked.

'What Baba? We've come here for Pereeie ...' Kisna pointed at her.

The lady said, 'Who Pereeie? All these girls belong to the Yonuba culture. They have come from Orissa, a part of India. See here is our God!'

We entered another small room. The lady drew the curtain from a huge picture with the strange face of a dark man clad in tribal attire. He appeared more of an embodiment of evil than a God. The sight scared me.

'He is our God Olodumare!'

She covered the picture with the silk purdah again and closed the door of the room as we came out.

'Why do you keep it hidden, if you worship and believe in Him?'

'Because we are forced to follow Christianity. We live in this settlement and work for them. That is why we cannot pray openly. Since you have come from India, I allowed you to have a darshan. Would you like to meet the reincarnation of our Baba?'

Pereeie brought us some tea and sat next to Kisna. He held her hand passionately. 'Pereeie ... why have you given up your research? I was so worried about you. I rang up your home many times but your parents refused to speak about you!'

Pereeie cried as she spoke, 'My parents don't want me back after what has happened to me. Baba saved my broken soul. He is kind. He has given me shelter ... let me live here ... I'm very peaceful here.' She cried and her beautiful face glistened with tears. She looked elegant and beautiful even in her dirty, unshapely dress.

'You can come back to your work, Pereeie, whenever you feel like. Call me up or I will come again.' Kisna tried to comfort her but she covered her face with both her hands and shrunk to one corner of the room and leaned against the wall.

The lady took us to the Baba's room. He was sitting on a rocking chair – with one very fat black man sitting next to him. When we folded our hands, he greeted us with a strange sound like 'Okun-o-baba' and shook his head. It was how they greeted each other. The camphor lamp in that room had a flickering flame and the fumes filled the room with shadows, adding to the strangeness.

I was feeling suffocated.

'Baba, do you believe in the God "Olodumare"? Is He real – Hindu or Muslim?' Kisna asked.

'He was Allah's light first and then Oum and then His light. All human beings are part of His creation. Because of His light, the entire Being came into existence! He is part of our heartbeats. He is the One who guides us to understand what is good and what is evil.'

Pereeie said, 'Baba is very kind, Kisna. He supported me when my family disowned me after that horrible incident. Now, I've become a member of "Afugbin African Society". I'm very peaceful.' The stress on the word peaceful agitated us.

The fat man said, 'We are all members of this society. One of our ancestors – Bro Jacob 'Jake' established it for the tormented souls and the slaves … for all those people who have not been accepted by their community.'

'But He is here. He fills our jholi, our laps. It is He who has filled our jholies with everything,' said the Baba.

'Okun-o-baba,' the fat man said. 'Okun-o-baba,' repeated the lady. Pereeie only wiped her tears and propelled us towards the exit.

We came out of the room saying, 'Okun-o-baba' … leaving behind all those listless figures who were still sewing shiny brass buttons on men's shirts with mechanical hands and stitched lips. When there is not enough light or desire or perhaps future … the whole thing faded into a mystic camphor smoke. I don't know why but I felt that the attires of all those women were slowly turning into the outlines of shrouds.

8

When I entered the large reception area on the first floor of that building I was greeted by the smart receptionist. Though her face appeared very familiar, I couldn't place her. Very sophisticated, she was dressed immaculately in a business suit. When she saw me, she immediately got up from the chair and hugged me, saying, 'Hi! Welcome to our office. But you don't seem to remember me?!'

I was still not sure where I'd met her. 'I'm Bano. I know your family very well. Jivesh and my husband Ismail, are good friends. We attended your reception too, now do you remember?'

'Oh! Yes … I remember! How nice to see you here!' I was genuinely happy to find someone known to the family.

'I have been working here for a long time.' She smiled. Her eyes shone and her face seemed radiant which drew me closer to her. She had an oval face with deep-set eyes. Her long eyelashes seemed to provide a thick shade on her cheeks as she fluttered them.

'I'm sure you will like this office. Everybody is friendly and helpful,' she encouraged me. I appreciated the concern before my interview.

When I entered the main office, I was awed by the sophisticated interiors of the office, done in the typical British style. The entire set of furniture was intricately carved and shone in its dark brown polish. All the chairs were upholstered with fresh leather that added to the ambience. Two men sat across the beautiful office table decked up with rich brass accessories. A smart computer lay on top. There were fresh flowers in a tall vase which somewhat relieved the formal atmosphere of the room.

My future lay in the hands of these two men. One of these was the boss, Phillip Warren, the chairman of the company. The other was Mr Subramaniam, the managing director. I was told that Mr Subramaniam was the person in charge of operations. He was a qualified architect and worked in partnership with Mr Warren – who mostly lived in London. They were both very well dressed in. I wore a simple silk sari which I'd thought was befitting but which looked so out of place there. I became self-conscious and concerned about my very ordinary appearance in that stylish and posh office. I sat in the chair with a thumping heart. My hands trembled when I passed my file to the most good-looking men I had ever met in my life. I missed a heartbeat when Mr Phillip Warren opened with the file the remark, 'We still think of India as a place of stations – never as a place of destination. Where people don't live in proper homes or live a civilized life.'

'I'm shocked, sir, with your remark, as India is known worldwide for its architectural wonders like the Taj Mahal, Qutub Minar and thousands of Mughal and Rajasthani palaces and temples. We are proud of not only our brilliant architectural beauties but the rich culture which is based on a value-based, spiritual philosophy.'

'Still … India is many years behind the times.' He spoke with typical British arrogance.

I remembered Jivesh had warned me, 'To be put on a job and requested to get on with it, it is very important Anvita – never to argue with a white boss, even if you have a different point of view.'

'What do you mean by value-based philosophy? How can it help you in an architectural firm?' the other one asked.

'I personally believe in human relationships which is one of the basic principles while dealing with the clients, your ability of being whatever you are, is empowered with a value-based philosophy at a workplace. I feel you cannot achieve high quality in any field till you gain a high degree of trust from others.'

Mr Subramaniam looked me straight in the eye. I was spellbound. Though he had a wheatish complexion, he possessed unusually deep blue eyes that were like a deep ocean, in which anyone could drown easily. I was again mesmerized when he said, 'As you know our country is going through a profound metamorphosis throughout its society, and is passing through a thin pathway to bring the political stability. How do you think an architectural firm can help it?'

'Sir, I feel that we have to win over the confidence of our clients through our sincerity. It can only be done by creating something very different from the old paradigm of white superiority or the darkness of apartheid. What I believe is that one has to establish a psychological approach in the relationship between the company and the client.'

I looked at Mr Warren very apologetically and said, 'I'm sorry Sir, if I've said anything wrong!' Tears welled up in my eyes. I was sure I'd be rejected. But for me, to speak the truth was very important. It had become an habit. The bitterness of my past life had established some principles of constancy within – and truth was the primary among them. Suddenly, Mr Warren's cell-phone rang and he got up from his chair and walked out of the room with his narrow-minded outlook and plain snobbery.

Mr Subramaniam again looked at me and said, 'Your remark was very harsh Miss … but tell me why did you say that?'

'I'm sorry, but I will tell you what happened the other day. I visited one of my husband's relatives who lives in a state-funded housing colony. Firstly, the houses were very small, barely one or two bedrooms with tiny kitchens and toilets. The other disadvantage is that they are very far from the main city and it takes hours to reach the office or other places of employment from there. By the time they reach their destinations, they are too tired or drained out either to cook or work. Have you seen them, Sir? I'm sure if you see them, your company will not opt for repeating such a mistake.'

'Ok, miss …' He looked at my file. 'Yeah, Anvita, we will let you know.' It was a signal to leave. I picked up my file and came out. Bano offered me a cup of coffee as we sat in a small coffee area of the office. She told me that the company dealt with town planners and had built small townships in many suburban areas of Durban and Cape Town. In her conversation, she praised Mr Subramaniam and his way of dealing with employees as well as with white clients. He could express himself with boldness and apparent candour that appeared pleasant though, unusual among the South African Indians.

We walked out together to board a bus to go back. She agreed to come with me as I was not sure of the route. On the way, she narrated many incidents that can happen while travelling in these buses. She told me once she was travelling alone with a few Indian boys. 'The Africans started singing filthy, anti-Indian songs. They were drunk. One of the lighties had a mes (knife) and stekked (stabbed) one of the Indian boys. He asked them not to misbehave. The other one – who was trying to protect me – was seriously injured … Luckily for me, the bus stopped at some place. I threw out my purse at them and ran. Do you think I'll ever forget that incident all my life?

'Last Saturday, did you read about that incident in the newspaper?' Bano had re-entered the trauma of the incident in the bus. 'The newspaper related an incident where a young white couple and their two kids were travelling in their car from Gauteng for a weekend to Kwa Zulu-Natal's north coast. One of the kids needed to pee and the father pulled the car the side of the road. They were attacked there by a gang of black youths who shot dead the white parents. The children were left to fend for themselves in the bitter cold. It was also raining. A passing highway police patrol vehicle stopped and found the children sitting and crying near their parent's bodies. They arrested the suspects from the neighbouring camps. The arresting officers were whites and Indians. Allegations were made that the white policemen wanted to shoot all the suspects dead and then claim they were resisting arrest. But the Indian policemen apparently did not agree to the plan!'

'So is it happening everywhere … everyday?'

I shivered within. That day, I walked all the way towards our home on Hatfield Road. Before entering the house I spent ten minutes sitting on the bench of our garden reflecting upon the day. I went over my job and incidents that Bano had narrated – what Jivesh wanted to keep away from me. I was driven by both logic and instinct to maintain a balance of head and heart. I've crossed so many seas to reach this place. Was it for love? Or was it for my own rootlessness or just the challenge? I could not exactly figure out what it was. Anyway, I decided, one should not be disheartened by what people say. I will use my instincts to handle the situation.

But the palpable sense of insecurity was equally true. One day Pratapji told me, 'We Indians who are born and brought up here in

Durban do not feel the same sense of security as the Africans do. We live in a constant state of fear while waiting for a day when we can trade, walk around freely and live without feeling intimidated as an ethnic minority.'

I noticed our house had an electrified fence and the entrance door had two locks with strange numbers.

9

It was a Sunday, but a different sort of Sunday. I was alone. Jivesh was travelling for one of his training programmes. This Sunday, I was not allowing myself to think of the inevitable frustration built up within me by not getting a job for so many months. I did not want to be reminded of the noticeable tensions in the house that crept up in everyone's behaviour including that of Jivesh. Finally, the dilemma was coming to an end. The day had come. I was to join Mr Warren's office from Monday. When I informed Pratapji and Leelaji, they were very happy and excited. They suggested that we all go for some shopping followed by some spiritual discourse.

I preferred going to 'Bhoolabhai Grocery Store', for daily necessities, as it was a shop with a difference. Baba Bhoolabhai, the old man, always inspired me. I remember Pratapji telling me that the old man had grown from a very humble background to a fairly well-established position. He'd started a shop with a very small investment, selling only basic necessities like soap and toothpaste. Now, the shop was fully equipped with expensive perfumes to 'Ready to Eat' packets. Bhoolabhai spoke very little, but used a lot of Hindi words in his conversation like 'achha', 'meri kismet', 'chup raho'. I developed a bond with him when he greeted me with the word 'bahurani' and called himself a 'fakir'. Pratapji was very friendly with him. They used to sit and chat together while Leelaji or Jivesh picked up the groceries. Bhoolabhai's son, Manish did the running around.

One day, when I'd gone alone to the shop, Bhoolabhai wasn't there to greet me with his usual address of 'bahurani'. Suddenly, Manish asked me, 'Anvita, do you know what a fakir is?'

'Frankly, I don't know much,' I admitted.

'You've come from India, I'm sure you have lots of fakirs there.'

'May be there are, but I've not met any. Perhaps, they are the people who are detached from the world and believe in an abstract god who does not live in a mandir but lives in one's heart.' I was speaking Jo Jo Uncle's words, not mine.

'Oh! That's why?' Manish exclaimed. 'Anvita, these days I see my father crying in a hidden corner of the house many times. He's becoming quieter by the day. He doesn't talk much. When I asked him the reason he answered, 'It's very difficult beta, to live in this country and to maintain a balance between the soul and body.'

'But Manish, it's the unavoidable consequence of everyone's life. Especially for one who is struggling for survival.'

'I don't understand philosophy. But I know that my father cannot forget or forgive the past. Anvita, in the past, the unwritten norm of the work contract of the coolie was that a new bride was forced to sleep with the white sirdar on her wedding night. If they refused, they were brutally harassed and not given any food for days. Baba could never forgive my elder sister because she was born with very fair complexion and golden hair. He never loved her and more misfortunes were added when her daughters inherited her golden hair and blue eyes.'

'We have so many people like that – especially in Punjab – fair complexioned and blue-eyed. That doesn't mean there is something wrong. They lead a perfectly respectable life.'

'Yet, I feel that Baba is becoming quieter in trying to maintain an equilibrium – with one foot in hell and the other in heaven. He is in great pain as he's not a hypocrite. I don't even know if there is anything like perfect freedom.'

'How about your mother? I hope she could help him?' I asked.

'She died early,' he answered briefly.

When we reached 'Bhoolabhai Grocery Store' Baba was quietly sitting on his low chair. After shopping for a few things, Pratapji invited Baba to accompany us for the spiritual discourses. He agreed readily.

When we entered the room for the spiritual discourse, we were greeted by others with hands folded in a 'Namaskar'. I noticed there was no furniture in the room only white mattresses were laid out. Everyone sat in a circle. Our group, including Bhoolabhai also joined in the circle. The reason for this form, I was told was that they believed in energy that moves in circles. There were people from all walks of life, South Indians, Hindus, and some Gujarati Muslims sitting together in the gathering. When the prayers started, all of them recited mantras loudly. While praying, they held each other's hands, right palm on top and left below. Guru Shrikant, with a shaven head, explained, 'The right hand is for giving and the left for taking.'

After the chanting of the mantras, everyone sat in a meditative posture. Guru Shrikant Manikchand explained the theory of Vedanta not as a religion but as a way of life. He explained that according to Vedanta, the entire creation emerges from and ultimately merges into the supreme cosmic force, the 'Brahma'. This supreme cosmic force is also accepted by modern physicists; they consider 'Light' as an aspect of the electromagnetic field which is part of cosmic consciousness in Vedanta.

I found it too difficult to understand but I saw Bhoolabhai engrossed in it. The discourse was followed by bhajans.

I learnt that the group called itself the 'Connect-Ticket'. They clapped together what they called energy. The 47-year–old Kaveri said that by clapping they are only trying to change the perspective – from despondence to something positive. They all clapped and it created a strange echo. I was told that people also mailed their letters to the Guru Shrikant – flooding him with requests for prayer for family members or suffering friends. Many members hadn't personally met but knew each other only through the email ids. All of them chatted and prayed. Some talked of their personal problems, ensconced in the comfort of unburdening to strangers. They talked about 'love'.

'We have a great deal of suffering in what is called love. Love as commonly known is "pleasure" or sexual love or the love for a person, country, idea and so on. When pleasure is denied, hatred, antagonism or violence occurs. Can there be selfless love not just between you and me but with others?'

'Yes. Without love, there is only suffering. Love has to flow in every heart.'

'Does our religion teach us how to love?'

'No, rather every organized religion has wrought terrible suffering ...throughout the world. There has been a great deal of harm – religious wars, endless persecution, burning and torturing of people – especially here in this country. Perhaps it's a gift of the West. In our group we talk of putting up with suffering, not its acceptance, which in any case is the emotional outcome of the social set up of this country. Through 'Connect-Ticket', we learn to come out of the suffering – to gain great compassion which is real bliss.'

A process called CV – creative visualization – followed the prayers. All of us sat erect, legs folded and with eyes closed. We visualized that the afflicted person is already cured after overcoming his or her problem. Sometimes, the person who was being healed had not even approached them and they were doing it by themselves. They even tried to help and pray for people they had read about in the newspapers. They visualized them and sent their positive vibrations to anyone who was suffering. They had done this many times, not only sending their prayers for people whom they had never seen, but also to places they felt were in turmoil.

Another kind of bonding occurred at the end of the three-hour session. They talked to the new members like me – exchanging phone numbers and philosophy over steaming cups of tea and samosas. They all parted from the place with the same words on their lips: 'I will pray for you.'

10

It was one of those very normal afternoons, when we all got together at our favourite restaurant. As we sat, Kevan started, 'Jivesh, don't you think our country is changing? Especially Durban. You don't see as many whites as earlier on the Victoria Street. Even if some of them do, most do not look at us with hatred.'

'Kevan, it was bound to happen one day. Our ancestors suffered so much for this day. I believe humanity prevails in every heart. It is infinite and affects every heart. It also affects human consciousness,' replied Jivesh.

'Jivesh, you always talk like a philosophy lecturer. But this too is true. Standing next to a white, can you forget that you were shunned during political apartheid? Thank God, finally they have withdrawn into a psychic exile.'

'Since when?' I asked.

'After losing in 1994.'

'Where is Kisna?' Kevan asked. 'Whenever I look at him, I sense that he can never forget or forgive his past. His eyes are always red with some kind of rage,' he added.

Ismail said, 'Yes, you're right. He can never forget his past. I remember, once he narrated a horrible incident. Let me relate that to you before he comes. Kisna's family owned a large house on the Queen's Street, where he lived with his parents, grandparents and aunts. One day, when he returned from school with his father, he saw a huge crowd assembled outside their home. The whites had raided the house – only because his family was well off and they were successful and were making a good amount of money through trading. They killed his grandparents .... saaley madar chod ... and Shobha Aunty too. Kameeney robbed all the jewellery and cash. The police did not interfere. They sat quietly and watched. How can one forgive them?'

Ismail had an ugly froth on his lips. Bano wiped it with her sari pallu and said, 'Ismail, please! Why are you abusing them? Why can't you stop using that language?'

'Bano, I'm not educated like you. I'm only a product of the university of the street. Whatever I've learnt and achieved in life is not through books or a college degree, but by mistakes and experiences,' Ismail was lost in his own reverie.

Bano came closer to him, held his hand and wiped the froth from his lips again with a paper napkin. Ismail was a devout Muslim. He prayed five times a day. Namaaz was his road to Allah's grace.

'Don't mind his language, Anvita,' Bano broke the silence. 'His grandfather started his life when he was only thirteen years old. He worked as a waiter in the white-owned Durban Club. He got the job because he was fair and was mistaken for an Arab – that made him escape the coolie taint.'

'And my father also worked in a five-star hotel where he dealt with a large clientele of white estate owners, ministers and maharajas. The abusive language was part of their speech, their way of calling people whom they considered inferior. So it automatically became our language, as we used it for them in our private conversations.'

'But your father started this restaurant. Didn't he?'

'Ja ... he started it with a white nominee. That ullu ka pattha used to take away a substantial part of our profits every month. Still we survived. Thank God, we were able to pay his share. Now we own this place.'

'I remember my father-in-law was a very blunt man, full of spirit and drive. Though he was not educated he could speak two or three languages like English, German and Dutch,' Bano added proudly.

'He was farsighted and calculating. He only believed in learning and for him learning was through hard work ... in doing things.' Ismail was almost normal.

Kisna entered with a few books. He settled down with a glass of beer and looked very serious. We began to eat our lunch in silence.

Kisna finally broke the silence: 'Have you seen the film *Love Actually*? I saw it yesterday. How do you react to it Mr Professor?'

'Yes. We saw it too. It has an unusual theme, especially for our country as it features a blonde marrying a black. And the best part is that the whole issue is portrayed with dignity and grace. At no point does the interracial marriage make any controversial point. Only the emotion overpowers. What we call love, is involved. When love is highlighted, colour loses its significance ... My dear Anvita, its love that matters.'

'That is why I was insisting in my personal observations that "change" has taken place, it is happening. See, today even the little kids express their revolt fearlessly and the film has the courage to project change,' said Kevan.

'Kevan, what you're saying is right. On the surface of our relationship, we feel there is a change. Love is gaining its footing in relationships. But at a deeper level, there are two types of Indians – those who're racists and those who aren't,' Jivesh commented.

Kisna again looked pale with furious red eyes. 'Do you know why, Kevan? When South Africa's democracy was born, the politicians never referred to the country as a multiracial society, rather it was termed as a non-racial society.'

'It was planned that way. It was simply to stress the fact that we should stop recognizing race. One of the fastest and easiest ways to lose credibility is to pull the race card as you're doing Kisna, with your writing. Your articles are very brave and provocative and a perfect satire on our socio-political system,' Kevan replied.

'Kisna, tell me how you feel about the Michael Jackson controversy and the child molestation charges? Were they racially motivated?'

'I feel that happened because the white America could not tolerate such a successful black superstar, though he tried to change the colour of his skin.'

'But it's also true that in spite of all his trials and tribulations, he did not lose his credibility. He was popular till the very end. Maybe that's because he worked hard for his shows ... and had faith in his own performances.' I wanted to share whatever I knew.

'Ja. Anvita, but everyone has faith in oneself, which provides confidence and helps one to move further in life, and that is the only thing which helps.'

'But racism is still racism and should not be tolerated,' Ismail was firm.

'But let's take your father, Ismail. He rose above the racist system and carved a niche for himself. We all feel proud of him for owning a chain of restaurants.'

'Now, let's enjoy the food. Forget what colour we are and enjoy other things … flavours. We have become global. So let's savour the Italian Pizza and Chilean wine. Let us live for ourselves and our friendships as every moment is precious,' said Bano looking glamorous in her new dress.

'Yes, Bano. We all deserve to be real, our original self, as most of the time we wear social masks to look different … to project what we are not.'

'Kisna, but it is very difficult to be real … or to be normal. Once you take up odd jobs as part of your profession … you will also not remain normal enough to enjoy your drink. What if I tell you that yesterday, I terminated the pregnancy of one of your students, Pereeie? She was three months pregnant ….'

'Evil … black or white, dark or bright, remains evil in every situation. Can you help it?' said Kisna.

11

In a seminar on 'human settlement', the acting chief director of the National Housing Programme, Julie Bayat, explained the concept of 'Integrated Human Settlements'. She said that the completely sustainable scheme incorporates an environment that sustains a fully functional community with the provision of housing, health, education, socio-economic as well as recreational facilities in an environment that serves the needs of a fully functional community.. She was emphatically against the vast, sterile, dormitory townships legacy of the past. It was encouraging to listen to her and know that the government was incredibly positive about social housing plans. There were many old photographs of the settlements in her presentation. These were provided as dwellings to inhabitants in the olden days. How primitive they were! One quotation struck me immediately: 'We were confined to the barracks … barracks which were the same everywhere, drab and dingy, with no sight of greenery to break the monotony. Just stands and stands and stands again …. the men could only wait and watch the shadows of the barracks creeping across the blinding white dust'.

Out of that white dust, human settlements emerged as a new concept and were appreciated by the people. Gradually, there were many moves all over South Africa either to upgrade informal settlements, or to correct the past errors or even to construct fresh new dwellings.

Bayat emphasized, 'The fact is that the future will not be a continuation of the past. It will be a series of discontinuities.'

Our company was awarded the 'N. 2 Gateway Project' on the outskirts of Durban. Mr Subramaniam drove me to the site along with one of the chief contractors. Moratiwa Naso was to carry out the construction work. With sufficient experience he was a successful businessman. He must have been in his early fifties, very gentle with extremely good manners. Though he had not formally studied architecture, he understood the intricacies of the designs and implemented them perfectly. Now, we were to work together on our project called 'Cosmo City' where 12,500 residential units were to be developed for people of different income groups. We were also going to build schools, churches, clinics, libraries, a police station, shopping centres, parks and common swimming areas. I was enthused by my job description as it was going to provide me a large space for self-expression – an expression of my ability. Mr Subramaniam had explained to us that the site in the countryside would even include some villages to form a truly integrated community within a single resort. It would be a challenge to translate continuity with change – a balance of opposites. However, he was worried whether the villagers would cooperate as he felt that 'since independence was proclaimed, South Africa has been adding layer upon layer of change. But the old racial conflicts have not absolutely disappeared. Let us try to sweep away the old and start afresh'. Moratiwa Naso was hopeful that the project would give employment to many of those who live in these villages and are not educated.

We parked our car near the marked area which was not very far from the village. We walked the narrow and uneven passage to study the work site and to get feedback from the people who lived there. We saw many people living in slum-like conditions. Some were sitting idle – aimlessly looking at the passers by on the main road, while others were sitting in groups playing cards, gambling or cooking food. There were heaps of very familiar garbage on the even more familiar looking unpaved roads. A few shops selling household goods and groceries completed the picture. Moratiwa Naso spoke to them in their native language. They complained of unemployment, hunger, unpleasant experiences like robberies and cheating. They recounted being traumatized, as some were stabbed or shot to death for small sums of money and their relatives and friends had disappeared in mysterious circumstances.

Moratiwa Naso convinced them that they would get employment and earn enough money to live in a better house with better facilities. There was some reluctance but the women appeared more supportive and enthusiastic. Some even promised to help. I don't know for sure to what extent they were convinced or influenced by our loyalty or seriousness. But they wished us in their Xhosa language, 'Hamba Kable' and 'Enkosikaikuyblu'.

12

This year on Diwali the family decided to celebrate the festival. Last year it was very quiet; it was like any other ordinary day, except all four of us visited the temple. We did not even eat at 'Gokul' which we normally did when we visited the Hare Rama Hare Krishna temple. This year Jivesh gave me extra money to spend and Pratapji enthusiastically invited his friends from 'Connect-Ticket' circle. He even brought a cheap wall hanging glittering with words 'Happy Diwali' along with some flowers and a box of sweets. Jivesh placed the wall hanging on the entrance door and helped Laura and me organize sitting space for the guests.

I prepared a typical Indian meal to go with the celebration – chhole, bhaji, halwa and puri, as it was cooked in Bua's home during various festivals. Bano offered to bring biryani.

At about six in the evening the guests arrived, some carried musical instruments like tablas and a harmonium. One of them placed the deities of Laxmi and Ganesh on a high table. We worship Goddess Laxmi on Diwali as she is supposed to illumine our life with hope and prosperity. When everybody settled down after a cold drink on the carpet, a group of ladies started singing bhajans. I was listening silently, spellbound, as the melodious words of the bhajans unfolded spiritual and philosophic truths with a simple note. Towards the end, an elderly lady in a beautiful yellow sari sang two bhajans alone in her deep husky voice; they touched the core of my heart with their spiritual affirmation. Leelaji told me she was Bhanumathi Somaru and was a professional radio singer during her younger days. Suddenly to my utter surprise I saw Phelela Casu entering our room with folded hands. After the 'aarti' was over I got up to greet her, she touched my shoulder and said, 'You have to pardon me for gatecrashing like this, as I have come uninvited. The vibration of this music was so powerful and inviting, that I could not resist. I hope you will not mind …'

'Oh, no Ms Phelela Casu, on the contrary I am very happy to see you, please take a seat and be with us.' I asked Laura to get her a drink, but did not miss the expression on Laura's face when she did so. Bhanumathi Somaru was getting compliments for her singing. She graciously smiled at Phelela and said 'But why have you come late, you missed the devotional part of the evening.'

'Sorry for that, but I was very hesitant, as it is not proper to come like this that also without any gift.'

'Your presence is a precious gift Ms Phelela.' I was really pleased.

'Festivals are not meant to give and take gifts. Festivals are meant to share love and happiness along with togetherness of friends and relatives,' Baba said, 'you have broken an age-old barrier Miss Phelela.' Pratapji was also touched by this gesture. I hurriedly laid the table and invited everyone for dinner. When Bhanumathi Somaru picked up a puri from the dish, she remarked, 'Leela, I believe your daughter-in-law is an architect, she cannot make proper round puris how can she design proper buildings?'

Everyone laughed, Phelela came to my rescue, 'Oh there is a tremendous difference in cooking food and designing buildings. Can't you notice the elegance, the way she has laid the table – there are rose petals around all the dishes, pretty oil lamps and candles are making it more beautiful and ceremonial.'

I was touched by the remark, before I could say anything, a young lady dressed in a faded sari looked at me saying, 'Don't worry about the shape of the puri, everything is delicious. After a long time I have eaten such good food. The halwa is lip-smacking.' She hugged me with unusual fondness.

'She is our neighbour Renuka,' Baba Bhoolabhai introduced her. But Manish came forward, and touched Phelela's shoulder. 'Anvita, you will be shocked to know that her husband was brutally murdered only few years back, by a bunch of black hooligans.'

'Why ...what was his crime?'

'His crime was that he was prosperous in his business and was driving a Mercedes Benz which is a luxury car, not meant for Indians.'

Before the atmosphere could turn into a bitter scenario, I hurriedly handed over a candle to everyone and asked them to light it and place it in a row on the boundary wall of the house, I handed one to Phelela too. Pratapji held his candle in his hand and with great enthusiasm raised it high in the air as a toast and said, 'Life is too short to nurse grievances and harbour grudges and resentments.'

I raised mine, 'For faith and love. Happy Diwali to all of you.'

Phelela, stood next to Renuka and said, 'Let us walk hand in hand. Happy Diwali to you.' They lighted their candles side by side. A strange flame of human intimacy flickered on their faces.

13

It was a shrieking sound – too annoying to bear and too loud to let anyone sleep. We both got up – shaking with fear. We ran towards the entrance door. It was open and Pratapji and Leelaji were already standing out in the garden. Almost all our neighbours were gathered near the house. An ambulance and a police car were making a maddening noise with their alarms and flickering lights.

I could see Pratapji and Leelaji were shaken up. They were trembling with some undefined fear.

'You know Anvita … my friend Bhanumathi Somaru … the one who was at our 'Connect-Ticket' circle, the one who sang bhajans towards the end, has been murdered!'

'Why? Who murdered her?'

'Her grandson. He is a drug addict.'

'They are such a nice family – wonder how he became an addict … how he got into it. The parents didn't notice where he was going … or what he was getting into …'

'Oh I just can't believe it. She was here only a few hours back singing beautifully, so vibrant and graceful her performance was.'

'She was the one who made the evening perfect, the melody of her voice, the fragrance of her breath is still alive in our living room … it is so difficult to believe she is no more.'

Something of tremendous disgust had happened and we were all plunged into an unbearable pain and disbelief.

Mrs Rajani Naidoo, another neighbour walked in. She was clearly shaken. Jivesh and I got chairs for everybody.

'Please sit. I will get you some tea.'

Mrs Naidoo unraveled the mystery further.

'You know Leela Behn … Ravindran had a seventeen-year-old girlfriend. She is also involved in the killing … they needed money for their drugs …'

'Oh! How sad.'

'Well, these drug peddlers are leading our children to destruction.'

'They are too young to go to jail … what a waste of life.'

'But where were the parents?'

'They lived separately. Ravindran lived with his mother and Bhanumathi who was his grandmother.'

'The problem is that this generation has very confused parents. Our elders had grown up in tin roof township barracks and no schooling, living under crazy laws.'

'Yes. We always lived under the shadow of fear of white people's superiority. And if we are not brave enough to be sincere, we stagnate in our views about life.'

'We can't help it. Because we grew up devoid of any philosophic tradition. Whatever it was, it crumbled because of the system.'

'Because of this sense of bitterness, bewilderment and frustration a profound anxiety about the intellectual-moral state has overtaken this country. We desperately need some spiritual guidance which the church and the tradition-bound conservatives cannot provide.'

'That is why there is help in the form of Ramakrishna Mission and Sivananda Ashram to help manage the modern pressure.'

'Our Connect-Ticket circle is also a very solid institution. It helps people to think positively, uplift us spiritually and changes the lifestyle. It helps one to live a contented and peaceful life.'

The forum may be weak, but it was an experiment to bring the people of a minority together. It is a group that is numerically inferior to the rest of the population, politically non-dominant and which is being reproduced as an ethnic category.

A more fundamental question is: can the boundaries created by race and class during apartheid be transcended by the creation of a new

African elite acting dismissively towards Indians and other Coloureds in affirmative action and by the rise in African power in the government? Does it bring about a new and more patriotic South African identity?

What shocked me more was the newspaper coverage next day in the *Fourth Column* by A.M.I. Nanakchand.

> *Tragedies, inevitably, if unfortunately, engender conventional wisdom. When the 57-year-old Bhanumathi Somaru was murdered by two young lovers to feed their craving for drugs, it is time to ask two hard questions: firstly, why is the government not protecting its citizens? second, shouldn't our pledge to uphold human rights – especially the paramount right to life – be reviewed?*
>
> *Both are "statist" responses from blacks and whites and, in this particular instance, Indo-South Africans. President Thabo Mbeki's belief that the perception of crime being out of control is fed by entrenched white racism – although plausible – carries the risk of making whites disliked as much as criminals.*
>
> *Whites and some blacks want the government to flex its muscles by using "Jackboot" tactics to fight the scourge. They also want all criminals convicted of serious and violent offences to hang for their deeds. Blacks generally want the nation to rediscover "unbuntu" or a moral code.*

Whatever the law claimed – the truth was that there were 18,000 murders every year. More than 5 million had HIV/AIDS in our country, along with millions of amphetamine addicts.

'So are we supposed to wait?'

'Yes. Time never stops – it flies. Time does not look at your pains ...but it heals ... embalms as it flows. Don't wait, break free from it to recognize what really is happening around you.'

14

'Anvita, why don't you call me Mom?'

Yes. Why haven't I ever tried to address her as "Mom" like Jivesh calls her? I wondered.

'I'm sorry. I didn't realize it.'

'It's been more than a year that you have been here, living with us. Do you still feel like a stranger ... or you think I don't love you enough to be called a mom?'

We were in the kitchen doing the dishes and clearing the leftovers. Jivesh was not in town so I was not in a hurry to go to my bedroom.

'The reason can be that I'm not used to this word "mom". But it doesn't mean that I disrespect you.' I washed my hands with the liquid soap and prepared coffee for both of us. We went to the living room.

'I think it's nothing else but my complex childhood. It has always created hurdles in my life. As I told you earlier, my father suffered from some sickness and died early. My mother was trapped in that marriage due to a dispute in the family. I was born in the very first year of their marriage. I never had an opportunity to see my father. My mother brought me up all by herself and with great difficulty. She did not go back to her father or to her in-laws for any kind of financial support. Why didn't she go to them? I wouldn't know. Maybe it was her self-respect that she wanted to protect. There was no income left. To support us she worked in a small handicrafts unit where she embroidered phulkari. She spoke very little. She either prayed to God, or was lost in thought, or stared at the ceiling of our room. There used to be frequent communal riots in Punjab those days. Once, when curfew was imposed, we remained hungry for many days. One day, she held me by my shoulders and drew me gently towards herself. Her grasp was frail and her hand was trembling. She turned her face towards me and said, 'Go Anvita. Go with this uncle. He will take you to your Bua, Rajrani. She will give you everything ... food ... education. Please study hard to achieve something in life ...' She handed a small suitcase of my belongings to a policeman who appeared to be human and friendly.

'She refused to look at my face directly, as if she wanted to hide something. But as I was leaving, she gazed into my face for a very long time. The blend of hope and sadness in her eyes is etched in my heart forever. I was only six years old at that time, but at that moment of parting, I understood many things. And within me, something very natural ... something very beautiful died. Maybe the term "Ma" or "Mother" with its manifold tenderness is dead forever for me.'

In the silence of the room, only our coffee cups rattled ... and the tiny sobs behind the tears ... but I continued. 'Though in India we say "Dharti Ma" (Mother Earth), "Durga Ma" (Mother Goddess) or "Gau Ma" (Mother cow), they are all names that evoke triumph of life and respect. Indian culture is full of images celebrating Mother. But for me, this word is horrifically hollow. When I came to know of my mother's death after a few days, I remember I used to sit on the cold stone of the window-sill through the night – trying to understand death and my own life ... looking up at the sky ... befriending stars in my loneliness ...especially the "Saptarishi", the cluster of seven stars – the seven hermits going in search of salvation.

'As I grieved for a few days, my Bua fed me with milk and hot paranthas, which I'd never tasted before. One morning, Bua and Jo Jo Uncle took me to a school. That was the day of stepping out of my own poverty ... or the beginning of the journey towards learning. After that there was no looking back.'

Leelaji was reclining on the sofa. She got up and hugged me. Her warmth was genuinely touching. But I still said, 'I'm very sorry, if you're hurt. I don't know how to respond to life, especially to love.'

But for the first time, I also held her by her waist. Something happened to me as I did so, stirring a different emotion somewhere inside the layers of my being. Perhaps it was my transformation or even a metamorphosis of my evolutionary soul ... moulding me into a human form ...

'Ok. In future I'll call you "Ma" and not "Mom" like Jivesh,' I whispered finally.

She cried. It was a genuine gesture of a mother who loves. I left her, as I wanted to be alone – to be with myself. I sat on the garden bench near the Bird of Paradise grove.

After many years, I sat like that – staring at the sky. There were many stars with a very thin crescent moon – Duj Ka Chand – we call it in India. Suddenly, I felt homesick for the streets of my old city and its people – for Bua's warmth, Jo Jo Uncle and Vati Aunty ... But there was nobody back home. Nobody calling me Annu – with a dew of affection in her eyes. I cried into the silence of my surroundings. Suddenly, I felt the long forgotten and unusually melodious mantras playing in my ears. Once my mother used to recite them. But it was so long ago in the past but still those mantras were like fragrant jasmine flowers, smelling of love. The mantras arose shy from the vastness of earth to the eternity of the sky where the cluster of Saptarishis were shining like a burning flame of guidance and reminding me of my past.

15

Unna, the small town near Hoshiarpur, had come alive the day I returned after completing my studies in architecture. I remembered the, ugly, scarred roof of the bus stand eaten away with rust, the rush of passengers caught in a web – the chaos of the cart pushers, tongawallahs, chhole-bathurewallahs, the temporary shops, iron nails bent under the weight of the hung handbags. Mundu scratching his ringwormed thighs at 'Amrik Singh ka dhaba', dal boiling over in the shiny brass-pots, skinned chicken strung on iron rods – all spiced up as usual, and the pushing and jostling of the passengers – I suddenly felt the crowd had increased a bit too much.

Retracing my fleeting glance, I reconnected my memories to the scene around me. Hurriedly, I sat in a rickshaw. I remembered Gali Shyam Lal. I recollected the lane curving left of the street from the Gol Darwaza … and the meandering row of shops beginning with Chajju Halwai. The crowds still broke the kulhars in the drain after drinking their pedha (sweetmeat) topped lassi. Emaciated stray dogs still licked these mugs as they did so many years ago. The pigeons still sat on the same old, blackened pots hung on the railings of the upper storeys of most houses. Everything was the same as it was when I used to trudge through these galis while going to school. Every colour, each shape and the 'oldness' was the same as it was – so what had changed? Maybe four years was not such a long period to change things.

Preeto's door was still half open as always … and that scene came back … of her husband lying dead after being hit by a bullet in the communal riots … her only son dying because of lack of medical care … of even proper medicines. The dead bodies lay there for two days. After the curfew lifted, a swayamsevak (ostensibly a volunteer, in reality a political worker) had thrown the two bodies nonchalantly into a mass cremation. We could watch the flames rising and falling in Preeto's eyes till much later … and then her inner flame dying out and getting mired … what was left were her screams that shook the soul.

Some new shops and pucca houses had come up in between … and then that three storied house with a nameplate that still proclaimed in half erased letters – 'Jayant Jai Singh' … my Jo Jo Uncle. I paid the rickshawallah. Didn't even think of asking for the change … my breath had stopped. I stopped and stared at the house for long … and then turned my gaze at the haveli opposite it. Its door bore the legend 'Damyanti Chawla, District Magistrate'. A man with gigantic moustaches stood at the gate as if he were a part of it. His heavy booted footsteps spelled terror for us children – even a fly couldn't enter the house without his express permission. I didn't know how many knew at that time that Jo Jo Uncle had a mysterious relationship with the house.

I remembered that I could have an unobstructed view of that haveli from my bedroom. I could see it clearly from my window whenever the lights went on … or off. I also heard my Bua cursing the entire time that the light was switched on … 'Kanjrey na ho toh sirsiriye (she is no less than a prostitute)!' Uncle spent many evenings there. Earlier I didn't know the meaning of my Bua's curses … but later after passing my Class Ten exam, I knew what she meant. Perhaps because of my uncle's evenings out, his own children had left for hostels in Dalhousie and later for studies abroad.

Namrita or Nony as we called her, seemed to know a lot about those evenings. In fact, she thought a lot of herself. Whenever she came back for her holidays, she looked at me as if I was a worthless piece of furniture or a maid in her house. Even after Bua and Uncle upbraided her, she never accorded me any respect – I was always just a maid for her. She always tried to distance herself from me. She didn't talk much to Jo Jo Uncle even. Her brother Sanju's behaviour was just about tolerable. Whenever he came back home, he used to study. He loved his 'mom'–

my Bua and perhaps for that reason took her out shopping during his free time. He talked to her for long and even showed her some movies … yet I was never included in any of these. When – and if either of them introduced me, it was always, 'She's my distant cousin!'

So that's what I was in that house … a poor orphan girl who was being fed and allowed to live in the house for her own security. Bua would only call me when she needed help in the housework. She managed the household.

I used to study sitting on a cane moora or stool. When I told about the happenings in the school to Jo Jo Uncle or showed him my homework, corrected and accompanied with remarks of 'Very Good' in red ink in teachers handwriting, or informed that I'd come first in the class … or showed him the paper upon which my teacher had showered me with praises – he would be very happy. He would tell Bua, 'See Rajraniji, how intelligent she is … your brother's daughter has come first in the class – this girl didn't even need tution classes … And our Nony needs tution to even scrape through. We had to send her abroad as she didn't get admission into any good college here … I don't know how others pass with 90 per cent … You will see that Annu will pass with the best grades.'

'After all she is our family,' said Bua proudly. At that time I became her relative … her close relative.

At such moments, I would've given anything to wrap my arms around her … to say, 'Thank you, Bua,' it was so essential at that age … but Bua didn't like physical closeness … or closeness of any other kind.

The sabziwali would arrive and I would collect my books to get ready for school. Jo Uncle Jo would call out, 'Anvita, just recite: "*Khoob lari mardani woh toh Jhansi waali Rani thi*" for me. And I would readily recite it as clearly and properly as I possibly could in those circumstances. And then he would ask me to study a few books and relate their meaning later. 'Don't forget it … haan! It describes good and evil very well …!'

'Why do you need to know about good and evil – just look at your own character!' My Bua would pipe up … 'You shut up!' Jo Jo Uncle would retort and move away. When I'd come to the verandah in the evening, holding the cup of warm tea with my dupatta, I'd find Jo Jo Uncle all decked up wearing a new safari suit and emanating a magnificent, expensive perfume. Hurriedly, he'd cross the street and trot towards that haveli where the mustachioed guard with heavy boots would welcome him inside, as if he were a maharaja.

Bua would sit on the charpoy and intently knit on the two needles she held with trembling hands. 'You're young Annu … after you grow up you will understand that when someone rips your heart out – it is not too pleasant. Listen girl … you grow up, study hard and get established, earn a lot … you or Nony should not have to face any injustice from your husbands – that's my only prayer to my Rabb, my God!' She would join her palms in prayer to her unknown Rabb.

'Yes, I promise you! I will become a doctor or an architect, definitely. I will sit for the entrance exams.'

I could see the inside of Ms Damyanti Chawla, Magistrate's haveli very clearly from my window. There was an open space with the rooms on the one side and on the other side the kitchen in the corner. There was a tiny wash-basin on the outer wall of the kitchen. It leaked, always. A servant used to sit on a bench outside it. As soon as Madam Damyanti Chawla the Magistrate called out, he would enter the kitchen and come out with a tray with ice and glasses. He would swagger as he walked in and place the tray and the glasses on her bedroom table. Jo Jo Uncle would then pour 'whatever it was' liquid and mix the given ice … I understood 'whatever it was' liquid only later. Then the two would talk late into the night – tinkling their glasses … gesticulating and laughing … and then the door would close and lights go off. When uncle returned, Mohinder would quietly open the door; steady his swaying body before depositing it on the bed. He would also feed him and change his clothes. Bua's lights would go out at that moment. Only the lamp on my table would glow … and I'd turn to making notes as if nothing had happened.

Even in this environment, I somehow topped my board exams and won a scholarship to study architecture in Chandigarh. Jo Jo Uncle later gave me some money and Bua got me some clothes … but the love that Sanju and Nony received when they visited was a bit different.

Chandigarh became the city of my learning. This was the first time I had gone to a big city from a small town. The atmosphere at the college was very cultured. I learnt table manners. I also learnt to wear clothes that hid my rusticity. I learnt self-confidence, learnt to be self-sufficient and acquired self respect – I had to become something. This was the first step. I also learnt to laugh heartily, if ever.

Once when I visited 'home', I found preparations in full swing. Bua and Jo Jo Uncle had gone to Delhi and when they returned, the verandah was brimful with shopping items. I was told that Nony had entered into a court marriage in Delhi … only the pheras were left to be solemnized. Nony's husband was to come after a few days with his family. Halwais had already started preparations for a feast. When I asked them whether foreigners eat our sweets, I was informed Nony's family was indeed Indian.

All the pre-wedding rituals were duly completed – from praying, to the hearth's fire, to the oil ritual. Nony participated in all these with joy. Sanju joined wholeheartedly in the preparations. Bua gave me some of her old saris to wear.

On the day of the marriage a huge shamiana was erected. white flowers were used to decorate the vedi. The tables were piled with mouth-watering goodies. The flower-laden gate – the toran … everything was a new experience for me. It was the first time I was part of any celebrations.

Damyanti Chawla also attended the wedding. Swathed in an expensive sari and weighed down by her jangling, heavy jewellery she was beaming – and she had brought her three-year-old son who held on tightly to her fingers.

The wedding was finally concluded. The customary seven rounds around the fire were made. The newly weds Rajiv and Nony cut the cake followed by merriment and music. 'Who's she, Nony?' asked Rajiv. 'Just a distant cousin, an unfortunate poor orphan that my father is educating.'

That evening I collected all my belongings – even the books gifted by Jo Jo Uncle. After 'namastying' to Bua and Uncle I set out. My heavy study load was – I knew inside – only an excuse.

I kept away from prayers. As far as I remember, my mother used to go to the temple more often than needed. Bua also spent her time in prayers and fasting. She used to chant satyanarayan katha regularly and would make me listen to it. But look, what happened to her? It was so much humbug.

I returned to Unna after four years. By now I had become a full-fledged architect. I'd joined a firm in Chandigarh. I lived in a small guesthouse owned by the firm. A few money orders from Jo Jo Uncle and some letters from me – our interaction was limited to only that.

16

A sea of people dressed in white swarmed the courtyard Everyone had their heads covered. In the midst of this white-wrapped multitude lay the mortal remains of Jo Jo Uncle. A white enwrapped Bua had put her arms around the lifeless body – still like a stone, her lips moving but only silently. Seeing me life coursed through her limbs again. She stood up. 'Finally, you have come … after all these years … when your uncle has left us for ever.' She suddenly caught me in a despondent embrace.

Leaving others to take care of her, I rushed inside. I rang up Nony.

'Yes … Namrita here.'

'Nony didi, this is Anvita. Uncle … Jo Jo Uncle is no more. Please come as soon as you can … we cannot keep the body for long!'

I could hear her sobbing.

'Please don't cry … he'd a very peaceful end …!'

'I'm not crying … I'm not an emotional fool … just calculating … the earliest I can reach is the day after … Sanju stays even farther …!'

'Wh … what should we do with the dead body?'

'Cremate it … don't wait for us!'

It was evening when we reached the cremation grounds. Isharee and Mohinder helped in the final preparations. Jo Jo Uncle's body was kept on a raised platform. I arranged some flowers to be placed as a mark of respect to the dead. Bua was hugging the body's feet and crying inconsolably.

After the mantras, the Pandit asked, 'Who will perform the last rites?'

A deathly silence ensued. Among Hindus, the death rites can be performed only by the direct descendants – preferably male heirs of the deceased. Bua's face turned ashen. Damyanti Chawla stood aloof and alone from the crowd – holding little Arjun's, her son's, finger.

I said, 'Panditji, let him see his father's dead face – he couldn't see it during his lifetime.

'Yes, let him!' A shriek erupted from Bua. She was transformed into a statue as she wailed, 'She has won – in life as well as in death!' As Panditji helped him perform the last rites of his father, my Uncle Jo Jo.

Later I met Damyanti Chawla. 'Thank you for your support. If you hadn't been there, little Arjun would've been deprived of offering fire to his father's body!'

'Oh I didn't do anything. It was fortunate that Arjun was there. Otherwise, who would've offered fire to my dead uncle?'

'Anyway, thanks. Please keep my card – I'm in Delhi nowadays – posted as a member of the Planning Commission. I may as well tell you that your uncle always used to praise you very highly – he felt very lonely when you left for Chandigarh!'

The next day was not like other days. The charpoy had gone from the verandah. The subziwallah, vegetable vendor, too did not turn up. Only silence reigned. I ran upstairs and sat on my table with a thud. The table was a refuge from every disappointment, difficulty and despondency.

Suddenly my eyes caught a bundle of letters. The moment I saw the handwriting on the envelope, I knew they were written by Jo Jo Uncle.

> *Ever since you left, I see your photograph everyday – not just your face but your entire profile … this is like a spiritual exercise for me … I find your face so close. I can see the sharpness of the lines on your cheek and the bumpy mole on your chin … your complexion like burnished gold … if your husband had not fallen victim to that dreaded disease … perhaps you may not have accepted me … I would've lived out my life with my illiterate wife.*

I wanted to write poems on you, Vati ... poems of my love for you. When I was young, I wanted to become a writer ... I had an inclination towards literature ... I see the potential of a writer in Anvita... even architecture is creativity ... sort of ...'

Vati ... from Anvita's bedroom, she can clearly see your verandah and bedroom ... I don't know whether she has seen anything ... in any case nothing is hidden ... the day you told me that you had registered my name as Arjun's father, I was amazed by your courage ....'

Sometimes ... only sometimes, I feel like opening my heart to someone – I cannot find that someone. My wife doesn't understand me ... if only Anvita had stayed, she'd have understood me ... maybe ...? She's not like Nony, she's sensitive and human.

I could not read anymore. It was an eye opener about their relationship and a new valuation of my own being.

After Namrita arrived she hugged everyone – sharing their grief. Without even greeting me she asked, 'When did you arrive?'

'After hearing about his death. Didn't I call you?'

'Oh ... yes ... I remember I talked to you about the cremation ... and I came to know that you made that illegitimate son of my father perform the last rites.'

'I didn't even know where they lived, or Arjun was his son, everything came as a surprise, believe me!'

'Oh don't try to be too clever. I know everything and why you're here!'

'I don't even know how you can say this ... from the time I came to this house, I've been conscious of the obligations I'm under ... without Jo Jo Uncle's help, I couldn't have studied architecture or become an architect. I'm so grateful to him, at least I'm not likely to forget it! I am so grateful to him.'

'Grateful my foot! Why have you come here? What do you want now?'

Bua finally intervened. 'If Annu hadn't been there ... who would have organized the funeral ... I had gone mad with grief ...! She has been managing the house and guests since then.'

We resorted to eating silently to avoid the sensitive issue again. While eating Sanju said, 'Ma, a friend of mine from USA will come over. He used to study with us. He is interested in seeing the historical places in India.'

'I thought you had actually come to fulfill your duties towards your late father's tehrevi, so many things are still left. We've to observe the sixteenth day, immerse the ashes in the holy Ganges and you're thinking of visiting places …!'

While going back to his room, Sanju had turned towards me and said, 'Thank you for everything!'

17

'Ma, this is my friend Jivesh,' and then turning towards me Sanju introduced, 'and she's my cousin Anvita.'

I stood up from the charpoy. 'Hello!' He extended his arm. I took his hand into mine – it was smooth and friendly.

Arrangements began at once. The servant boy took the luggage upstairs. Sanju shifted to Jo Jo Uncle's room and gave his room to Jivesh. I went to make tea. Isharee went to buy some sweets from Chajju Halwai.

While drinking tea, Sanju began, 'Ma, Jivesh lives in South Africa …in Durban. He was studying for his Ph.D, but we have been sharing an apartment.'

Bua turned to Jivesh, and asked incredulously, 'Are you still studying?'

'No, we've finished. After my visit to India I'll return to my country.'

'But you look like an Indian …'

'Yeah. We're originally from here … many years ago our forefathers went to South Africa and settled there.'

'Any relatives here?'

'None that we know of. Times were such – we were focused only on survival …nobody looked for us …'

'Isn't Durban the same town where Gandhiji was thrown out of the first class train compartment?' I couldn't help myself asking.

'Yes, the same … we've even preserved the place. Every Indian wants to visit it.'

'What's your caste, son?'

'We're Brahmins by birth – from Allahabad, but my mother is from Agra.'

The talks meandered. He got up. I moved in the same direction as he was going. Outside the room, he said, 'Could I have a big bottle of water, I drink a lot of water Miss …?'

'Anvita, my name is Anvita.'

'What an unusual name?'

The expressions in his eyes were changing … something seemed to melt in them and waft towards me ….

Sanju had come home early that evening. Nony was trying to convince Bua about selling the showroom. Sanju made it a joint enterprise. Jivesh said to me, 'I was in Delhi for a week. I feel that a new consciousness is entering me after I came to India. Everything is very advanced here – especially women of the new generation – they are extremely aware. On the one side they are very advanced, on the other they are extremely industrious, they do all the household work too. They are not strident feminists. They are very compassionate and soft. You were saying that you're an architect.'

For the first time in my life someone had praised me – appreciated me – I was not used to this. Even here, I was at best a servant … at the worst a slave. Slavery had perhaps led to Jivesh's forefathers to South Africa.

'Oh you're so taciturn … please tell me something about yourself.'

'I don't have any history, Jivesh. I can only claim to be an orphan. I don't even remember my parents. I came to this house when I was six. I've grown up here. Bua is my father's sister, that is about all the relationship I've with this house. After completing my studies in architecture, I'm working with a construction company in Chandigarh.'

'Oh! I'm sorry to hear about your parents. But I am glad you have done well for yourself.'

During dinner Bua sat crying quietly in a corner while the others sat eating on the dining table. Isharee and I were serving them.

'Oh, won't you join us?' asked Jivesh.

'I'll eat later. Even Bua has not eaten.'

'The food's very tasty … and this pudding … what do we call this …?'

'Kheer-malpua …,' I replied.

'Its actually rice pudding … we prepare it with rice and milk,' Nony butted in.

As I went in to serve some food to Bua, I felt her fingers digging deep into my forearm almost pinching me.

'You go! Get lost – don't try to get into everything. This is my family!'

I was shocked. She'd never spoken to me like this. Was she losing her hold, her position in this house, like the pale reflection of sun as the moon does every night? Had she taken her cue from Nony?

I locked myself into my room. I could hear their voices from the ground floor. Bua was crying. Nony and Sanju were trying to convince her. I remained unconcerned … all relations had been sundered. Everyone was so selfish ….

Isharee had later whispered, when he came to my room, 'Behnji do you know what these Sanju and Nony are up to? They want to sell – Jo Jo Uncle's showroom and even the house – they want to take Bibiji away to America. At this age, how will she adjust there!'

'Shhhh!'

18

I was standing at the kitchen door – giving instructions to Isharee and making a list of vegetables when I saw Jivesh approaching. The refreshing smell of his perfume enveloped the entire atmosphere.

'Can I have some tea? Where has Sanju gone? He was supposed to take me around to see the old monuments of the city.'

'If he's said he will come, I'll ring him up!'

'Why don't you sit down, please. You're always busy with work. I want to talk to you!'

'It's not always like that. Bua is so disoriented these days.'

'In Delhi a friend of mine took me around, I saw the Rashtrapati Bhawan, did some shopping at Janpath. What fascinated me the most was what-do-you-call it? Three wheelers, yes auto-rickshaws! I'd never seen anything like that! I went to the Old Delhi too. Had kebabs from Karim's near Jama Masjid. Really that was the experience of a lifetime!'

Mohinder appeared from nowhere. 'Sisterji, Sanju is held up by the legal matters and some visitors. He is asking you to take his friend around the city.'

'Where can I take you? I don't know enough about the place!'

'Anywhere!' I could see a certain gleam in Jivesh's eyes.

After I got ready, we set out to see the city.

'Don't you have any river in the city?' Jivesh asked.

'No, no river touches this unfortunate city. This is not a city of dreams Jivesh – nor a city of promises. It's the city of my uncle's death. A saga of my parent's helplessness … of my slavery.' I'd been possessed by uncharacteristic boldness. I rode on it.

'Jivesh, there's a lake in Chandigarh where we can go for boating. Are you planning to go to Chandigarh?'

'Yes, I've to go to Chandigarh … will you take me?'

'Of course, I will!'

That day Nony and Sanju were relatively free and wanted to entertain their guest. They opted for *Parzania*. Jivesh asked me to join and I happily accompanied them. I rarely saw movies but I was spellbound during the screening of that film. The movie established that the recent riots were not caused by the Hindus' hatred of Muslims but they were engineered by powerful politicians of Gujarat for selfish gains. When we sat in the car after the movie, we were lost in our own thoughts. But Sanju broke the silence 'What a movie, yaar! It was an eye-opener to what is happening in India. Living in USA we are not aware of such horrible incidents.'

'Don't you think Sanju that the movie deals with the psyche of a common man, a man who is trapped in a conflict of globalization and mechanization of his nation. I personally feel that the absurdity and confusion has overpowered his thinking, he cannot react to life properly.'

'How can you say so, Anvita, when the whole struggle was based on religion? The Hindus hated Muslims and Muslims hated Hindus.'

'No, I don't think so. I feel the movie depicts a confused common man, a man who refrains from drawing rational conclusions and has no idealism.' I was clear about my point.

'Why?'

'Because for a "common man", his existence is the basic problem. To survive or "to exist" in this world is more important than to fight for a religious identity.'

'But they do have to prove their identity, Anvita, the Muslim man in the movie had to open his pajamas to prove his religion.'

'Yeah, they have fallen down to that level. Fear is the factor, fear of death.'

'But I feel there is still some humanity left within your common man, Anvita,' Sanjay remarked. 'In *Parzania* a Hindu, a terrorist, leaves a Muslim woman who hides under the table, alive.'

'You know Jivesh, even Anvita was brought to our house by a police constable when communal riots were in full swing in the interiors of Punjab.'

I was shocked. Nony always made it a point to put me in my place when I am more vulnerable. I was too shocked to say a word. I only thought of the past as I trembled with nervousness.

'Was the policemen Hindu or Muslim?' Sanju further ignited my agony.

Jivesh came to my rescue. He touched my hand softly and said, 'Do you know Anvita those police constables of your film resemble the "shite force" of South Africa whose only mission is to kill. Even in the film they killed everybody like butchers, Hindu, Muslim, Parsi – everyone. In my country they kill blacks and us Indians.'

'Haven't you noticed the uselessness of police? Till today they haven't found that young child whose parents are still waiting.'

'But Anvita was lucky, she could find a destination.' Nony was still trying to pull me down.

When we reached home, I hugged Bua and touched her feet in front of everyone, 'Oh Bua I will be indebted to you all my life, for all that you have done for me.'

Bua was perplexed, 'Pagal kuri hai tu, Annu – you are mad, Annu – what have I done for you? Nothing, out of the ordinary. I only gave you food and shelter, it was my dharam, my duty. You are my brother's daughter.'

'The education, Bua, an identity to a lost orphan child that is what you have given me. You have created a clear outline and given a real three-dimensional shape to a shadow which could have faded in that remote village of Punjab. You don't know Bua how thankful I am. I have no words to say anything more.'

'I don't understand your bhashan Annu, your lecture, your language is like your Jo Jo Uncle, like a riddle that can't be solved.' She lovingly made all of us sit on the dining table and served dinner. Biryani, along with makki ki roti and saag. The aromas were most appetizing and we all started eating. But Jivesh was still under the spell of the film. He said, 'Sanju I was always under the impression that there no such killings of innocent people here in India as they are back home in South Africa. We hated for the colour of our skin which is not our fault. We are born as what we are according to God's plan in South Africa. But in South

Africa people have suffered this hatred for ages. Our burden is heavy, drenched in the blood of blacks and us, the Indians.'

'Why do you live in a country where you don't have respect and security?'

'Many of the blacks and Indians have left the country. They have migrated to Australia, or USA. You may leave your earth and your roots, but they do not leave you. You miss your own country, even if you are happy or successful abroad. Some kind of vacuum always remains in your heart, enough to make you feel lonely.'

'Yeah, I remember Jivesh, when we went to see *American Blues* in Chicago. Anvita, all the musicians, they were black, they performed majestically. The melodious music was a treat, it was the experience of a lifetime. But we all could feel the mystical vibrations that lay under the surface of that shrill music. Many layers of suffering and loneliness revealed themselves in their own silent way.'

'Oh really,' Nony said, 'I was also there but I did not feel it the way you are describing.'

'I am surprised, Nony Di.' Even Jivesh was shocked with her remark. 'Nony Di, all those songs were a kind of escape from rootlessness, escape from pain of the past. The past which is full of harsh memories of their ancestors' sufferings.'

'But surely they can always go back. Why don't they?' I asked

'Because there is nothing left for them to go back for,' Jivesh replied.

'I believe now the blacks are ruling their own country,' Nony commented.

'Yes, they are, they are openly killing the whites to take revenge for all the humiliation their families have suffered. And even the whites are apologetic as they are suffering from a "white guilt",' Jivesh reasoned.

'But has it helped the economy?' I asked.

'No. At the moment the whole nation is going through a metamorphosis as the white estate owners have either left the country or have been murdered. The blacks are not able to manage the farms and sugar industry though they are trying hard. At this time the whole situation is in a very shaky state,' Jivesh replied.

We all ate in a strange silence, till Sanju said, 'Yes Jivesh, I remember one of the *American Blue* songs – "If I die in Arkansas".'

'What is American Blue?' I asked Jivesh.

'It is a kind of musical blend of both African and European idioms. Mostly blacks sing it, the blues are very sad, their sadness cannot be softened with tears.'

'Oh really?'

'I will sing it for you,' said Jivesh and he sang,

If I die in Arkansas, if I die in Arkansas
Do ship my body to my pa
If my papa refuses me, ship it to my girl
If my girl refuses me, shove me into the sea
Where de fishes an' de whales make a feast over me.

After that song none of us could eat the halwa which Bua served us lovingly.

Late at night, Bua called me to her room. Nony was sitting beside her. A little bundle lay opened before her. She held out a dirty looking pouch towards me and said, 'Take this … balliye. This is your property. Your mother had given this to me. I'd planned to hand it over on your marriage. But I'm leaving now … Rabb knows when we will meet again! I had kept your mother's possessions for you.' Then she took off four gold bangles from her arm. 'Take these Annu … it's your Bua's only blessing for you. Remember that I loved you like I loved Sanju and Nony!'

'I can't repay your debt even after seven rebirths!' I cried holding her arm. 'Bua, you're the only one I have!'

I went back to my room to open the little pouch. It contained a few pieces of jewellery – a necklace that was ensconced in the velvet box it had come in. There were two pairs of earrings. It had a touch of my mother … the red velvet exuded her smell, a smell unknown.

When I came downstairs early morning, I saw the main entrance door wide open and swinging wildly. Bua was not at home. I shrieked in panic. Hearing the noise, Sanju and Nony came down running. Jivesh accompanied them. They ran out searching for Bua.

After ensuring they were not within earshot, Isharee said, 'At night Nony had informed her that the deal is done, the showroom is sold. They will leave once her passport is ready. Nony wanted Bibi to sell her gold and silver jewellery as well as the utensils. But she refused … and cried out loudly, "I don't want to go there … I'll remain here … after marriage I'd come to this house as a bride ... only my dead body would leave this. You can take all the money ... I'll get by somehow ... Annu's with me, she will take care of me." I think Nony has got separated from her husband ... she's alone ... can't even earn much. But this is not the way to displace an old lady!' Isharee had tears in her eyes.

The dead body lay in the centre of the courtyard. Some labourers had found her. We found out later that Bua had laid down on the railway tracks.

Nobody sat on Bua's charpoy that evening. I just sat nearby. I wasn't prepared for the scenario changing so quickly. Jivesh came and placed a hand on my shoulder. 'You were asking me Jivesh, if an Indian woman had any legal rights. Bua put up with Uncle's extramarital relationship all her life, but she remained here meekly in this house. Uncle had put his children's name in the will – she never had any rights to the property – ever. Even her wishes didn't have any value ... everyone is out to safeguard their own interests.'

Next morning I got ready. 'Ok Sanju, I'll take my leave now. I don't know if we will ever meet in this life. Here is my address. If you want, you can send some letters or even e-mails to me ... even though I'm just your distant cousin.' I was crying.

'Don't worry, Anvita. Who would not like to maintain a relationship with a sensible girl like you?' Sanju replied.

Jivesh accompanied me as I walked out. His face looked strange through my tears. He took my hands in his, 'Do you know Jivesh ... just a few moments later ... a few minutes perhaps, I will get on that bus and will be alone again – an orphan, rootless – in fact, someone who doesn't have anybody in this entire universe.'

'Don't worry Anvita, there's always somebody for the person who feels he has nobody!'

TWO

1

I don't fear questions. But I'm afraid of doubts as these lead to misunderstandings. I could see the questions being formed in Jivesh's eyes as well in those of Leelaji and Bano's. Only Bano was aware that I was simultaneously working on two extra projects along with my official assignment. The time period was short and I had a long way to go. To design, to survey, to conceptualize not only needed research but it was also immensely demanding. I was trying to come to terms with it and also struggling to maintain equilibrium between my life and work. At this point in time, my job was playing an integral role in my life – I'd found this job after great difficulty and struggle. I was trying to hold on to it – in spite of all the emotional pressures … and questions. Also, I was genuinely trying to prove myself, as my mother's last words kept echoing deep within, 'you have to become something!'

Jivesh is the anchor of my life. He offered me a sense of security. But I was conscious of our financial status. I could not have asked for more. What I badly needed was a personal office with a computer and a library. I could then work on my own, even at late hours. For my extra work I was using our office facilities. It was holding me back till late. I used to board almost the last bus to reach home, sometimes walking long distances in unsafe conditions. Fear is an emotion I don't allow as my mission is my challenge. My mother's faith was alive in me like Saptrishi stars in the sky.

Whenever I reached home, I could see the family waiting for me for dinner. There was silent recrimination in their eyes, and a burden of guilt in my heart. But after a month of staying late, it suddenly stopped. I was relieved of the guilt. Jivesh sometimes waited patiently, but in spite of an understanding of the nature of my profession and the resultant workload, he used to be upset. As a college professor, his working hours were not so intensive. He had almost a set routine of five days of work in a week.

Upon returning, he went for socializing with his friends like Kisna, Kevan, Ismail and Bano. He must have been missing me in the gathering. But I missed him too.

The day I was to make a presentation of the layout designs of the new colony, I was very nervous. For two months, I was working hard on the project. Ignoring what was going on in the outside world, I concentrated on ways to elevate my work to a fine art. It was as if my soul, my very consciousness, was to be revealed in front of the judges in the near future.

To an architect, history means a lot. To understand the historical facts about the nation is vital, for these give a context and a perspective. But the future is to undertake a journey without maps. In a sense, the architects are futurologists – they predict and they create – they help a nation develop. I'd gathered that historically – and tragically – the blacks could not experience the whiteness, with all its implications and layers of meanings. Similarly, the whites could not feel the blackness or the human aspect of being black. Both the races maintained a distance from each other's humanness and psyche. In South Africa, there was a hardened line of demarcation between the two colours. The rulers had remained in their white zone, a quarantined glasshouse of the elite which was so remote that they could not even see or feel the miseries of the coloureds.

The coloureds continued to be confined to 'Grey Graveyards'. But in the mid '70s, during the era of Bantustan independence within the country and the guerrilla movement, an era of black-white dialogue on federalism emerged. It was an era of reemergence of mass black activism in the form of strikes within the labour force. The clerk working in our office informed me that he was raised in the hostel of the 'Helping Hand Club'– a kind of orphanage of black people who belonged to 'The Pass Law System'. It was riddled with irregularities adding to the injustice. At that time, there was immense frustration of the newly privileged class – who were actually the unprivileged class, the blacks.

Considering the heavy and often unbearable past, I wanted to create something which was pleasant and unwinding, projecting a dazzling future. Something that makes you want to belong. When I displayed my designs to Mr Subramaniam and his team, they looked at it carefully. Then he remarked, 'Anvita, I feel the township looks as attractive as a resort. But do you think it is viable … economically?'

The residential houses in my plan were facing an artificially created small oval lake surrounded by an oval garden. To match it, I had designed the roofs into a sloping curve. It was were different from all the normal stereotypical British designs that common there. A double-storied building that was to function as a school and a church were similar in appearance. These were near the residential colony and stood out from a distance. They were elevated from the ground level and looked majestic. I could sense the entire team was discussing something that they thought ought to be there. Someone said, 'Please rectify and make a flat ceiling as this is not very practical.' Mr Subramaniam suggested that I had projected my Indian self into the whole project while the new generation of consumers including Europeans needed to be satisfied.'

'But, Sir,' I defended myself, 'our demographic structure is a positive factor for South Africa. The new generation is engaged in a process of learning. To help them emerge from their past and make them experience a phase of liberalization, we have to provide them with something that is different, something that not only brings comfort but accords them a feeling of dignity. That is why I've elevated the plinth.'

'Why do you always dream, Anvita?' I looked into his deep blue eyes. They were strikingly unusual.

'Dreams have played an important role in my personal growth. I feel nobody can do without them because dreams become vision and the vision transforms into a mission. Only a mission can lead you to achieve difficult goals. And sir, this is a goal oriented project for me. I've put my heart and soul into this project …'

'But Anvita …' His eyes seemed to possess an intriguing gaze.

'Sir, don't forget that the township is different from a settlement, and it is for those who are at the bottom of the pyramid, those who are destitute, whether blacks, mixed or whites. I'm trying hard to provide them an upliftment – an opportunity to identify with a living, sensuous soul.'

All the other panelists grilled me for hours. I was confident they will not be able to ignore my enthusiasm or my perseverance. And, of course, these discussions help in building mutual trust which not only improves official work but contributes in building relationships.

I waited till they approved my designs. I had tears in my eyes when they said, 'OK Anvita. Congratulations for a very nice plan. We will submit it to the town-planners as it is … then we will let you know.'

'Thank you, sir!' I could not control myself from trembling … my tears mingled with my achievement.

While I was leaving the office, I could hear Mr Subramaniam telling the rest of the staff, 'Anvita is courageous. I feel she is very real and sets an example for humanity, besides being a good architect.'

I thought of my mother, Bua, Jo Jo Uncle, Sanju … my past. What an uninformed, unimpressive neglected clump of clay I was … was this my metamorphosis? Or was it coming back to my self? The pleasure of creating something by fusing mind and soul was a kind of magic, it made me feel as if I was floating on clouds.

My bus was taking me back home where Jivesh would be waiting. I started reading the names of the shops across the road. 'Regent Tailors' (for the world famous BT drape cut), 'Dattar Tailors bespoke tailors and customers'; 'Jagan Bros – for the man of distinction'. A few shops had Gujarati boards and invariably displayed gold jewellery in their showcases. How surprising – I pass these shops everyday yet had never noticed their existence. I looked at my own clothes – my crumpled salwar suit was old and faded. Suddenly, I realized I had been here in South Africa for the past two years and had not bought anything for myself except for the bare necessities. Bano always commented on my appearance, about my 'behnji looks' I know what she meant. I counted on her opinion – though our personalities did not match. Yet, it was she who had provided me with that insight. Why hadn't Jivesh mentioned it? I could not reveal it to her but I was handing over all my earnings to Jivesh like a dutiful wife. But maybe today I will tell him that I needed to shop. To buy a computer was a priority … but I will buy some business suits too, like the ones Bano and other girls in the office wear.

When I reached home Leelaji opened the door. 'Oh! Anvita! You have come home early!'

'Yes, mom. But where is Jivesh? He normally comes back by this time.'

'Jivesh has gone to Johannesburg, … hasn't he told you?'

'No, he didn't. I was in office … I tried to call him on his cellphone but it was switched off constantly.' I did not want to have the usual thoughts – not raise suspicions … didn't want to disillusion my relationship. I wanted to think of the horizons – positive and affirmative.

I remember Bano once telling me, 'Don't spend your entire life waiting for other people to respect you. On the contrary, you have to snatch respect from others. Come out of that outdated shell. Start living in the present – it's a world of opportunities out there. There is nothing wrong with striving to improve your life situation.'

I asked Laura to bring me some tea and a samosa. I'd forgotten to take my usual lunch of a sandwich to the office. She looked at me in a strange way. Was it because I'd asserted myself as a member of the family for the first time? Which made me wonder if I was unaware of myself as a family member?

The television showed the same news repeatedly. There was a strike in the city of Johannesburg. It was overpowering. All the teachers, nurses, doctors and others were collectively demanding a 12 per cent raise in their salaries. They were interviewing a 31-year-old teacher from Soweto, Johannesburg's main black township. She was struggling to make ends meet as a substitute teacher in a state school during the day and teaching at the adult education centre at night. She earned about 4,000 Rands a month to support a family of ten members. She looked frail and worn out – about ten years older than she actually was. I know Jivesh was getting only 6,000 Rands, and he was supporting both his parents and me. On the TV, they said they were struggling to be heard. They were talking about nurses and doctors who were disillusioned with low salaries and difficult working conditions and had left the country's well-known hospitals – leaving too many vacancies unfilled and a large mass of patients unattended. As they knew that the African National Congress was about to announce a new policy and scheme with an increase in wages, the impatient public sector had launched one of the largest campaigns in the country's recent history.

There was a huge crowd all around the place. They were not unruly nor were they shouting slogans. They were just holding posters of their protests. Somewhere in that crowd, I could easily identify Jivesh. But before I could say anything, Leelaji said, 'Oh! I can see Jivesh. There he is with Kisna! See there he is wearing that blue striped shirt!'

'Yes. Yes! I can see him … he is busy talking to that white girl …'

'Ja … Ja. She is Julia … his friend. She teaches literature in the same college.'

'But Jivesh teaches Science & Technology …?'

'Yes, but they are fighting for the same cause. The outcome of the earlier strike was that they were offered 6 per cent raise plus a revised salary structure and better benefits. But the agreement was not fulfilled. The Trade Unions also downed tools for a day in their support. But nothing came out of it.'

From what I know, Jivesh was in the department of Science & Technology. He was working on Science Education, which could help at the core of national development. He was engaged in developing policies and programmes for attracting talent for the study of science building career with a focus on rejuvenating research in universities. He was trying to build up a trained workforce that could help in maximizing productivity. He was also trying to identify different categories of workers like those involved in construction or the furnishing industry or in retail. His objective was to develop a sufficient level of skills among the workers through programmes and to conduct rigorous training at college level. For the vocational training programmes, they were preparing interactive media platforms, satellite, Internet and radio.

Jivesh mainly worked on theory-oriented courses. Another group of professors were working on lab-centric sciences. He was very involved – travelling to Cape Town or Jo'burg for identifying industrial belts for training people.

After the strike, he reached home tired and exhausted – and very upset about the system. I also gathered from reports in the papers that the general sympathy of the people was with the strikers, mainly because they all knew that the economy of the country was doing better than ever. As I read in one of the reports, the economy of South Africa had grown by about 5 per cent a year over the past four years. The stock exchange had given handsome returns and the government was running a budget surplus. The booming sectors of the economy such as construction and retail had contributed to the creation of over half a million jobs in the past one year. It was a record of sorts. But trade unions declared that many South Africans do not benefit from the rising prosperity and that the big business gets a disproportionate share of the cake. Many new jobs were casual and a third to half of the population was still doomed to be abysmally poor. The official unemployment rate was reportedly slowly dipping from its peak of the early 2000s, but still continued at a higher side of 25 per cent. However, if we took a broader definition, it worked out to be around 40 per cent.

2

That evening, I got an opportunity to go back to the city with Mr Subramaniam. When he offered to give me a lift in his car, I immediately accepted. There was so much to be discussed about work plans. The multitude of questions in my mind was making me restless. The working patterns were magnifying the many difficulties about what was to be implemented or modified. We discussed it for almost an hour, focusing on rectifying many aspects of design plans. He was very clear about his ideas – very conscious of his thought patterns. He answered all my queries patiently. Though our portfolios contained completely different jobs, I needed to connect, as I could not handle it alone. Above all, I needed some kind of personal security in our professional relationship too.

Suddenly, he said, 'Ok. Anvita, enough is enough. No more discussions about your architectural plans. Learn this in life – never shy away from any kind of struggle … as it is a never-ending process. But try to make the struggle a gift, a gift that adds certainty in one's life.'

I looked at him. I was touched by his affectionate smile. Though I had never focused on his appearance, I suddenly realized that he was very sophisticated and had a touch of elegance in his manners.

He gave instructions to the driver to stop near a cluster of very modern-looking buildings.

'Are you fond of art, Anvita?'

Caught in a zone of 'no mind' and yet totally aware of the question, I didn't know what to say.

'I don't know sir!' I blurted.

'Come. We're going to an art exhibition and I'm sure after working all those long hours, you will like it. Do you know Indian art is appreciated greatly all around the world? Have you seen Husain's or Tyeb Mehta's paintings? They are prominent artists of India.'

'I'm sorry sir. I don't remember seeing their art. At this point of time sir, for me, my career and my survival are my priority. I'm not even sure of my likes and dislikes.'

'But I like to be surrounded by art – that is why I've collected some.'

His condescending tone was opening a mystical door in my heart.

'You know Anvita, art is extraordinary in an ordinary life. It elevates your thinking and transforms your aesthetic spirit to make you a realist and a humanist.'

'I'm sorry – I'm not much into art, sir. But definitely today is my life's new beginning.'

We entered a fairly large hall which contained a few paintings on the walls and an artistic display of ceramics. Like us, there were some visitors going around the exhibition and getting photographed with the artist. I followed Mr Subramaniam when he paused in front of a painting to look at it from various angles. I too did the same. I could gather that all the paintings were symbolic of some kind of painful void created through some tragic loss. Most of the human figures were skeleton-like, sitting amidst dark shadows with broken plates and empty eyes. The paintings filled me with an invisible sorrow and a strange, inexplicable tension. The artist was black. One of the paintings greatly impressed me. It was of a crying child who sat on a torn cloth with an empty bowl. One of his hands was raised towards the sky. The title of the painting was *'Uthi kle! Wemah kle! We mah!* (You hear me cry: O mother, I break. O mother.)

I could see that Mr Subramaniam too could not take his eyes off the painting. When the artist came towards us, I could not help saying, 'I must congratulate you … I'm sure, this is your masterpiece.'

'Thank you!' he had a deep and penetrating voice. His expression was also very philosophic when he continued, 'Thank you. Actually, this one is a transformation of a satirical nursery rhyme that serves as an entertainment to the black children. But for me, it only means hunger and loss of the mother, only she could have filled the empty bowl.'

'Most of his paintings reflect dark and tangled motivations, where politics and psyche struggle to accommodate in the South African personality,' Mr Subramaniam informed me. 'These ones,' he pointed at one cluster of paintings, 'depict a biting but elegant attack on the white complacency.'

'Oh!' I tried to grasp his words. It was a new area of learning for me. For the first time in my life, I realized that a pot or a utensil which we use everyday for serving, or eating food, can become a work of art. Simple clay transformed into divine imagery to provide it an identity. For me, the whole experience was overwhelming and unusual.

When we came out of the exhibition hall and walked towards the car, I realized Mr Subramaniam was very serious. Was he deeply immersed in art? I wasn't sure. Suddenly he said, 'Would you like to see my collection of art, Anvita?'

I wanted to go home. It had been a long, hard day. I was very tired and hungry. But Mr Subramaniam's serious face made me reply, 'Why not, Sir? It will be an honour for me.'

As we sat in the car, he said, 'I think, Anvita that our duty as builder is not only to fill gaps in the bridges, but we also have to provide people a bonding between races, cultures and nations. And you cannot do it if you don't understand the psyche of the people. Any kind of art – visual or performing – offers you an insight – to help distinguish the light from the darkness – the darkness of light. Art is almost the romantic conviction that there is a hidden philosophy under the cover of life – which we should understand to create a new visible world.'

Mr Subramaniam's living room was filled with a variety of paintings and many black and white photographs framed in beautiful silver frames. I had not seen any room like this in my entire life … yes in all of my thirty-seven years. The whole room was bedecked with Victorian furniture and covered in expensive upholstery. I was awe struck as I'd never seen a picture perfect room like that before.

'I've inherited some paintings from my grandparents – and some I've collected. Now I'm used to their presence around me – they break the circle of my solitude.'

'You look at them every day, Sir … with the same emotions with which you bought them?'

'No, Anvita. Not always. But slowly, they have become a part of my life and consciousness.'

His servant brought some coffee and cookies for us … I wondered where his wife and children were.

I asked, 'Your wife is not around, sir?'

'I'm not married, Anvita.'

'Oh!' I sipped the coffee and ate something to remain calm – but there was an inevitable inquisitiveness quaking in my heart and making me restless. I could not shake off my eyes from a portrait of an old lady. She was sitting elegantly on a chair, clad in a delicately embroidered black and white sari. Her sea blue eyes enclosed a cold winter – looking at them sent a shiver down my spine.

'Who is she … Sir?'

'She is my mother, Anvita. She died in an asylum.' His words epitomized his feelings of isolation powerfully. A simmering silence gripped both of us, as we sat in that dimly lit room.

'I'd a very traumatic youth, Anvita. My father was an Indian and my mother a German lady. Firstly, my grandparents never forgave them for their marriage. Then my father was sent to jail as a political prisoner, where he died. My mother could not reconcile herself to all of this and became insane.'

My mother was an only child. So my grandparents lived with us for a while. But they hated me because of my colour. When my mother was sent to the asylum, they secured my future by admitting me to a boarding school. I studied architecture in Cape Town. But when I came home – intermittently as it was – I couldn't stand the distorted face of my mother, who was a beauty in her younger days. I was also disgusted with her condition and avoided seeing her while she was alive. Circumstances deteriorated to such an extent that I could not even bid her goodbye when she died. Maybe I relived the horrors of my childhood experiences – when my mad mother would howl, burn me with cigarettes and sometimes lock me in the room at a time when all I needed was love and attention. She was beyond the realm of emotional understanding.

'Now I when contemplate the life I've lived, it seems to consist of a series of sensations. I can recall my father's smiling face only in a family portrait.'

Mr Subramaniam had – figuratively – left the room. He'd wafted into his memory lane. I could feel his footsteps far away in the corridors of time … while his mother's portrait continued to haunt me.

'Isn't it the agony – Anvita – of dying human beings struggling to articulate some last thought, wish or even regret – yet not succeeding in expressing themselves … and the words die on the lips of the dead? My father in his heroism, or cowardice, wanted to convey something to me. Or take my mother in her saner moments, she may have wanted to express her love. But seasons changed so fast – death overpowered the rhythm of life. Many years have passed but I cannot share a normal attitude towards life or death. I feel without love or friendship life is a disillusionment.'

'It must have been very difficult to live alone in such horrific circumstances and still remain as human as you are. Sir, I really appreciate your courage.'

'Anvita, I wanted to tell you about one more thing. It's my complex about life … I never had a mirror in my bedroom. I only see my face while brushing or shaving in the bathroom. I'm not self-obsessed, nor have I ever tried to lean on others for support to overcome my loneliness. It was always my inner self or inner voice that guided me while taking life's decisions to make me what I am. Fulfilling my physical needs was not my mission. I mainly believed, and worked, for my profession.'

I looked outside the window to hide my tears. It was pitch-dark. The sky was washed clean by the heavy rains. Again the silence enveloped us. We sat quietly in the realm of thoughtlessness, unaware of time. I began wondering, why was my every experience a discovery?

3

When I reached back home, I could sense a peculiar tension in the air. Jivesh was watching television with his parents.

'Hi. How is everybody?' I waited for a response.

Jivesh looked at his watch. 'It's 9 o'clock. Where were you Anvita?'

'Coming straight from the worksite. You know how far it is, Jivesh. I had to change three buses. Have you all had your dinner?'

'How could we? Laura has not come. Mom has a terrible headache.'

'Oh really! Don't worry. I will cook something!'

I had bought a few things from the supermarket. I often used to buy some groceries from the 'Bhoolabhai Store' on my way back home. Those were usually things not stocked in the house such as juices, curd, chilli pickle, some vegetables and brown bread.

I kept the grocery bag in the kitchen and my office bag in my room, washed my face and hands and prepared myself to cook for the family, though I was not good at it. But being the daughter-in-law, it was my duty to do so. Before commencing cooking, I opened a large bottle of juice and offered it to all of them. I filled a glass for myself. Neither Leelaji nor Jivesh offered to help. I got ready to cook all by myself. I made use of all the four burners of our cooking range. On the one side, I kept rice for boiling and on the other I placed the daal. The third was being utilized for making baigan ka bharta, while I fried some onions on the fourth along with some peas for the pulav. When everything was on the verge of simmering, I laid the table with plates, katoris and curd along with my chilli pickle, glasses and water. It took me 45 minutes to prepare the food. Leelaji looked at me with surprise. They ate well and enjoyed the meal. Pratapji praised my bharta and Jivesh loved the pulao. But Leelaji ate very little. Dinner at this late hour for her was difficult to digest.

After dinner, I was drenched in sweat and fatigue from washing all the dishes. My legs began to tremble. When I entered my bedroom, Jivesh was already there in his night clothes. There was new Hindi music playing on the tape recorder.

'Oh my office suit has become dirty. I forgot to take it off before cooking.'

'Oh yeah! Anvita. I was about to comment that you look very different and professional in this dress … when did you buy this?'

'When you were travelling for your strikes. I bought this with Bano's help as everyone had started commenting on my "behnji" look. I also became very conscious of my drab Punjabi suits when I travelled with Mr Subramaniam in his car. He is so sophisticated – dressed so elegantly all the time! So after we visited the art exhibition, I promised myself to buy some new clothes.'

He watched me while I was removing the counterpane. He stood up, came near me and said, 'Ok, madam architect, can I undress you to reach my wife?' His hands were unbuttoning my dress. I looked into his eyes. I could feel a compelling desire floating under his eyelids.

'Can I take a bath, my dear husband? I'm sweating and smelling of food.' He was about to kiss my neck but stopped. 'Yes … yes … but be quick.'

Even though water is usually therapeutic, but it couldn't wash away my tiredness. I knew my body was supposed to perform marital duties and even if you don't want it, you have to show you are in love. I wrapped a towel around my wet body and entered the bedroom.

The music was very suggestive. I could feel the life in the air beckoning me for merriment and joy. The melodious voice of Lata Mangeshkar enhanced the romantic atmosphere of the room. I slipped under the sheets where Jivesh was already waiting for me. The smell of his naked body was intoxicating. The way he moved his body, his gestures and flexibility were unusually sensual, sensitive and provocative. But it was strangely different. He started from my feet. He kissed and licked each of my fingertips, my toes and then my trembling legs for a considerably longer time. It was not his usual way of making love. My fatigue disappeared. My heart started to pound with desire. We lay clinging to each other for I don't know how long. But when the tape started playing again, it worked potently to quicken our desires. We had to go back to the pleasure – and joy – of our bodies. We could not help ourselves.

'I've already taken a second janam with you darling … within this life … and you're aware of it.'

'Yes,' he said, 'I, a Brahmin married to a Punjabi Khatri as you put it. Haven't I elevated your status? You should be grateful!'

I looked at him in surprise. Why did this reference to caste inequality crop up between us? And that too at this moment. I did not want to think of anything … just could not … I wanted to sleep … I don't know why.

When I got up, it was still very dark. I looked at the watch. It was 5 a.m. Jivesh was fast asleep. I went straight to the bathroom, took a shower. I had to work. I had to finish an article for *Architectural Digest* about our 'N. 2 Gateway Project'. Mr Maratawa Naso was very keen that it should appear in the earliest issue of the magazine. I settled on the dining table with a cup of tea and began to write:

Location: Outskirts of Durban

Client: City Planners

Area: 258,000 square metres, 2.4 million sq. feet.

Structure: Laminated timber, light steel.

Material: Aluminum, blue stone, quarry tiles, polished granite.

I began to sketch. I used modern clean lines with lots of open spaces around the row of houses. Every house had a curved ceiling, an element that echoed the mountains. The mountains provided a picturesque backdrop to the colony.

Homes are our most intimate structures. When we live in such a building we look for comfort, practicality and privacy. I had created an artificial oval lake with an oval garden to evoke the dreams and aspirations in the three realms – living, working and for elevating the spirit.

There was a touch of Indian imagery in my design. I'd provided small verandahs in front of each house overlooking the small private garden and then the larger one in order to incorporate a sensitivity intended towards uplifting one's individuality. I knew that listening to the sounds of nature like the ripples of water, the rustling of calm forest leaves reduces stress. All the elements we were going to use were simple, natural, functional and accessible and were designed to flow with the natural terrain.

We were going to provide many other structures and facilities for this row of houses including schools, hospital, church along with tennis courts, gym, spa, swimming pool and a huge business centre.

In one hour's time, I had only written three or four pages. My output was very little. With a computer, I could have finished the article by now. I promised myself I'd buy one that very day.

Jivesh rushed in to demand his cup of tea. I saw Pratapji getting ready for his morning walk. I had to leave my article abruptly to prepare tea for them and for Leelaji.

'Jivesh, I've to buy a laptop. I can't function without one. Will you help me get one?'

'Why can't you use your office one?'

'My workload has increased and I've to work extra-time. With a laptop, I can operate from here and increase my productivity.'

'But where is the money? You've already spent a huge amount on your clothes!'

Bano's advice kept on ringing in my ears. 'Anvita, maintain your financial independence and identity by keeping at least one bank account of your own!'

I could gather from his tone that he was not going to help me. In the past six months, I had given him most of the money I'd earned. My clothes were essential for my work identity which may have chafed him.

I got up and collected my papers. I could see some questions were welling up in his eyes.

'Don't worry. I will earn much more when I'm equipped with a proper office of my own. To begin with, I will ask mom for the room in the basement. I will convert it into my office.'

The telephone bell rang. Jivesh picked it up. I got busy in preparing some breakfast and lunch for the family. I also started thinking. I'd walked away from a lot just for Jivesh. I'd changed my country … changed my culture … and for what? Now a challenge is being thrown at me. I took a deep breath to handle it … Yes, there is no room for short cuts. I have to focus all my energies on my work.

'Hey, Anvita! It was your cousin Sanju. He is planning a trip to South Africa.'

'What? Sanju called after so many months … or is it almost two years?'

'Yeah! He said he will be participating in an art exhibition in Jo'burg. It is scheduled to be held next month. Besides, he wants to meet both of us.'

'Really? I'm very surprised. Firstly, that he is interested in meeting me. And secondly, that he has become an artist. Whatever I remember of him and Nony, they were both very practical and dry people … not sentimental enough to believe in emotional ties or to become an artist. Art is an expression of human emotions, which they both lack.'

'Anyway …he is sending all the details of his programme … and love to you.'

'Oh … love.' All the past memories started to well up in my mind. Our backward town … the market … Chajju Halwai's sweetshop … Sara Baji's bangle shop … her language … kites … All the colours of the past cast an interesting rainbow of images in my mind. My article got swept away by the rush of those images.

4

On the first day of the earth-breaking ceremony, I insisted that before starting the construction, we must perform some kind of puja. When I was in India, I noticed that newspapers daily announced the ritual of Bhoomi Puja for a new building before they started any civil work on the site. But nobody really understood what it meant!

I gathered a few things from Pratapji as he was more religious than Leelaji. I borrowed a book of Vedic prayers, roli and some rice for tilak. I also obtained a metal diya with oil and cotton and a box of sweets. I picked up a few roses from the shop near the bus stop. When I reached office, I was told to go to the site with Mr Naso and Bano. I was not aware of the social norms of this country, but I was introducing something that I believed in myself. I wanted to create an emotional ambience of peace and harmony as the dominant viewpoint for the people who were to occupy these residential apartments. I didn't tell anyone of my plans. I was concerned they would discourage me.

When we reached the site, I carried my bag of puja items to the spot where we were going to commence the digging. There were a lot of people from the villages, some people from the town planner's office and our own office, and of course Mr Naso's crew which was to carry out the construction. We all waited for Mr Subramaniam to arrive.

When he walked towards the place, I hurriedly kept my puja items on a flat stone and lighted my diya and aggarbattis.

'What are you doing, Anvita?' asked Mr Naso and Bano.

'I'm preparing for Bhoomi Puja. I'm sure you'll allow me, sir?' I looked at Mr Subramaniam, as I quickly applied a roli tikka on his forehead, without even waiting for his answer.

'You're amazing, Anvita. Always charged with unusual aspects of human nature!' His blue eyes had a magnificent gaze enough to mesmerize anyone.

'But why do you want to do it?' Mr Naso seemed very perplexed.

'Mr Naso, in India we believe that the Earth is not just a mass of soil – but it is a living expression of God … we call it Dharti Ma. It provides us everything including food. We have to seek her permission through this ritual before we dig even an inch of soil.'

'It is really unheard of here. We're not aware of it. But of course, I remember Aristotle saying "Nature does nothing uselessly".'

'Even in our Muslim mythology, we believe that nature is a living entity – it feels and senses everything and responds to human being's feelings,' Bano commented.

'Yes. That's why we believe in Bhoomi Puja. It is for praying to Dharti Ma for her blessings – as we all know Dharti Ma belongs to man and man belongs to her.'

'OK … now, let's start Anvita. I'm impressed with your faith – which is always deeper than ideas.'

I made the holy Swastika sign at the place where we were going to begin the earth breaking. Then I lit my diya and incense sticks, spread a few rose petals along with rice and from the prayer book started reciting mantras for the well being and benign influence on many unknown lives. I bent towards the earth with folded hands and touched it.

Mr Naso clicked a photograph. Suddenly, I became nervous and concerned about the disparate interpretations of the puja. But I was sure everyone was quite attentive and the fragrance of the aggarbattis was evoking a certain kind of intimacy in togetherness.

It was indeed a humble step to create a positive world through Indian values. As it is said 'Men may come and go – but a generation (that is going to inhabit) goes on forever and ever.' I was just trying to make it happen.

The work had started. They were digging up the land to lay the pipes and the roads. As it was to be a newly developed residential suburb, we left the site half surrounded by a few old family settlements. These were built on a hilly area and by the embankment along the railway tracks – so that the old character could be maintained.

Maritawa Naso and I, along with two other people were going to the site together in our office car. While on the way, we discussed the various alternatives and implementation of work plans. Mr Naso had earlier undertaken field trips to study indigenous villages in various parts of Natal and Deloga Bays. His interest was reflected in the design. He emphasized that the need of any building was to reflect spatial relationships. It should also reflect family and community relationships.

When the discussions ended, he switched on the music system in his car. 'Are you fond of music, Anvita?' He pronounced my name with a very heavy African accent.

'Not really, Mr Naso. But I'm learning to enjoy and appreciate fine arts of life. A few days back, I visited an art exhibition with Mr Subramaniam and was impressed with local art. Since then I'm trying to figure out how philosophical gravity of art and and music plays a role in one's life.'

'If he ever invites you again, don't miss his private collection of art … and old family portraits … they are all priceless!'

'Oh really? I'm only aware of popular Indian music, mostly from our old films … the popular numbers that were played in our home when I was young. As far as I recollect, they had considerable literary merit.'

'If you hear our old songs, you will find that they are humming with the harsh realities of life … not the humour or beauty of life … and a nameless, incomprehensible pain.

'Let me tell you something very interesting about the relationship between art and music, Anvita. When I was about ten years old, I was taken to the caves in Lebombo Mountains by an old friend of our family. These caves are located in the northern part of Zululand. That guide was an old woman of about ninety or more. She said that the caves were there even when she was a child. Those were used as a hiding place during the wars and endless battles fought between the Zulus and Swazis. Some of the dwellers in those caves were my ancestors who fled during the war after Shaka's army invaded Ntabankulu, the ancestral home of the Mtshali clan. She told us that her forefathers had settled in the Northern Zululand and Swaziland. I was very young at that time, Anvita. But, I can never forget that exciting bit of history. I still remember it vividly, as if that old crone had related it only last night. I remember seeing the timeless relics of my past, like clay pots, crude iron tools and the kiln where iron was smelted to imikhontho (forge assegais), izizenze (battle axes), occelemba (hatchets) and of amazeja (course hoes) for tilling the soil.'

'How lucky, you have witnessed a past that was buried in the layers of forgotten caves.'

'Ja ... whenever I visit a museum and see the excavated archaeological artifacts, as they call it – I try to collect the debris of my shattered culture and immortalize it in my designs wherever I can.'

My other colleague, Mr Parini, who was also with us added, 'The greatest tragedy that ever befell the black man in the southern parts of Africa is not that they could not invent the wheel, but that they could not write. But the cave paintings of our Abathwa people are still preserved in the mountains of South Africa.'

'Thank God for that!'

'You cannot ignore the most important contribution by our conservationists – musical instruments from various parts of Africa as an evidence of a great musical heritage of our country. And all the old songs and lyrics are still alive as they were passed down orally and not recorded. They are still as fresh as they were when our great grandmothers sang them. We are thankful to those who have preserved them.'

Along with art and music, we talked about the cultures to which Africa had been exposed through slavery, colonization and settlement.

'We Africans have lived in South Africa since time immemorial. That is according to indisputable black historical facts. The other version that we came to South Africa from the equator at the same time as the honourable Mr Jahvan Riebeeck in 1652 is nothing but fiction.'

Our team reached the school we'd planned to see for the township. While getting out of the car, Mr Naso said, 'I believe at the core of my heart that this world is created for all of us, whatever the colour of our skins. It's only we, our ability that can change the world.'

'So have faith in yourself ...'

The school was in Phoenix Township – a very simple building in red brick architecture. The building had a small garden in front where we could see a lot of children roaming around, clearly showing a lack of discipline. They all wore black trousers and white shirts, perhaps symbolizing its 60 per cent Indian and 40 per cent African division.

When we entered the visitor's room, it was amazingly different from what I had imagined. It appeared to be more of a railway platform than a school reception as it was plastered with posters. Most of these were mainly graphic illustrations against AIDS, sexual control, the responsibilities of a pupil in a classroom and advice against vandalism. There was a huge portrait of President Nelson Mandela and President Mbeki along with a new flag of South Africa. An Indian greeted us. He took us around the few blocks of the building. He said, 'Our educational programme is based on five courses of study that are meant to suit the needs and interests of each student. We conceived the school as a system of spatial layers. A great deal of visual and verbal communication is made possible between students of different layers of colour discrimination.'

He then talked about the teachers. He said that they believed in selecting teachers who are known to be humane and were multicultural. Because the need was to learn more about ourselves, confront the racism and biases as well as learn to see reality from a variety of perspectives.

While we were walking through the corridor, we heard a commotion in one of the classrooms. When we reached the door of that classroom, we saw a very big, oversized black girl kicking a thin Indian boy. Instead of resolving the scuffle, the teacher stood in one corner, frightened and trembling. What we gathered about the incident was that the black girl had not done her homework. When she asked the Indian boy who was sitting next to her for help, he refused. Infuriated, she got up and punched him on his nose then kicked and slapped him. She was so big that he could not do anything to save himself – she even appeared much older than him. The teacher was nervous. As soon she saw us, she almost cried. 'I'm powerless because I cannot even punish them. When we tried to defy apartheid, we had this utopian ideal that integration is the best way to solve apartheid's discriminatory policies. But the reality is very different. They form gangs and we have knowledge that they are armed and ready to fight, for our own safety we maintain a distance.'

Our administrative officer smiled at us. 'This is only a mild incident, in comparison with others.'

As we moved out of the school, I visualized our intended building blending abstractly – influenced by regional, local, historical and geological images into propaganda for the triumph of emotions over objective reality.

When I reached home late in the evening, I found a copy of *Architecture Digest* lying on my table. I opened it with trembling hands. I could not believe it. My article had appeared in the journal. My heart began to beat faster. I stood speechless with wonder. It was my name in print. It made me nostalgic. There was something about it, a strange beauty, a strange stillness – words, drawings, illustrations – full of my own self, yet unnamable. Maybe, it was because all my life, I felt I was born with an empty canvas – a canvas meant to paint for myself. Suddenly I was afraid, afraid of what I don't know. Was it a fear of success or fear of life? I didn't know.

I showed my article to Leelaji and Pratapji. They were happy and blessed me and wished that I achieve more. I missed Jivesh – he was in Cape Town. I called him late at night and told him about the article. He congratulated me and told me that we would celebrate when he come back. I later wondered about the meaning of his remark, 'You're really beyond what I know of you – Anvita!' Was I different? I didn't know. But I could feel that life was becoming more challenging and more meaningful.

When I reached office the next day, Bano congratulated me. I could see genuine happiness in her eyes and words. When I entered Mr Subramaniam's office, he was going through some papers. But he got up immediately from his chair, walked past his huge table and hugged me. There was an unusual perfume exuding from his body. The aroma instantly reminded me of some exotic flower and the beauty of a large tree laden with thick green leaves that provides solace and peace. In that moment of silence – numerous unspoken words were conveyed. I almost felt as if I was sitting motionless near the bank of a beautiful river. It was strange. I had never felt as significant as I felt at that moment. Without uttering a word, I walked out of his office.

Everyone wanted to celebrate the event, especially Bano. So we all decided to go out for lunch. Bano was assigned to ask Mr Subramaniam to join us. He graciously agreed.

All of us got into one car. I could see that the monsoon had set in. The sea was almost black under the dark and heavy clouds. The trees near the seashore swayed in the breeze. How I wanted to walk on the seashore and touch the gigantic sea waves with my fingers! But I knew

I could never do it, it was not safe. Bano said, 'Today's newspapers said that it will rain, rain for a few days, torrential rains …'

'Yeah. I'm aware of the weather forecast. Let us go to the Blue Water for lunch!'

We entered the small lobby of the hotel. I remembered I'd come there with Jivesh for some book launch. Mr Subramaniam held my hand when we walked towards the restaurant – the roughness of his fingers mirrored the softness of his heart.

While we were walking, some people greeted Mr Subramaniam. He was quite well known and respected. After we'd settled down and ordered food, Bano said, 'I'm glad to be a commoner, for there is power in being able to publicly misbehave and speak loudly without anyone noticing or remembering it.'

'But today, you can't do that Bano as you're with someone who is known and one who is going to make a name.' Mr Naso looked at me with a meaningful glance.

'Oh … please … it is a very simple and ordinary thing to write an article … look at those who write volumes … novels … poetry or paint masterpieces!'

'One can create masterpieces in architectural designs also, Anvita. You should aim for that.'

'Oh, Mr Naso … don't give me so much importance. I've just begun to breathe.'

'There is a saying "it is better to have loved and lost than never to have loved at all",' Bano said as we ate out food, 'try Anvita, and you will reach heights of writing, I'm sure.'

Mr Subramaniam said, 'What I like about you Anvita is your simplicity. I cannot handle the ladies with heavy makeup. They put me off. I feel I am with someone who is not real. They are artificial, but you're real. And your beauty is your intelligence. I thoroughly enjoyed the way you performed puja at the site.'

'Thank you, sir. I'm always open to constructive criticism. You can tell me freely about my flaws.'

'I will. But only when there is a need.'

'Hey Anvita! Enjoy the food and celebrate your mind because it can take you to greater heights. Celebrate the world around us,' Bano enthused.

It was a beautiful day. It became even more beautiful when we received our monthly wages. I kept some of the money in my purse and some I hid in my office files. When I stepped out of the office, I didn't realize it was late. It was about 8.30. The last bus dropped me at the nearest stop to the Harfield Road at about 9.30. Many a time, Jivesh had picked me up from the bus stop in his car – but he was not in town. When I got down, there was hardly anyone on the street. I started walking briskly towards our home. Suddenly I saw two African men following me. I started running but they got hold of me. I shouted for help but there was nobody around. I struggled, tried to save myself, but only for a while. I remembered seeing one of them holding a very sharp knife in his hand. I fainted.

5

When I regained consciousness, I was in a hospital. The light was dim and hazy but I could see Jivesh sitting on a chair next to my bed. I tried to sit up but could not due to the immense pain in my stomach. My head was also spinning. I cried out loud in pain and against the humiliation every time I drifted into consciousness or came out of sedation. Why did it happen to me, especially on the day I was supposed to celebrate my success?

Jivesh told me that I was stabbed in the stomach twice. As I fell unconscious – they took away my purse which contained money for my laptop.

'Thanks to my 'Connect-Ticket-Circle', Mrs Patel was returning from with her son and she recognized Anvita. She and her son rescued her from these monsters. They ran away with her purse and even shoes .... but they managed to save her office bag. She was the one who informed us and helped take Anvita to the hospital as Jivesh was not here. Her son was kind enough to go through all the formalities,' Leelaji announced with great pride.

'Don't ever come so late, Anvita. You overwork. Every time I tell you this, you just laugh. It is not India, it's not safe here,' Jivesh said.

'Even a hospital which treats Indians is far from our house,' Pratapji added.

I silently reflected how it was scary to be on one's own in a country one doesn't belong to. After that disastrous incident, I was trying to figure out what had happened to me. But I could not remember anything except passing out into a deep darkness. I could not ask anyone … I could not even speak. I spent my time looking out of the window where many small birds sat on a telegraph wire very quietly and close to each other. Their calmness helped me come out of my immense shock.

Bano and Ismail came to see me with Pereeie and Kisna after they heard what I'd been through. It was nice to see all of them concerned. When Pereeie remarked, 'You should thank your stars Anvita that you were not raped,' her words were soothing like a balm. I felt reassured.

Her words echoed in my ears and my immeasurable pain was also somehow reduced. In the quietness and silence of my heart, every movement of thought became still. My existence was gaining profound meaning and beauty all over again.

When we reached home there was a gift lying on our dining table. I opened it. It was a laptop with a note: 'Write more articles and design masterpieces … for you Anvita. – M. Subramaniam'

I sat alone in our garden for a while, looking up in the sky. The sun was fading and before it became dark, a very shy moon showed up alone. Only one star was shining next to the crescent moon, symbolizing beauty and hope. Maybe beauty was not an apt description, it was an emotional response to moon's enchantment. Spellbound, I was meditating on an unknown image of God in my heart.

6

Jivesh brought the packet of medicines and my belongings, gave them to me and disappeared. Not a word of sympathy. It was as if nothing had happened. From my bed, I looked outside the window. Two crows were squabbling in the air – cawing and tearing at each other. They could not find a foothold in the air. So they tumbled down to the earth, struggling with each other. Leelaji brought me a cup of tea. 'Thank God, you are all right Anvita. Life is precious.' She sat with me for a while, enquiring about my health, while Jivesh watched a cricket match on the television.

At night, I waited for him – his sympathetic touch, love and warmth. But it was not to be. Just a few words. Formal, non-formal, stiff. To my surprise, I felt he was not there at all. He was somewhere far away. I did not even know where he was at that moment. I tried to put my arms around him saying, 'Jivesh! I need you! You don't know how much I missed your love!' But he stood strangely aloof. He passed several critical comments based on his often false assumptions. He was criticizing others. How strange human beings are!

I tried to kiss him, saying, 'Hey, love has no distance … don't go away from me Jivesh. Or I will die … and Jivesh! Do you know I was not raped? … if that's at the back of your mind …'

'I know that …,' he replied, not looking into my eyes.

'Then why this distance? Distance only exists if there is some sort of reason or accusation, inward or outward. If there's nothing, why is there this tension?'

All his explanations were a means of escape – turning away from the reality – whatever it was. But it mattered to me. Why was he searching for the reasons and wasting his energy? I was tired. I could not argue anymore. So I swallowed my sleeping pills and just merged into my unconsciousness. It was the only remedy I could think of at the time.

During my recovery from the injuries and helplessness I discovered many things. That our family was not a traditional or stereotypical like Bua's. The women here are supposed to build their own fortunes, make money and look after their own interests. At this moment of pain and distress, I needed Jivesh's extra care and love. But he remained aloof. I'd thought that by now our marriage had reached a stage of friendship and understanding over pure lust. But that is what Jivesh seemed to want.

One day I asked Jivesh, 'Are you satisfied with my recovery? Don't you think I need to consult another doctor and get some vitamins and nutritious food? I feel weak and worn out …'

'But you are taking all the medicines the hospital has prescribed. Next week they have asked you to come for a check up, then you can review your medicines again.'

'How about some nutritious food?' I wanted to know.

'How much of it can our family afford? You must adjust.'

I was shocked. Shaken to the core. Adjust to what? To anything; to cruelty; to your blindness; to snubs; to lies; to unprovoked hostilities; your overpowering whims; as if you happen to be the sole breadwinner of the family?

'Its more than a year since I started working, I gave you whatever I earned … and you are telling me to adjust! Isn't it your duty as a husband to look after me?'

'The problem with you Anvita is that you have become too demanding … not only that, after your achievement, you have developed a very individualistic super ego. What do you want to prove … tell me?'

He got up from his chair, and shook my frail body. I could feel some blood oozing from my wound. Still, I maintained my equilibrium and remained calm to understand the situation.

'Jivesh, I'm a dreamer and listen, I'm determined to reach the pinnacle of my career, before I turn forty.'

He looked at me with utter disdain and said, 'I had to clear your huge hospital bills. First, pay back the amount when you get back to your job.' He had stepped down to his objective reality which I was trying to avoid identifying. He left the room to go back to Cape Town for his classes, leaving me behind in incomprehensible pain. I felt cheated.

I could sense that there was tension in the air. To mitigate the humiliation, I needed to become financially independent and self-sufficient. I was left alone to myself. It was important to be alone in that solitude to hear my intense inner silence. It was important to understand how materialistic human relationships are.

Next day, I rang up Mr Subramaniam. I thanked him for the laptop. I rang up Mr Naso to ask him to visit me if he could and hand me some more work that I could do from home. He promised he would do so. I thanked Mrs Patel for saving my life. I called up Bano and asked her if she could organize somehow to take me to the doctor. She promised to come.

I had to review my wardrobe. I had to choose a lifestyle that was distinct and professional. I thought of Phelela, my neighbour who epitomizes an independent woman, who fearlessly speaks her mind and does exactly as she pleases. I hardly possessed any so-called wardrobe. There were a few saris which Vati Aunty and Bua had given me. My salwar suits were worn out and faded. Among my belongings, there was some jewellery, which I'd kept in the locker. I decided to sell some of it and open a bank account with that money. Suddenly, I came across an old velvet bag full of letters. They were by Jo Jo Uncle and Vati Aunty – the ones they had written to each other. How they loved each other, each word bespoke their feelings. There was a strange aroma of old paper and jasmine emanating from those crumbling letters. I touched it to my eyes, my tears also mingled with those tender love lines.

Leelaji woke me up for lunch, which I found quite insipid. Then she announced she was going for her Connect-Ticket-Circle. I requested her to take me along as I needed a change. Pratapji drove us and on our way to Mrs Kaverie's, he treated us to an ice-cream. The bald Guru started chanting with synchronized breathing. It opened a very new spiritual route for me as I felt breathing and chanting together helped me develop patience. And when he said, 'It doesn't matter what cards you are dealt with. What matters is the way you play your cards. So don't waste time complaining, focus on something positive and do stand up for yourself with your own help as the outside world is ruthless. It is not interested in your success.'

I was awestruck. I looked at his closed eyes. How does he know I was seeking an answer to my inner turmoil? When he got up, he gave me a small copy of Bhagvad Gita. I was touched. He said, 'Even a little of this practice of chanting will shelter you from great sorrows!'

The sound of Sanskrit chants had a strange effect on my mind. Almost all of them were chanting collectively and the walls of that room seemed to be vibrating with their echoes. I was wondering what the function of culture is? Was it to heal or totally transform men?

The sky had lost its colour and just over the horizon a new moon shone – young, shy and tender. On the road, everything seemed to be moving. Near the moon, there was no star.

At night, I tossed and turned fitfully on my bed, pondering over the events of the evening. It was a form of torture for me to be alone after such an experience of turbulence.

When I woke up in the morning, I felt very weak and my wound was oozing. There was nobody to help. Jivesh had already left. Lying helplessly in my bed, I thought of many things. I was analyzing matters better than ever before. I was almost convinced that I understood my life but I definitely needed a certain clarity on our relationship. It was causing me untold bitterness. In this city that had become my destination unknown, I was wondering about my alien husband. How much do I know him? Has he gone to earn some extra money or fulfill some commitment? Who knows?

Bano and Ismail took me to a goldsmith where I sold my four gold bangles. Bua had given me these and I'd even worn them during my college days. With the money I got, I opened a bank account. After that they took me to a doctor that they knew was necessary. The doctor was shocked to see my condition. He prescribed medicines to guard against infections. I had to struggle to survive. Help from Bano and Ismail meant a lot as I now knew they were friends and mentors I could bank upon.

Suddenly, I felt ill, shaky. Bano looked at me. It seemed that my skin was turning purple, the colour of eggplant. With ebbing consciousness, we entered the nearest restaurant. I was in severe pain. I thought of Bua – her words echoed in my ears. 'Nanak Dukhiya Sab Sansar'. Pain is part and parcel of every human experience. Lord Buddha had also said 'dukkha' exists and persists in all our lives. But if we are powerful and live within our true selves, the pain may be mitigated. The positive thoughts and a cold drink saved me from fainting. I ate the food as if I had never seen food all my life. I'm sure Bano and Ismail were amazed by my appetite.

While eating, we saw two young men sitting on the table next to ours. One was dressed in a deep pink shirt and the other had a long ponytail. They were enjoying some alcoholic concoction – colourful and frosty. The way they talked and gestured were very different. Ismail said, 'They're top male models of Durban. This is 'gaydom' – a deliberately chosen new way of life. There are a lot of them in the fashion circuit.'

Bano said, 'One of my distant cousins had to go in for a live-in relationship with a city-based designer when he opted to become a model. He succeeded. But once he confessed, "to gain something, you've to sacrifice something. My relationship was to attain a foothold in the industry". As far as I remember, he'd a steady girlfriend before he entered the fashion world. And they were on the verge of getting engaged before he moved to Cape Town to become a fashion designer.'

'You walk into any fashion institute and you will find that most men are effeminate. A lot of them affect gay characteristics just to fit in.'

'They're even proud of it. They ask what's wrong if two men are in love? We're considered as special couples, they claim.'

'Many of them have signed a legal pact. This pact or certificate is to declare that they have become civil partners and that allows them the legal right to travel together as spouses.'

'In some countries like France, homosexuality is legal. And maybe, it is fashionable to be in love with a person of the same sex … who knows?'

'Moreover some NGOs and trusts actually support them. Many organizations are also becoming gay friendly.'

'It's an amazing world. How unusual I feel … as if I'd not lived at all … isn't it?'

'No, Anvita. You're more than what you think about yourself. You will go far.' Bano hugged me with affection. 'Now you need to go home and rest. Come we will drop you.' It was soothing to have a supportive friend.

While we were turning in the lane to go towards the car parking, I saw a beggar sitting quietly on the steps of an dilapidated building. She had a paper glass filled with water in her hand. I was taken aback when I saw that she was dipping a piece of dry bread in the glass and eating it while humming a satisfied tune. I don't know whether Bano and Ismail noticed it, but I kept on looking at her till she disappeared from my sight.

When I reached home with the bag of medicines and a few other items I needed, Leelaji looked at me with surprise, 'Where were you Anvita? And all this shopping?'

I knew what she meant. 'I sold my gold bangles as I needed money to recover, to go back to work.'

'Oh really!'

I remember once she'd asked me why I could not call her 'Mom' as Jivesh did. I'm sure she was more surprised to see me eating rice and dal without raising an eyebrow.

7

I was taken aback when Pratapji told me about the death of his dear friend Bhoolabhai. I could not believe it. I had met him only a few days back. At that time he looked absolutely healthy and fit. After the prayer meeting Manish held my hand and said, 'Anvita, you remember that incident with the white lady?'

'Yes, I do remember it.'

'That evening Baba sat for his puja as he normally did everyday. After that he said, "Beta, all my Fakir friends are calling me, I think now I have to go. But you don't worry, I have asked them to bless you. Their blessings will protect you all your life. Don't worry, nothing will go wrong with you." After that night he did not speak. He lay quietly in his bed, closed his eyes and just got merged with his world of Fakir's and silence.'

'He was a true Fakir, he was chanting mantras all the time and spoke no ill of anyone,' Pratapji missed his friend.

'Yes, I am also convinced, uncle, as he has taken away all my problems, my fear with him leaving me free from all the confusions of life.' Tears rolled down his cheeks.

'Manish please, I hope you don't feel I am responsible.'

'Oh no … no Anvita.'

'Why are you saying so?' Jivesh wanted to know.

I narrated the incident to him.

'The other day I was at his store, to purchase a few things. While Manish was packing my goods, one very smart lady walked in very authoritatively and demanded all the attention. Manish, conditioned as we Indians are, left me waiting and attended to her. She ordered her stuff, Manish made a list and packed everything. While she paid the bill, Manish realized that he did not have enough change to return to her. While he was looking for it, she became impatient and started saying, "You bastard, black coolie, you are pretending that you have no change, you thief, don't waste my time. Return my money."

'While Manish stood perplexed she threw all the packets on the floor and tore them with her sharp nails, mixing up rice, sugar etc. Then she got up and snatched the money from Manish's hands and walked out. But instead of Manish, I felt humiliated and ran after her. I got hold of her hand tightly, and shouted, "Who do you think you are? What was his fault? You had no patience. Come inside and pay his money and apologise or I will call the police."

'The white woman froze into a statue, as my furious face was enough to terrorize her. She mechanically took out the money from her wallet and gave it to Manish. While she was turning to go out, again I shouted, "Wait, pick up your stuff too.' She picked up whatever she could from the debris of her purchases. I handed her the remaining change from my purse and said, "Now you get lost."'

'The chaos of anarchy and changing social order has conditioned our behaviour, isn't it,' Pratapji analyzed the situation.

'Yeah, Manish was scared when I stopped her. He felt that she would take revenge.'

'Yes, it happens, Anvita. Pratap Uncle, you remember the Nathan-Barber shop case?'

'Anvita, you don't know. Nathan's only fault was that during the process of shaving a white client, he accidentally nicked his skin near the neck. Bus, that Gora came out of the shop shouted for help and collected a lot of people and claimed Nathan was trying to cut his throat. In no time the whole spectrum changed and a few of his white friends brought a tin of petrol, threw it on Nathan's shop and set it on fire. The police is also indifferent, they did nothing to protect Nathan.'

'It is self-created filth, everyone is looking for an opportunity to take revenge, no matter whether they are white or black.'

'Why assume the worst?'

'Don't worry Manish, times are changing,' Jivesh consoled him.

'Yeah nothing will happen, as Baba has taken away my problems with him and left me safe. He was a real Fakir. His blessings are with me.'

I wondered if I was responsible for Baba's death, or was he spiritually detached both from good and bad.

8

Whenever I reached home around 6 o'clock, I always found Pratapji and Mom praying to Sri Krishna, actually a cut-out from an old calendar. They were seen in almost in the same posture every day. That day, they were reciting their favourite *'Vasani jeernani yatha'* from *Gita Vihaya* which was part of their evening ritual. The fragrance of incense always reminded me of my mother, especially when they were reciting.

I joined them and folded my hands. Suddenly, I noticed a stranger standing next to Jivesh. He was tall, handsome with a beard lining his face. He was dressed in khaki trousers and a black leather jacket. After the prayers, he wished Pratapji and Mom by touching their feet. 'God bless you, son!' They looked very happy to see him.

Jivesh introduced him to me. 'Anvita, meet my cousin Bobby Singh. Bobby, my wife Anvita.'

He hugged me. 'Pleasure meeting you. Sorry, I couldn't attend your wedding reception … anyway, we will catch up … I'm here for two-three days.'

'Bobby lives in Cape Town and has come to take part in the Phoenix Settlement celebrations … we will all go together.'

'He is my brother's son, Anvita. He was an integral part of the African National Congress (ANC). Because of his participation, he was put behind bars in Apartheid's Alcatraz, the Robben Island, which is about thirteen kilometres from Cape Town,' Pratapji said.

'Let him sit and have some tea.'

Laura brought in a tray of tea and cookies.

'How are you, Laura?' he asked.

'Fine ... and you? Still living alone and unmarried?' Laura touched his shoulder with real fondness.

'Yes ... and very happy. And you Laura? Your son? Still in and out of jail?'

'No ... no ... he's quite settled now. Lives with his family in Soweto.'

Bobby had a very deep voice. When he narrated the incidents of his life, gentle movements of his face accompanied them. I was struck by his mannerisms but could hardly believe that he had lived in jail for ten years, that too with the famous Nelson Mandela. I asked him many questions about his emotional balance and his thoughts during his incarceration. 'How did you manage your studies and maintain your equilibrium living in those horrendous circumstances?'

'As far as I know, before Robben Island was converted into a jail, it was a dumping ground for lunatics and leprosy patients. Women and white prisoners were barred from there.'

He looked at me with a smile and said to Leelaji, 'Chachiji, you have a smart daughter-in-law. I must say, Jivesh you're lucky to have her.'

'She's just won an architectural competition, for designing a colony,' Jivesh said proudly.

'I'm sure she will achieve much more. She has an intellectual insight, which few people have ... they only ask the obvious questions.'

Bobby said, 'I was very young at that time, an ordinary student at Sastri College ... when the movement started. I will never forget those days of intense humiliation. I vividly remember the news which appeared in the *Leader* on 29 January 1949. It went something like this: 'Those Indians who have seen their homes destroyed in front of their eyes, those who had seen their life savings go up in smoke, those who have seen their children hacked in front of them and those who helplessly watched their daughters being raped will not – cannot forget. The generation that lived through the night of terror – January the 14th and the 15th will never forgive Africa. At least for two generations, the embers of hate will smoulder.'

'Yes. Even our family was a part of it,' Mom said. 'The honest Africans and Indians perceived it as a betrayal of their own principles … but escape was illusory.'

Pratapji added, 'As none of us could accept the misfortune, so we revolted. That was the time when Gandhiji emerged as a torch bearer – inspiring people to fight for their rights.'

'Gandhiji was dealing with two opponents at the same time – the Boers and the British. The enemies joined hands and their leader was the wily Jan Smuts, the commander of South Africa. He had perverted dreams of ruling a 'white only South Africa'. It was to be accomplished by rejecting all Coloureds – Indians or Africans. As a result, most of the courageous students joined African National Congress (ANC) and were arrested during a protest march. But we continued our political education even in Robben Island where as many as 4,000 prisoners learnt to read and write and eventually graduated.'

'How creditable …' I was impressed.

'No. It was not creditable, but a chilling experience to live behind cold stone walls – carrying on a conflict against warders and vicious killer dogs.'

'Have you ever been there Jivesh?'

'Yes. Once very long ago … with my college friends …when Nelson Mandela was released.'

'Yes, Anvita. The cell no. 5 hides a dark chapter in our political history. Mr Mandela lived in a 2.5 m x 3 m cubicle where he slept on a cold cement floor for almost fifteen years, till doctors prescribed him a bed. Now, when you go there, you will find a hand-written script of Mr Mandela's '*Long Walk to Freedom*' pasted on the wall of that cubicle.'

'How strange! In India, we're not aware of what has happened here – the painful history of South African freedom. All of you walked on the thorny path called life, while for this world, liberty is taken for granted.'

'With determination and by focusing on right thoughts, one can move mountains. And hope is humanity's quest for betterment. We are fortunate it happened. We are able to leave a proud legacy for the next generation.'

We were all spellbound, as not only his face, but his entire body imparted an unusual aura of human dignity and grace when he spoke.

Pratapji proudly showed me the invitation card that the family had received.

'On the occasion of the centenary of the Phoenix Settlement we invite you to attend the celebrations on 17 September 2004. The President of India, His Excellency, Dr Abdul Kalam will grace the occasion.'

'What is the Phoenix Settlement?' I wanted to know.

'It is a settlement established by Mahatma Gandhi during his stay in South Africa. He tried to inculcate community feeling amongst people. At that time, many Indians shifted to the Settlement with him. He also started a printing press there which rolled out the first daily Indian newspaper, *The Indian Opinion*.'

'You know, the phoenix is actually a bird that never dies. If it's killed, it reemerges from its own ashes.'

Pratapji and the family seemed to be staunch followers of Mahatma Gandhi and found an inquisitive listener in me.

9

We crossed the Kwamashu Highway leaving behind an old graveyard on the left. We were all going together in a minibus – Pratapji, Mom, Bobby Singh, Jivesh, Kisna and Pereeie. My compulsive inquisitiveness kept me involved in asking questions or interacting with people from different walks of life. Just survival or material acquisition was not my mission in life. I also believed that knowledge trains one's mind to analyze, investigate and realize the quintessence of life. Not to submit to blind faith or superstitious belief was an axiom. The route to Inanda Heritage wove a rich tapestry of past and present. Immense historical significance welded with natural beauty here. The vast, sprawling township had mushroomed with the settling down of sugarcane farmers near Durban.

Bobby Singh informed us that 'Inanda was named after an Indian trader Nanda – one of the first farmers to settle there in the latter part of the nineteenth century. In the 1980s there were political and social demonstrations and the great majority of civil disobedience campaigns were of a very different nature being based on unemployment and the Gandhian concept of 'Satyagraha' and 'passive resistance' – they led up to the first democratic elections.

'But it took a long time. Only on 27 April 1994 did the first democratically held post-apartheid general elections were held. I remember a friend of mine was working with a news agency at the time. And he always used to tell us that the media helped immensely in creating the required climate for free and fair elections. My friend even kept a cutting of the *Daily News* (3 May 1994) which published an article with the impressive caption: 'ANC ELECTION WIN FOR THE PEOPLE'. Not only South Africa, but the whole world was surprised to witness the first non-racial general elections taking place, with minimum violence and it also gave birth to the "rainbow children of God".' Bobby had a spark of brightness in his eyes as he spoke of those days.

'Did it happen because of Gandhi? Did he guide the elections in spirit?' I was now part of the stream he was floating in.

'Gandhiji left South Africa around 1914 never to return. But, undeniably everything happened because of his inspiration and guidance. That is why even today, South Africans and Indians celebrate not only Satyagraha and Phoenix Settlement Day but also the famous Dandi March.' Bobby Singh helped me widen my horizon and gave me a perspective of the historical background of South Africa.

We reached the very humble entrance gate of Phoenix. As we entered the settlement, I could see a very simple, ordinary building complex spread in a small area. We all went near Mahatma Gandhi's imposing bronze statue placed under a thatched gazebo. Along with it, was a map of South Africa surrounded by a metal globe symbolizing the world. One could not miss the small obelisk saying, 'May Peace Prevail upon Earth'.

I held my breath when I entered the room where many old photographs of the Mahatma Gandhi with different politicians and at important social gatherings were displayed. They provided an adequate and meaningful insight to a person like me who was totally ignorant about this chapter in Gandhi's history. On the wall were pasted quotes and extracts from Gandhi's speeches.

In one of the rooms, the old printing press which had once rolled out the *Indian Opinion* newspaper for many years was preserved. 'There are many dreams that disappear in the dust of time, but this was preserved like a pressed flower – as a saviour of a dream which came true.'

Pereeie was immersed in taking notes and clicking photographs, as this was a part of her research. She even hummed the bhajan along with others, 'Vaishnava jan ko tene kahiye, jo peer parayee jaaney re' which all the visitors standing near the Indian flag sang. It was a beautiful experience. I could see Pratapji trembling with emotion during the ceremony. Speeches from various people who participated in the Gandhian movement followed. Everybody was spellbound when the president of India delivered his speech. From what I gathered he said, 'Such rare breathtaking beings are not born, they just happen. To name but a few on the eternal list of God, the deathless ones on earth – whose influence passes into the lives of generations in which they resurrect – keeping evolution alive – Vivekananda, Sri Aurobindo and Mahatma Gandhi – are the perhaps choicest contribution of Heaven to Earth.'

The environment was totally permeated by the culture of the freedom struggle and contribution of immense sacrifices by people who followed Gandhi. On one wall I read: 'DEDICATED TO PEOPLE – I HONOUR YOUR SACREDNESS, YOUR HUMANNESS. I ASK YOU TO HONOUR MINE.'

On our way back, we even visited the Ohlange Native Institute which was meant only for the black children. We could see many of them in their black and white uniforms.

When we reached J.L. Dube's house, Kisna told me he was not only a politician but a philosopher and an eminent writer who had written *Amazana Abantu* (1911) in Zulu language. He also played a significant role in the freedom struggle against apartheid. He focused on health and education of the children.

The first president of ANC had visited J.L. Dube's graveside in Inanda's Languliablilele before casting his vote. After that, the president-elect Nelson Mandela declared himself ready to work with other parties for the upliftment of South Africans to heal the old wounds and end deprivation. Such gestures made Mandela the Messiah for all – and many began to recognize him in that light.

When we returned to our bus, I showed Jivesh and others some copies of the *Satyagraha* tabloid and a few other papers that I'd picked up. One article was addressed to 'Her Majesty Queen Victoria and Natal Indians.' It was an extract from the document from Colonial Secretary's office, Natal dated 1893 and outlined the essence of their 'fair and just policy' for the British Indians. It went like this:

Majesty Queen Victoria and Natal Indians.

With regard to the position of Her Majesty's Indian subjects in Natal it is the desire of Her Majesty's government that the

Queen's Indian subjects should be treated upon a footing of equality with all Her Majesty's other subjects.

It was an eye opener for me, how a human was turned into a subject. Jivesh took my photograph while I was holding all the papers.

'You appear to have the sensibility of a research student, Anvita. Now snap out of it, my dear. I agree there are struggles in life, burdens in life – who will know it more than us – but there is immense joy too – come let us have some lunch. Let us celebrate our freedom, our life.' Jivesh hugged me with immense fondness, especially when he whispered playfully in my ear, 'Let us celebrate your body – you have gained health – after all the illness, and let us lose ourselves in love'.

'Yes, dear, it's been ages. But one has to satisfy the mind too – because it can lead you to places of greatness. Just read this:

> *The Indian gentleman with all self respect should not enter into a compartment reserved for Europeans, any more than he should enter a carriage set apart for ladies. Although you may have acquired the habits and manners of a European, have the courage to show that you are not ashamed of being an Indian, and in all such cases, identify yourself with the race to which you belong.*
>
> – *H. Hardless,* The Indian Gentleman's Guide To Etiquette

I'm sure the forgotten darkness and humiliation of yesteryears had come alive in everyone's minds. We all became serious. As a shiver ran down my spine, I couldn't resist crying.

Jivesh hugged me again. 'Be yourself, my darling Anvita. Why are you so sensitive – please don't!'

I could feel the vibration of love from his subtle, emotional language and gestures. I felt victorious – like Gandhi.

10

As we were getting ready to leave for office, Jivesh told me, 'Anvita, this Saturday we will go for a 'Westlife' concert. They are going to perform at the Westbridge Stadium. We can't miss it. After that we will go for a drink to Evolution night club. Julia has organized a fashion party there which is going to be one of its kind.'

'That sounds like a good line of events! I hope Kisna and Ismail are also joining us.'

'Yes, they are. But please wear something smart. Don't wear anything shabby.' He left without looking at me, but I could see a hint of a joy in his eyes. What was it, I wondered.

Office was hectic as usual. Mr Subramaniam discussed a new project in Jo'burg. It was a huge shopping mall. I was very excited for getting another opportunity to express myself. He also suggested that I should visit the site. Soon arrangements for my travel plans were made. I was thrilled to the core. It was another challenge … and challenges always fill me with a new kind of energy. I collected all the papers and said, 'Thank you, sir … I'm really very grateful!' I'm sure I had tears in my eyes.

'Don't be emotional, Anvita. The work is allocated to you because you have potential. And please prove it. Don't let me down, Ok. All the best!'

I broke down in front of Bano. She was happy and wished me growth and stability in my career. And then we decided to go for some shopping. Pereeie also joined us. I was suddenly reminded of Jivesh's remark. I remembered that when we had married, Jivesh epitomized the many influences in my life. He had subliminally persuaded me to make radical changes in my personality. But now, his being was not that blanket of security that it was earlier. Rather, friends like Bano and Pertie were a greater influence, changing my behaviour by intimately participating in my life in many ways. I thought of the days when I had no friends, nobody to share my thoughts with. But now at this stage, I was almost living and breathing a slice of togetherness with Bano and other friends. I had realized that we need friends, not in order to stay alive but to feel human. A person who can genuinely be trusted and who can point out one's faults while encouraging one's visions and dreams is a true friend.

We were crossing the corner of Grey and Queen Streets. Whenever I looked at the Jumma Masjid from this corner, it reminded me of Jamma Masjid of Delhi. The magnificent architecture of both the mosques was so similar. The minarets and the domes here too followed the Mughal style. Just as the Emmanuel Cathedral with its historic gracefulness enwombed the Catholic culture.

As I saw a lot of children around with school bags, I told Bano, 'This madarsa in the mosque inspires me. I'm sure, it provides a mixed culture of collectivism for South Africa.'

'Yes, Anvita. It's a sort of an internal agreement. We've solved the problem of discrimination for being a Hindu, Muslim or a Christian. And now we believe in one identity for healthy development of minds and morals. That is, our identity as South African Indians – and this gives us a lot of emotional confidence.'

'Pereeie, what happened to your religion? You were following something very mystic and primitive?'

'I don't know how I reached there, Bano.' I could feel the pain in her solemn face and bright eager eyes that were facing me. 'I was working very seriously on my thesis. I wanted to become a professor like Kisna but destiny had different plans for me. The frightening, humiliating, incident happened in a moving train. Afterwards I lay unconscious on the platform I don't remember for how long. When I reached home, my parents could not reconcile themselves to my condition. I had no place to go to hide myself.' Tears trickled down her face. 'Wherever I went, I felt people staring at me with lustful eyes. I used to feel groping, disembodied hands all over my body all the time … even when I sat on the church bench. I felt horribly exposed. I even felt completely betrayed.'

'Pereeie, you need to overcome the horror of that experience. Everyday many innocent children go through this nightmare. There is no pretext, not even a provocation. Pereeie, whatever you have gone through cannot be undone. But now, you try and come out of it – or learn to live with it. Do try to rise above it. I know it's not easy – but try! Don't forget, at least some of us like Kisna were really concerned – very worried. He has very high expectations from your abilities – regardless of the incident. I'm sure his support will heal you.'

'Yes. His unconditional love is the biggest moving force of my life. His magnetic healing touch, his concern helps me pull me out of that trauma. Otherwise, I might have committed suicide.'

'Yes. Love sees things as they are. I'm sure he will help you to see and realize your own abilities rather than dwell on "what happened" …'

'Why don't you marry Kisna? … It will provide dignity to your crushed individuality' Bano asked.

'I'm not sure of marriage, Bano. I feel marriage is like a jigsaw puzzle. When all its pieces fit well, it works. Otherwise, it crumbles and pushes you into a mess.'

'No, Pereeie. I believe in love. At least, it has played a great role in my life. For an introvert like me, it helped me take a bold decision to land up in this country. I'm just holding Jivesh's hand to walk on the uncertain ground of unknown, unforeseen possibilities,' I tried to reason.

'If it comes to choosing, what would you choose, Anvita – career or marriage?'

'At this time, it is difficult to decide because I'm still in love. Love has happened for the first time in my life and Jivesh's love has helped me grow into a completely new individual. His love has given me confidence which I lacked during my childhood. But, of course, career is also important in life. And now that I've created a niche for myself, I've discovered a whole new side of myself which I was not aware of earlier.'

'That is what I wanted to know, Anvita. We all are striving for economic independence rather than economic protection, not following the iconic women of yesteryear. We are also striving away from the rules laid down by our own mothers and the men ... but my struggle has a long way to go.'

'Don't worry, Pereeie. Have courage and determination. You definitely have the potential. You only have to discover it within yourself.'

When we reached the shops, we found a mind-boggling variety of dresses, skirts, frilly lacy gowns, four-inch stilettos, attractive designer bags, trendy stuff. But we only concentrated on trouser suits with matching blouses in sober colours to prove to our male compatriots that at this point of time we only mean business.

11

It was early morning when we left Durban. It is the city of hills and sea, where the green and the blue combine. But the grey smoke of chimneys had already begun to swirl against the crimson red of the sun. It was the sun of new hope rising in the sky, leaving the black world beyond the veil, striving towards self recognition amidst its strife in the world below. It was like a wheel within a wheel – grinding poverty and crime with its own kind of social consciousness.

As we passed through the scattered, box-like cabins of the poverty-stricken slums surrounded by lush green trees, churches and half-ruined houses, I felt the air had become very heavy. The air contained an unusual aroma of the dawning future that seemed impossible so recently. Even today, South Africa grapples with communal, colour, caste and ethnic conflicts. It has to deal with the pulls of inter-religious disputes, secessionist tendencies and sub-national aspirations. Is this the reason, I wonder, that even the idea that South Africa could continue as a modern, democratic and tolerant nation was widely dismissed as a utopian dream?

Is South Africa finally on the path to claiming its rightful place in the comity of the nations?

Jivesh's cell phone rang. He spoke to someone in a hushed voice.

'Who was that?' I asked when he finished.

'Office. They wanted to know where I am.'

I looked at the watch. It was only 8 'o clock in the morning.

It was only a couple of years or so that I had taken my life into my own hands. I remembered our college art classes where many students painted canvases and worked on stones. As they hammered off the last few chips of the marble, the figure took shape and came alive. A dead piece of stone had begun smiling a magnificent, serene smile. How about me? Haven't I made an extra effort to transcend myself to take the direction desired? I took the first step and married Jivesh. It just happened. I don't know how it happened, that too to a person like me – an insecure girl from a small town in Punjab. I don't know how I took the next step to reach this part of the world as my destination.

I don't know who or what set me in this direction. Nobody had guided, nothing had forced me, except love. And it happened miraculously. Nothing but destiny could have made it happen.

Jivesh was so quiet that I was a little perplexed. 'Are you not happy to come out with me, Jivesh?'

'Of course, I am. This is the first time we've taken a holiday together since we got married.'

'Yes. And I'm excited to be alone with you and away from my daily routine.'

'I wonder how Sanju will react …'

'Well … I don't know. But I'm sure he will be happy to see you at least – if not me. After all you're a friend, while I'm just a relative. We can't choose our relatives, but friends we can.'

'It happened with us, didn't it Jivesh? Remember how we met … two complete strangers … but love dissolved the distinction and we've become one in love.' I kissed him.

He kissed me hard. It was a realm of calm delight. It was another kingdom of bliss.

'Let's plan our day, Anvita. Let me know what all you want to do – besides meeting Sanju.'

'I want to do some sightseeing. I want to feel and understand the city as I've to take up a new assignment here. Mr Subramaniam has asked me to visit the site. Mr Naso will call me tomorrow for the visit. I've given him your cell number.'

'So then, today we can walk around the city. Maybe, go to the flea market – do some shopping and eat at some nice place.'

'That's a good idea. Two of us alone … oh! Jivesh, I'm so happy.'

'Anvita, sometimes I feel you're drifting away from me. You're too involved with your work.'

'It's true that I'm very involved. My work is such. Please try and understand. It's not only demanding, it's also very challenging. And I have to prove myself. I can't stop at the bottom and be satisfied. I've to move with the drive. For that I've to work very hard as there's a long way to go.'

'I understand. But I feel rejected.'

'How can you say that? You're my first priority. Not only you but your family. For the first time in life, I've found a home – an anchor. Besides, you also travel so much. But I believe in you and my faith is my strength.'

'I love you for that clarity of mind,' he said when I slipped in to his arms in our hotel room.

It was very dark and hazy. There was also a thick, overhanging mist that made my vision hazy. I was not even sure where I was. It was a full moon night and there were a lot of thick trees. Maybe there were some hills nearby. There was a dense, wild aroma of pine trees, sharp and nostalgic. Gradually, a human figure emerged from the mist. It was a lady in a white salwar suit with a long flowing dupatta of richly embroidered phulkari work. She walked towards me gracefully. I was taken aback as she was moving close to me. I stood and watched – feeling her burning gaze on my face. The moonlight fell on her face. I could clearly see her eyes. They were bright and lined with kohl. Those two eyes stared at me with a burning curiosity – emitting a brilliant light from the helpless tears that trickled down from them. She did not speak a word. But I could feel the gravity of her presence. I don't remember how long we stood like that. Suddenly, there was lightning in the sky. She hurriedly handed me something wrapped in a cloth. Her cold fingers touched my hand. I tried to grab her but she stepped back with alacrity – turned and walked away. Her flowing hair glistened in the hazy moon light. Her dupatta caressed my body. A smell of old forgotten 'ittar' touched my nostrils. She turned and looked at my face with the same meaningful burning stare and disappeared. I stood motionless, speechlessly watching the smoke turning bright and a cave melting into the mountain. Within minutes, the whole atmosphere was changed. The sky became bright and clear – a dark hue of blue, and peaceful. There were lots of stars and a crescent, no longer a full moon.

Recovering somewhat from that encounter with darkness and the half moon, I unwrapped the dark green brocade cloth bag. I could clearly make out an old photograph of a building framed in an ornamental golden frame. It was a picture of an old building. It was hexagonal with Gothic columns all around. Each of the columns was perfectly round and graceful, bedecked with the head of a celestial god on its shoulders. It was amazingly beautiful – an unusual combination of the old and the new. I looked at the vacuum where she had stood, to say thank you but there was nothing. There was no hill, no tree. Only warm wind blew swiftly. I wrapped the photograph back in its velvet cover and brought it near my forehead and eyes. But as soon as it touched my eyes, I was conscious – awake.

I found myself in my hotel bed – lying close to Jivesh. I searched for my precious possession. But my hands didn't touch anything – and the spell of a latent sense of danger and silence was broken.

12

He was standing tall in the hotel lobby, wearing a light pink shirt and black trousers. Normally, I wouldn't have recognized him. He looked more mature and serious than how he looked when I met him last at Bua's death. He had lost some hair near his forehead. He even looked pale and thin, but his eyes glowed brighter with an unusual sense of seriousness.

Sanju hugged Jivesh first.

'Hi, Jivesh, brother-in-law. How are you doing? And you … Annu? You look different in this smart dress. Are you happy?'

The tone of intimacy in his voice touched the core of my heart. He'd called me Annu – that's how Bua used to address me. Secondly, his approval of my new identity – his acceptance of Jivesh as his brother-in-law was too much to comprehend as it implied he had owned up his relationship with me. He hugged me softly too. Maybe we were meeting for the first time as relatives.

The three of us settled down for breakfast. Jivesh and Sanju talked about their common friends during their college days. I was mostly silent, watching him closely. When he wished to know about me, there were volumes I wanted to share. Jivesh told him about my new achievements. I was touched when he said, 'I always was aware of the spark in you, Anvita … in spite of all the difficulties of your lonely childhood. I remember how you suffered from all the neglect silently, especially the humiliating discomfort of your surroundings. Nony's rough and rude behaviour was shocking – even I was not very supportive. I always feel guilty – guilty about our rudeness towards you.'

'But I'm very grateful to Bua and Jo Jo Uncle as they took care of a poor orphan like me and provided me with the finest things on this planet, my education and self-confidence. These are the real wealth of my life today.'

'But it is an Indian characteristic to care for your relatives. Ma and Babuji believed in it. But we two, under the influence of American education – could not comprehend it. But our mother committed suicide after Babuji's death and Nony sold everything, pulling out all the roots of our past and our childhood. Even now, I feel very guilty for letting her do that. I feel ashamed of myself. As time passed, I felt uprooted with nobody to go home to. Why I was not able to understand my mother's emotional attatchment to the soil where she spent her life with Babuji? Don't you think, Annu, that Nony and I were responsible for her death?'

All the old incidents, forgotten dreams, fragments from Bua and Jo Jo Uncle's daily routine lost in the past appeared before my eyes like a slide show. Everything had changed in a few days.

'Yes, Sanju Bhaiya. I agree with you. Things should not always be seen in terms of gaining benefits. Human emotions, respect towards one's heritage, matter in our life. These are different for Indians as compared with the Americans. Unselfconsciously, we see the world with our ancestors and kin … please forgive me if I've hurt you.'

Suddenly, I'd changed back to what I was in Bua's house. I'm sure my face – even my physical chemistry changed.

'No, Annu. Go on. I miss this kind of conversation. In my materialistic life – this closeness of bloodline – the warmth … I really miss it. As time passes, I miss Ma and Babuji – you and our small town where all three of us grew up flying kites and eating fresh barfi at Chhajju Halwai's shop. The celebrations of all festivals, Diwali and Holi … oh … How I miss them!'

'Isn't it strange I'm meeting a very different Sanju. When we were in college, you never spoke about missing your family or mother … nor the rituals and festivals you are talking about.' Jivesh also noticed the change in Sanju's personality.

'The heart hath its reasons that reason does not know … A French philosopher said this and I believe in it.'

'But friends are also God's compensation for relations. I believe in that Sanju. So let's be friends and relatives both.'

Sanju handed me a big brown envelope. 'Here are some letters and Babuji's diary. All these old pages speak of traditional bonds between families. Read what Babuji thought of you Annu … and how much Ma depended on your emotional support. And see this …' He took out an old page from the diary where Jo Jo Uncle had scribbled with green ink – '*Matacha Parvati Devi, Pitadevo Maheshwara Bandhava Shivabhaktauya Svadesho Bhuvanatrayam.*' My mother is Parvati, my father Shiva, my kin their devotees and the three worlds are my country. These were his feelings about India. And in one corner Jo Jo Uncle had written, 'Now, I feel I made a mistake by sending Nony and Sanju to America for higher education …. they no longer understand or interpret our own heritage … what have I done? But, I'm sure Anvita will remain our pillar of strength – in our old age she will support us. At least, we will have someone – someone our own … Anvita mein apnapan nazar aata hai.'

'What is "apnapan" Anvita?'

'"Apnapan" is an extension of one's own self – considering the others person very close to heart.' I cried. 'I wish I could … I never got a chance to do so … to do their seva (service for them) … Oh Sanju I wish I could …'

When I cried, Sanju got up from his chair and tried to comfort me by caressing my shoulders. We ate for a while and sipped coffee quietly. Suddenly, I realized we had not talked about Nony.

'How's Nony?'

'She's fine. She's married a very rich American this time – after her divorce. I'm sure she's happy with all the money around her. We hardly meet as she's busy attending parties in a socialite group. Also she doesn't approve of me as an artist.'

'Are you not working with Digital anymore?'

'Yes, I'm but still I like my creative freedom.'

I was almost astonished to meet his new avatar – a brand new Sanju. It dissolved all the barriers of my past resentments.

13

I received a call on Jivesh's cell phone from Mr Naso. He said, 'I'll pick you from the hotel lobby for the site visit.'

'Yes. I'm ready – waiting for you. But where's Mr Subramaniam … isn't he coming?'

'He will join us at the site. He's busy with the G8 Meeting.'

'OK. Come. I'm waiting.' As I was handing over the phone to Jivesh, I saw two missed calls form Julia. The phone started ringing again. Jivesh snatched the instrument hurriedly from my hand and went out of the room.

I switched on the television. They were showing the footage of the summit.

'The presidents and prime ministers representing the G8 countries are already under pressure after months of publicity for a campaign calling on them to "Make Poverty History" …

'The campaigners pin their hope on a doubling of aid to Africa. Tony Blair, who was hosting the G8 Summit, has put the continent on the top of its agenda. Two significant reports from the United Nations Millennium Project – led by Jeffrey Sachs and from Mr Blair's own commission for Africa provide numbers to back the appeal.

'But none of the signal events in the recent history of poverty eradication depended on the generosity of strangers. Some said aid is useless. Some said it is worse than that. Economists worry that it crowds out export industries by, for example, bidding up the price of skilled workers. And aid makes governments dependent on their paymasters in the rich world, not their tax payers at home.

'Money was given on the condition that prices are established, markets be liberalized and industries privatized. But the early reforms had already been achieved and the tough ones were intractable. The vogue now is for "ownership" and "partnership". Countries are supposed to devise their own strategies for fighting poverty, in wide consultation with something called the civil society – and then invite donors to back them.'

But a question lingered on in my mind: 'If aid rarely buys growth, can it buy the reforms too?' The questions hung on my mind like an interminable mist.

Tony Blair admitted he had no idea of how and why Africa is the way it is.

> *The sorry state of Africa is reflected in three core aspects – the tribal ties of the rulers, which go beyond what we would normally understand in the West; the fundamental premise of government – which is rarely democratic capitalism and the Rule of Law. It is viewed very differently here. Success will come when the population forges its development without the shackles of tribalism (and accepts that democracy builds a stake in the welfare of their country) and when the ruling elite of each country implements the basics of democratic capitalism. Until then, Africa will continue along the path it has followed for at least 350 years.*
>
> Colin Swarder

Schabir Staik – a financial advisor to the Deputy President, Jacob Zuma – was on trial in Durban for alleged fraud. Fighting high profile cases matters. If junior officials or policeman see big time crooks punished, they may decide stealing public money or harassing motorists for bribes is not worth the risk. For different reasons, corrupt and honest South Africans alike will be watching with interest if any MPs are jailed over the travel scam.

Mr Naso took me to the site. It was very far from the main city at Lanecia. It was a kind of Indian locality where 90 per cent of the inhabitants were Muslims. We saw the allotted land and it was huge.

We were supposed to build a shopping mall with multiplex cinemas and office accommodation, along with service apartments. As I concentrated on the details Mr Subramaniam was conveying through his facial expressions, I was trying to remember all that Sanju had said in the morning. My past was alive with him but every exit is an entry into something new. New achievement, new world.

Mr Subramaniam looked at us and said, 'I want you all to put as much effort as you can in this project. I strongly believe that every human being has a dimension of consciousness far deeper than what he thinks. So bring out that in your design and in your quality of construction.'

'We will try our best, sir,' Mr Naso said. I only looked at Mr Subramaniam's face. How elegant he looked even in that authoritarian mood!

He said, 'I want my team to dream of an environment that is free from the ghosts of the past. I want you to work more creatively so that we can build a country we had imagined two decades ago.'

There was a blue dream in his blue eyes.

14

The name of the Art Exhibition was the 'House of Memory'. The participating artists were Caerlos Capetan and Jan Hafstrom from Sweden, Clifford Charles and Doug Anwar Jahangeer from South Africa; Sanjeev Malhotra from New York and the only lady participant, Loulou Cherinet, also from Sweden. The bright red and orange pamphlet carried the profiles along with the photographs of all the artists.

The name of the exhibition held a special significance for me. I was really walking down the memory lane – translating life into different dimensions. Sanju was waiting for us near the entrance as we reached the venue. He hugged me.

'How delighted I am, really delighted to see you Annu – and of course you Jivesh! Come, let me show you my work. '

We walked with him as his special guest.

There were beautiful paintings uplifting us with their associations with colour and a variety of moods. Every artist was different – even the realism of landscapes was depicted differently by them. It was like an interesting journey into other people's emotional consciousness – or maybe even their traditions. I could not believe my eyes when I saw Sanju's paintings. They were almost a pictorial autobiography of our life in Punjab. He showed urban elitism as a challenge. There was one huge painting depicting our narrow gali – with all the shops including

Sara Baji's bangle shop; Chajju Halwai's with different sweets arranged in large baskets and of course the kite shop – which used to be Sanju's favourite haunt when he was a kid.

'How realistic these are, Sanju! It seems as if we are back in India. The boundaries seem to vanish. What remains is the sensation or the vibration of being in the midst of it all over again!'

'Look at this Annu. Do you remember the angan of our haveli – Ma and Bhagwanti sitting on the charpai … and the sabziwaali with her basket of vegetables'. Devoid of any colours, the black and white in the painting was titled *Rajarani*.

'How realistic it is … the whole image of those good old days reveals the message and the meaning without the diversion of colours. Only two colours maintain the dignity of the traditional Indian home …'

I had tears in my eyes. Bua was there in the painting, with the possession and dispossession of her role … graceful with the purity of her being, as she was. 'Yes, Sanju. You did the right thing by not using any colours … as her shadows have become more significant when you look at her with a calm mind. You have uplifted her image.'

I could see that he also had tears in his eyes.

This was the essence of Sanju's portrait as an artist. Many of my unresolved thoughts and anxieties were resolved. I felt not only a part of his exhibition, but a part of the life that he was cultivating today at this point of time. Was it his individual transformation or a revival of the past life which he – along with Nony – tried to wipe out from our lives?

One of the onlookers was saying, 'Art is a product of man's subconscious integrations – of his sense of life – to a larger extent than of his conscious philosophical convictions.'

The other award-winning artist, Jan Hafstrom from Sweden, had also painted his childhood images with traces of Russian icons. The paintings were almost a symbolical wreckage of his dreams. When someone asked him, he replied, 'An artist, like any other man, seldom translates their sense of life into conscious terms. This is how I relate to life.' Sanju was full of an artist's enthusiasm.

'You enjoy painting as it is a sort of a reminder of your past life,' I commented.

'Yes Anvita, I love the journey of creation – there's something new you learn each day …'

As an artist, you pour out all your energies and your imaginations to create – to work … with the shades of your dreams. When the canvas is ready, you feel fulfilled. With paintings, one lives several lives … in this birth.' Sanju appeared a different person as an artist.

15

It was a dewy fresh morning. There was a slight nip in the air. But I was still rocking in my dreamboat. The art exhibition, those pictures of the past and all the meetings and discovering a different Sanju overwhelmed me. I was trying to get to terms with the whole experience. All his paintings were sketches of the past incidents; past life; shadows of us … our family … dead relatives. They had stirred the memories of my childhood. There was a mystic terror of the consequences that was rising above everything like a distorted vision thwarting life.

And then the spell of the old world was broken – bringing me back into the hotel lobby … where Sanju was standing as tall and graceful as he was yesterday.

'Annu … where are you? Day dreaming, as usual?! I've been standing here for almost ten minutes!'

'Oh … sorry! Sanju … I was just thinking of your paintings – how realistic they are!'

'Let's go sight seeing. Where's Jivesh?'

'He's not interested in sightseeing. He has seen it all. He's gone to meet some of his office friends.'

'Come then. The bus has come with the guide. Let's take the front seats to get a better view.'

The guide was a young black girl. Her name was Maria. She wished us 'Good Morning' and 'Molo' in Zulu as we settled down in the bus, with other tourists. Like a tape recorder she started in a singsong voice. 'Jo'burg is the 'City of the Gold'. It's about a hundred years old. It's the largest city of South Africa and is the capital in all but name. Its the largest city in the continent south of Cairo – a brash fast growing and often ugly infant with just three redeeming features – wealth, energy and a beautiful climate.'

For the poor and the ambitious, Jo' burg has an irresistible lure. In the last official census in 1985, the population of greater Jo'burg was 3 million – 2 million whites and about a million blacks, coloreds and Asians. At first appearance, Jo' burg looked as just another anonymous big Western style city.

'It looks like any American city,' Sanju remarked. 'It's clean and has so many skyscrapers. Very modern – ready to meet global challenges.'

We passed through 'Riviera Road', African Life Park, the Munro Road and Elmstar Road. The guide informed us that the 'Helgrow' was a white area. It had large modern houses protected by electrically-charged barbed wires. Our guide told us that earlier no black was allowed to walk on these roads after 7 pm. If caught, they were punished. But it all changed after 1994 as blacks also bought houses in this area and shifted.

I was completely engrossed in the scene and so was Sanju. We were walking on the historical past of a city that was unknown to us. Maria was taking us inside the 'Constitutional Hill' (1896). It was built on the site of the Old Prison Complex – commonly known as the Old Fort or Number Four. The whole place revealed how pain and the past were transformed into hope and future.

There was evidence of extreme human torture all over the place. It stank of desolation, repression and grinding torture through law to suppress the human spirit. The list of crimes that were punished here included breaking the pass law, curfew law, job reservation law, drinking law. There were many cells for those who broke these petty laws – small and dark cells that allowed them only to sit alone – to be reduced to nothingness in these four walls of extreme deprivation. It left man only to himself – in desolation and repression – so that he could undergo emotional turmoil by himself.

There were many walls pasted with black and white photographs of all those who were incarcerated here for demanding amendment of the law. The photographs had faded with time. The walls even had extracts from their speeches which they might have given on various occasions in spite of not being permitted a pen or paper.

Humiliation is fundamentally an experience which sometimes gives us courage or impels the analysis of a situation.

> *I've a call, I must answer. I must deliver my message to my people. This humiliation has sunk too deep in me to remain without outlet. I at least must act unto the light that has dawned on me.'*
>
> Solo Simon Gama (1908-1913)

'What is a Pass?' Sanju asked the guide.

'Well it's an identity of survival,' Maria informed us in a deep voice. 'People like you cannot even imagine how difficult it was even to breathe freely at the time of white rule. Every day was a challenge – not only in the physical sense but also spiritually, mentally and otherwise.

'It was an era of dialogue on black and white federalism – an era of Bantustan independence. Everyone was required to carry a Pass – which was a sort of identity card. Without this, nobody was allowed to cross the roads where whites lived. The whites could not tolerate blacks anywhere – no black was allowed in their restaurants or clubs. Anyway, those who were caught without a Pass were humiliated, beaten and were forced to live in these 'Khulukuthus' or isolation cells.

'Evil deeds were perpetrated here. The young boys and girls were sold to the gang bosses for sex.'

'I thought these cells were for freedom fighters.'

'Yes. Even Nelson Mandela and Gandhi lived here. This photo is of Prem Naidoo, Martin Panyaza Subanguz, Khela Shubane and so many others. They were part of the freedom struggle. This prison was used to break their spirit and their will to live. There was no electricity, no proper drinking water.

'It was extreme human torture to sit still all the while, to allow your life to be reduced to nothing inside the four corners of a cell and just sit still. Read the description in a poem:

Cement grey floors and walls
Cement grey days
Cement grey time
And a grey susurration.

It was a very depressing experience. With an effort, I prevented myself from vomiting.

We reached the Gandhi Square. It is the spot where in 1907 the Dutch handed over the keys to the British without any bloodshed. Sanju took a lot of photographs.

After a long drive, we reached the Soweto area. Maria said, 'It's a line of physical colour demarcation as it's the largest slum of South Africa – where 90 per cent of blacks live below the poverty line.'

As we walked on the road, we could see the sturdy, idle, uncouth country folk, walking or sitting in groups and laughing loudly. Most of the women were busy with household work – either washing clothes, utensils or tending to children. There was a market too, displaying heaps of cheap goods, clothes and candies. But nobody seemed interested in buying them.

Finally, we reached the street where Nelson Mandela and Bishop Desmond Tutu lived. Both of them were later awarded the Nobel Prize. Standing in front of a humble house, Maria proudly announced – 'This is Nelson Mandela's house – and this street is the proud Vilaklazi street, where the lion still roars.'

Photographs of his three children and his first wife Evelina, who divorced him, adorned the place. There was another with Winnie Mandela who worked with him in his political career till the end.

There also was a huge portrait of Nelson Mandela by Cardiss Collin and a poem:

A man,
Just a man,
But a man that moved
Mountains and mind,
With principle and perseverance
And he paid the price.

'Compared to the White House, it's like a log cabin,' Sanju referred to his American past. 'But he suffered. He spent twenty-seven years in the dreaded Robben Island – faced Ghetto Acts and many other political clashes. He stood for his beliefs for the anti-apartheid movement, he was a real man. Then there were the Anglo-Boer Wars or Zulu wars. A lot of black blood was soaked by this soil.'

Everybody had become hungry by that time we finished the tour. Maria took us for a very authentic South African meal to a restaurant, 'Wandie Place – African Delicacies', which catered especially to the tourists.

Unable to decide on what to eat, we came out of the restaurant with two cans of Diet coke each and a packet of biscuits. We sat on a bench outside. There were some locals sitting at a little distance and staring at us. Sanju began talking about his life.

'Every morning when I get up and make my cup of tea, the bhajans Ma used to play on her tape recorder echo in my ears. They uplift me when I feel forlorn, hopeless or insecure. With the help of these bhajans, I overcome my restlessness. I brought with me Ma's idols from her puja room. I've created a special place for them in my two-bedroom apartment. And I recite my Gayatri Mantra every morning.'

Overcome with emotions I hugged him. How much he had changed! He was no longer the arrogant, abusive and irritable Sanju.

'Though I'm pretty successful as a Chartered Accountant and I've had enough to keep me busy with parties and social life something within me always gnaws at me – it is the guilt of not looking after my parents. I even feel responsible for my mother's death. Why did I get carried away by Nony's selfishness?'

He looked far away where there was nothingness – no trees; no shacks … no sun … only a vacuum – shunya.

'I'm a loner. I've to paint. Perhaps one can do that only in solitude. That is why I live alone.'

'You get married Sanju, and have children. How Bua wished to see her grandchildren! At least now you can fulfill her dream.'

'No, Annu. I won't be able to adjust with anyone. First Babuji's affair and Ma's suffering. And then Nony's cruel, selfish personality – these have affected me so deeply that I'm not able to like any woman!'

'No, Sanju. Don't close your mind to the possibility. Look at me. I married Jivesh for love. I've found parents and a family I'd always wished for. I'm satisfied with whatever god has bestowed upon me.'

'I'm happy to hear that. Because your humiliation and the decision to shove you out of the house is also a part of my guilt. My repentance had made me so uncomfortable that I was almost on the verge of losing a sense of potency in my life. I even felt soulless despairing of my joyless existence. Then suddenly my ability to paint and to create helped me. It established my being in myself.'

'Don't do that Sanju. From my side there are no reproaches. All my life, I felt indebted to Bua, Jo Jo Uncle and you for providing me with education and a pattern of settled and respectable life. And also to Vati Aunty who helped me get married. She even performed my Ḳanyadaan, like a mother.'

'How is she and her son?'

'Arjun? I'm sure he must have grown by now into a handsome young boy. When I left India, he was just a kid. But I'm in touch with them. I do speak to Vati Aunty sometimes. She is not well … she has cancer I think.'

'Maybe it's her karma accumulated from the past.'

'She's a nice person, Sanju. She's told me everything – about her husband's illness and her relationship with Jo Jo Uncle. If you read those letters, they are so lyrical – like a long poem. I feel like writing a novel based on them.'

'I've given you Babuji's diary. Please keep it. Write about their lives if you can – maybe it will be our homage to them. In future, we will maintain a two-way openness to give and receive emotional support from each other. As someone said, "A sorrow shared is a sorrow lessened and a shared joy is a joy increased a hundredfold."'

'I'll feel honoured. It will give strength to my future and my life. But whenever you go back to India, try to make up with Arjun, if not Vati Aunty. He's your own blood, Sanju.'

Before he could say anything, a lady came and sat next to us on the same bench, her head was draped in a bright red kerchief but her grey hair peeped out from behind her ears, like unspun cotton. Her face and hands were dark, merging into the solid wooden bench we were sitting on. She kept on mumbling something in Zulu – then started crying and pointing towards a tree not very far from us. We could not understand any of her gestures.

Fortunately, Maria came to our rescue. She explained that the old woman's only daughter was a nurse in a hospital. She was also the only earning member of a large family of seven children. She was repeatedly raped by the doctors, who later declared her mentally ill and had her shifted to an asylum. She was said to be haunted by the ghosts of two of her children who were hacked to death by their father earlier – before she was raped. The man was sentenced to death. One day she sneaked out of the asylum and hanged herself from that very tree.

The old woman cried helplessly. We collected some money and gave it to her.

'The problem is,' Maria pointed out as we were boarding the bus, 'that even today blacks are classed with and treated like the lowest of the low, simply because they are black. That is why the social conditions are not improving. The main cause is prejudice. The whites and the blacks both reciprocate in the sequence of cause and effect. Both have to change by using both intelligence and sympathy across the colour line.'

When I returned to the hotel, Jivesh was in the bathroom taking a shower. There were a few small shopping bags lying on the bed. I opened one of them. There was a beautiful scarf in one and a few shaving accessories with a big bottle of foot cream in the other. He came out of the bathroom, almost shocked to see me. He didn't appear too pleased.

'Oh … you are back. How was your day?'

'Very nice. We saw a lot of Jo'burg as well as Soweto … Nelson Mandela's home …'

He snatched the shopping bags from my hand and shoved them in his suitcase.

16

Sanju was keen to watch an evening show of traditional music and dance. As it was the last evening we were to spend together, Jivesh and I decided to accompany him. Maria arranged to take us to the place that was especially designed for tourists. It was a typical mud hut with a thatched stage. The only modern interventions used were the lighting, the music system and the enormous speakers.

When the show began, there were about fifteen people on the stage, including three drummers and a lead singer. They wore sarongs and short-sleeved vests on their well-built bodies. Their faces were painted with black or white stripes to impart a tribal look. They even wore small bells around their feet and an 'onugandu', a small piece of bamboo with horizontal grooves that produced raspy sounds by scraping them together. The songs were of romance and heroism or satire on the white rule. As the song reached a crescendo, one or two dancers lengthened the wild movement with their frantic drumming, ending in a trance. The performance was called 'Body Beru or Baburu Lava' developed by the sailors from different ocean regions. The songs were sung using the rhythms of the older strains.

There were some other performances called the Fathing andu, jehan and langiri where the actors wore long black gowns. Four black women sang with their babies tied to their backs with a cloth. It's said that black people wrap their babies to their bodies while singing so that they can feel the vibration of their mother's heart. It is believed to be the first music that a black child hears and becomes aware of.

The last performance was also inspired by the times when the enactment of the Pass burning campaigns of the ANC were performed. In the actual incident, many women and children were killed by burning tyres thrown around their necks, or in course of police and military action during the event.

Suddenly, the stage became pitch dark and a man appeared in a round orange spotlight. Wearing a dark brown robe, he recited a poem in his harsh voice.

The child is not dead
The child lifts his fists
Against his mother
Who shouts Africa
Shouts the breath
Of freedom and veldt
In the location of
The cordoned heart
The child lifts his fists
Against his father
In the march of generation
Who are shouting Africa
Shout the breath.

The narrator's voice melted in the silence as he said, 'This poem is dedicated to those people, the Hottentots for whom life was nothing but a series of tragic accidents. This is a humble effort to light up what is dark. Again, the stage became pitch dark and pervaded with a strange silence. One very small earthen lamp flickered with a weak light at the centre of the stage.

It was a mystic experience beyond description. We got up with a heavy heart trying to recover from its spellbinding impact. On our way back, Maria related many incidents and stories about the psychological divide of the colour boundaries. Now, it is almost an infrastructural challenge for the country to rise above racial discrimination. While focusing on what she was saying, I was reminded of a story Bua used to tell us – about the discrimination of the caste system in India.

It was about Adi Shankara, who was the most learned of all saints. One day, he was on his way to the bathing ghat at Kashi, when an outcast chandala (low-caste) with four ugly dogs yapping around him appeared at the spot which Shankara needed to cross. Shankara yelled, 'Dooram Gachha! (Go Away)'.

'Why? Where shall I move?' the grimy chandala asked sweetly. 'My body is quite like yours – made of the same elements. My soul is also as immortal as yours – then why am I a chandala and you a sanyasi?'

Shankara understood his fallacy and realized the chandala was Shiva himself accompanied by the four Vedas. He was testing him. He fell at Lord Shiva's feet and begged pardon for his lack of understanding.

'But in this country nobody is asking for pardon for not understanding the pain of the deprived ones. They only fear punishment which overpowers all the actions,' Maria said.

'No, Maria. Times are changing. The whites are also realizing mistakes of their past – the cruelty of their ancestors. They even suffer from what we call "the white guilt".'

'The framework of social life is being altered, gradually being modified,' Jivesh clarified.

'There is also a desire to take revenge – the blacks are taking revenge for what they have suffered during the course of time. That is why there is so much crime – rapes and murders.'

Finally, we reached the 'Trade Route Mall' which catered more to the Indians than the locals. With a sigh of relief, we spotted 'Copper Chimney' the famous Indian restaurant. We ate to our heart's content, bringing back memories of Punjab.

When Jivesh went to the rest room, Sanju told me in an intimate whisper, 'There is an envelope with some money, and a letter that Ma had left for you. Please take it.'

'But why?' I was again getting emotional. 'I don't need money, Sanju. I earn enough to make ends meet …'

'Please Annu. It was Ma's desire – and my gift. This is for you.'

Jivesh came out in the meantime.

We parted with tearful eyes.

'OK, Sanju … Enkosi kakublu (Thank You)'

'Thank you, my brother, thank you for bringing back the family to me. It makes me complete.'

'And all the best for your art.'

17

I was thinking in existential terms. It was an absolutely new dimension in my life. For the first time, I felt I had some worth. As Sanju gave me those five thousand US dollars, a gift not only in terms of money, he had handed me a relationship, a connection to the past which was more relevant than anything else. It was very significant for an emotional person like me. Strange is the phenomenon called life, how it changes colours and transforms with time. I tried to figure out – was it his success as an artist ... sale of the maximum number of paintings ... or very encouraging, complimentary reviews on television and newspapers? Anyway, whatever it was, it made our meeting very memorable. He even spoke to Vati Aunty and Arjun over the phone, which I felt was gracious. On the path of life, we do need others to walk with us – not in order to stay alive but to remain human.

When we parted, he very generously gifted me one of his paintings. He asked me to visit California where he lived – or plan a trip to India together. Though we had tears in our eyes, there was so much left unspoken in our hearts that I could not throw my arms around him or hug him. We wished each other a formal goodbye and turned away. I wasn't sure of the state of his mental consciousness. But I was afraid of the intuition within myself – images of a strange awareness that was attracting me to an idea rather than to the corporeal reality of a kin in flesh. Suppressing my instinct, I clutched Jivesh's hand tightly before sitting in the car.

As we drove back, I remained quiet. I had been lost in my past for the last three days. All those moments of beauty and gratitude had strengthened me with an expanded vision. In my quietness, I wanted to include all in my new definition of self sufficiency. I did not tell Jivesh about the money that Sanju had given me. For once, I wanted to live up to my intuition that was guiding me to a new direction – on a road where my work would be my first priority. But, I could not ignore Jivesh and the love, a power that feeds passion and unfolds so many worlds. I looked at Jivesh with concern. But he was lost. He looked like Jesus crucified. I realized that in our first ever holiday together we did not make love even though for Jivesh it was as important as having a meal. Why was that?

'Are you feeling well, Jivesh? Or are you upset about something?'

Maybe he was not prepared for a direct question.

'You had no time for me, Anvita. You have been too busy visiting places – or meeting your cousin. Was it a holiday or was I needed as a driver?' He made an obscene mockery of all those cherished days.

'Why are you saying that, Jivesh? Was there any moment when I showed disrespect towards you? My work of course takes me away for long hours – or maybe in future, it will be days. But is there any need to feel insecure? Please have faith in me. Don't torture yourself with needless negative thoughts ….' I tried to hug him but noticed that his body was burning with fever.

'You're not well. Are you running a fever?' I tried to feel his pulse by holding his wrist – he was definitely unwell.

'Jivesh, we could've rested in Jo'burg today … or meet a doctor before leaving. How will you drive all the way in such health?'

He sulked even more and used a strange, abusive language which I had heard for the first time. I wanted to switch on the CD player in the car for reducing the tension brewing up between us – but he didn't let me.

We remained quiet for some time. I was trying to analyze what went wrong. Was I not attentive to his masculine and physical theories about what a woman should be? Or some insecurity had struck a blow to our physical communion?

He was feeling giddy by now. I gave him some water and tried to soothe him by rubbing his back. After a while, he came out with the truth.

'Anvita. I've lost my job!'

'Oh is that the reason? Is that what is troubling you, Jivesh?'

I was relieved inside – as my thoughts had taken an ominous turn almost killing me. 'Don't worry. I'm sure you will find another one. You're qualified. How many people have an MBA degree? This is a passing phase. But please don't harbor doubts about my character. I'm committed to you. I love you and will always remain loyal to you. If you've not understood me, it's not my fault.'

'How about all those days that you abandoned me, like dirty linen?'

'Don't ever even think about that. It was my commitment – and I've to work, please understand. One thing should be very clear – in future, never discuss my work or my long hours. I don't want to spell it out every time. You know how demanding and time consuming architectural designs are.'

I don't know how much and how deeply I reached him. But, it definitely triggered strange feelings in my heart. There was an indefinable something else – I sensed something changing in our relationship. I could sense – it was not about losing job – position or money – it was about losing faith in life.

He felt giddy again and wanted to throw up. He wanted to stop the car immediately. We turned towards the nearest stop. It was a dilapidated church like structure. We drove towards a corner and he threw up the 'Copper Chimney' food he had eaten, the night before. The water bottle didn't have any water left. I tried to look for someone who could help me find water or some medicines. While Jivesh rested on a very rusty iron bench, I peeped inside the half-opened door of the church. There was a dim light at a distance. I entered quietly, as the etiquette of a church demands. It appeared to be an unused old building with a few dirty wooden benches covered with dust and torn papers. The place looked detestable, the stench of rotten food swirled all over.

Suddenly, I saw a few bare bodied children working with tools and hammers in very dim light. The light was not enough to figure out the shapes but it was sufficient to know what was going on. They appeared to be black children, who may have been trafficked from nearby rural areas. They were most certainly engaged in slave labour.

Mirroring my shock, they appeared to be in grief and shock themselves and were shouting strangely from all sides. From a corner of the hall, a hefty middle-aged man appeared suddenly with a whip in his hand. I couldn't follow what all he said but I could see the children were crying and shouting in a strange language. I turned and ran back with all my strength to Jivesh and the car. We drove back.

I wondered why there was a statue of Jesus in that church – tight lipped, bleeding, nailed to the cross in silence, adding to the stillness of that gruesome absurdity of life.

THREE

1

There was a silvery glow of early morning light just about to illumine the dark shadows of the night. I was happy to be up as I like the morning freshness of my body. It maybe because Bua used to get up early and sing this bhajan:

Uth Jaag musafir bhor bhai
Ab rain kahan jo sovat hai
Jo sovat hai so khovat hai
Jo jagat hai who pavat hai

Awake o traveller its dawn,
Night has passed,
Why do you sleep?
The one who is asleep, loses
The one who is awake, gains.

I believed in this theory because at this early hour, my energy levels were better and that helped me work efficiently. I normally worked on the kitchen table as I could make as many cups of coffee as I liked. Coffee stimulated my working.

I was going through Jo Jo Uncle's diary and love letters. As I read them, I felt the account of the private journey of an ordinary man – and a lover – was written so vividly, that it appeared as a great narrative. Yet, it maintained the delicacy of emotions. It was amazing how they shared a secret life and lived every moment of their privacy together. How they tended to each other's dreams, hopes and fears so lovingly. On these pages were written, not only their intense desires, but even the facial descriptions that became soothing lyrical poems. Going through those old pale pages, I entered an unusual world of love and wonder. Was it real? Or was it a fantasy?

Jivesh was different nowadays. He spoke less during love-making. He exerted his physical abilities but forgot to express himself in loving, tender whispers. But I could not complain, that was the only love I knew. Recently, I felt it was becoming harsher and more demanding. While comparing with others, I wondered if he was too intent on proving himself, or was it pure passion? Jo Jo Uncle had lived a pretty quiet life in a small town of Punjab. Perhaps at that time the problems of existence and maintaining a lifestyle were less taxing than they are today. In this country, to survive or to earn money is not only very hard but nerve wracking, and it leads to a lack of true intimacy between a wife and a husband. Laura interrupted my thoughts.

'Good morning, dear.'

'What's the time?'

'It's 10 o' clock. What should I cook? Are you home for lunch?'

She not only interrupted my stream of thoughts but brought me back to reality. Earlier, she never bothered to ask me for anything but ever since I started paying her salary, she acknowledges me as a family member.

'We've to go out for lunch today. Laura, you better ask Ma what they want.'

'But Jivesh is sleeping, isn't he well? He doesn't eat properly and even throws up sometimes. Take him to a doctor.'

'Yes, I will. Thank you, Laura. Make some tea. I will wake him up.' I collected my papers and went inside my bedroom. Jivesh was up. He looked very pale and worn out.

'Are you feeling fine, Jivesh? After the fever you've not recovered fully. Let's go see a doctor today.'

'I'm fine. I'm taking medicines. I only overslept. Maybe I was tired.'

'And why did you tire yourself, dear?' I kissed him on his forehead with a tender look. 'You know Jivesh, I read somewhere about marriage? It's falling in love anew, every day, always with the same person.'

He suddenly looked radiant and handsome. As he laughed all the problems disappeared. Laura came with a cup of tea and biscuits.

'Get ready Anvita. Bano called. She will pick us up at twelve to go for lunch.'

'How about the car?'

'Ma and Papa are going for their 'Connect-Ticket' circle meeting.'

'Fine, but tomorrow, we will definitely see the doctor. Jivesh, don't ignore your health.'

'Jesus said "No man can achieve anything by worrying." So please leave me alone, Anvita. I will recover. I have spoken to Bobby Singh – you remember my cousin? He has assured me a job, maybe in Cape Town. He will call me in a day or two. Then we will decide.'

When we reached our destination, Kisna and Pereeie were already there along with Bano, Kevan and Ismail. They were watching rugby on the big screen in the restaurant – especially installed for the tournament. They were happy and had joined others in the audience in applauding the South African team that had won the Rugby World Cup in France.

'Which is our team?' I asked.

'Those in the white dress – there with Jack White, their coach.'

'But all of them are fair or should I say white-skinned. Is it the South African team?' Kisna commented.

'Yes. The sad reality is that the blacks are not included in the team though they make up about 80 per cent of the South African population.' Kevan said.

'But we always talk about the country's racial rainbow. Who selects the players – this coach – Jack White?'

'What an appropriate name!' I was amused.

'And just see how our president, Thabo Mbeki, is going out of the way to hail the event as a victory for all South Africans,' Jivesh clarified.

'He forgot that some of his lieutenants in the past have demanded that the country's top teams field more blacks than whites.'

'South Africa shows both the good and the bad side of affirmative action, like the government policy of "black economic empowerment" which aims to shift more of the ownership and leadership into black hands,' said Kevan.

'I'm sure this will lead to the creation of a super rich black elite well connected to the ruling party – while making the investors nervous,' Bano surmised.

'But a feeling still lingers that rugby has not yet shed the predominantly white sport tag that long symbolized apartheid at its macho worst.'

Kevan clarified: 'The South African Institute of Race Relations says that making sports is more important than the national team's success but their racial makeup is really unfair.'

'Now leave all this rugby talk. You all are behaving like press reporters or what do you call them – swift-legged paparazzi,' Bano interrupted. She was speaking for all of us who felt ignored.

Pereeie announced that she was carrying an original recording of music by some Sufi singers from Pakistan as well as some Rajasthani folk music from India.

Kisna suggested that after lunch we could all go to his apartment to listen to the music. Everyone agreed but Jivesh was keen on the movie *Kabhi Khushi Kabhi Gham*. I was sure some of his perspicacious companions knew about his job – or the lack of it. To cheer him up, we all opted for the movie. But there were no tickets available. So we all trooped to Kisna's flat for Sufi music. Kevan and I sneaked out to his small balcony with our cups of tea.

'What are you doing these days, Anvita?'

'I'm busy with a new assignment, a huge project in Jo'burg which is going to be something worthwhile, the project of a lifetime.'

'What's more mysterious, she is always writing something when its pitch dark outside. Come early morning, she sits at the dining table and writes like mad,' Jivesh also joined us.

'That's right, Kevan. It's strangely meditative. It all started when my cousin Sanju handed me a diary that belonged to my uncle. It is record of a mystic world of love and hate; passion and fury – amazingly strange. But when I want to write, I feel it's not an easy exercise. It's challenging – more difficult than any of my architectural designs.'

'Don't forget the people who are facing greater challenges, Anvita,' Jivesh was in a sarcastic mood. 'There are many things you avoid on your one-dimensional diagram. There are so many things which cannot be expressed in lines, or words.'

'But Jivesh, as a writer, my own experience is that by writing one learns to observe the rules and regulations of the game called life. When we create our characters, we associate with or assert our ideas in their life. Initially, we also change according to plan – mentally if not physically. It happens subconsciously. It happens. The quality of life changes.'

Kisna joined in our conversation. 'Change and growth is a sign of life.'

'What I feel these days Kisna, is as if I'm living in an ancient world – where my relatives are locked up in some sort of velvet-lined strong box but are possessed with very unusual, shocking characters. How their love was ever patient, forgiving, loyal and trusting. What surprises me is that even in the suffering, it only gives without the desire of receiving.'

'While writing fiction, one learns to figure out many things. Like I could handle my misfortune. I took it as a blessing. With that, I feel so close to my own self – my own life.' Now Pereeie was also with us.

'What I feel is that writing is a poor man's art,' Jivesh was in a foul mood.

'No. It's the essence of the shloka of life. It's the contentment of soul.'

The Sufi music was over – but we were still merged with the secrets of the divine.

Kisna said, 'You know Maharshi Dwarkanath Tagore, Rabindranath Tagore's father used to begin his morning with the reading of the Upanishads and Sufi poems.

Bano added, 'Say Allah, Allah when with a Muslim. Ram-Ram when with the Hindus. That's the way of life.'

2

I reached the dining hall of the hotel and found that they were already there. Phelela was dressed in an elegant long silk dress clinging to her body. Her expensive perfume and fine diamond jewellery were oozing professional success. But it was making me conscious of my own rather plain appearance. I wore a simple black kurti that I'd picked up from the flea market during my last visit. I had worn it over my black pair of trousers. The only ornament I wore was my pearl string with a dangling gold Om in the centre. We had been in Jo'burg for months, working non-stop for the completion of the project. I could not afford to go back to Durban to pick up any of my clothes and other belongings as the work was extremely demanding. Mr Naso had shifted base to a small flat here with his entire family. It was very close to the work site. But I obviously could not ask Jivesh to do the same. His parents were alone – and then, his new job was in Cape Town. I missed him – especially in the loneliness of my nights. Though I spoke to him everyday on my cellphone – it was not the same as being with him.

'What will you have? White, or red wine?'

'Whatever,' I was perplexed with my own ignorance – not knowing the difference between the two. 'Okay red!' as soon as I saw Phelela opting for it.

'Cheers,' Mr Subramaniam raised a toast. So did Phelela – taking her glass near Mr Subramaniam's. I also did the same. It was my first experience of a sophisticated evening like this. With Jivesh, we had only gone to some affordable restaurants where people like Bano and Kisna ate with their fingers after discarding spoons and forks.

'So finally, you have found a ground on your own dear, here in South Africa ...'

'I'm not sure – for me hard work is my passion and also my guiding force.'

'I'm sure somebody is guiding you in the right direction. Otherwise, just college education is not enough to reach the space you're standing on. I remember when I met you for the first time – you were so raw – not at all aware of the world.'

'But she always had the potential, Phelela. The first day we interviewed her, she spoke of her dreams so confidently that we were convinced. We could assess – it now seems correctly – that she was bold and intelligent.'

'Anvita, I also read your articles on and off in the *Architectural Digest*. How do you manage to do so much, who helps you?'

'Phelela we're all here to determine our own destinies. Nobody helps anyone. I grew up motherless and neglected – there was no one I could complain to. So I created my own norms of life. I thrive on challenges. I strongly believe in my inner self – or my own self which guides me through the wrong and the right turns. As for my career, I believe that the purpose of my life is to create the best I can.'

'You know why we all have become selfish and self centred after our own political independence?'

Mr Subramaniam reignited his cigar and refilled his wine glass. He looked very sophisticated in his beautiful tie and well-tailored black suit. I thought of Jivesh. He never wears a suit, none of his friends did. They wore casual clothes and were not particular about their appearance. Nor were they female-obsessed Casanovas. They were simple beings making their own choices.

'But my theory of life is different, Anvita. My mind is full of demons – they keep troubling me. I'm very restless at times. Maybe it is due to my past – my mother's madness, fear, insecurity and helplessness which overpowers me when I'm alone.'

Mr Subramaniam went pale as Phelela stopped and looked at him. 'How I tried,' cried Phelela with her seductive smile, 'to lure you! We could have got married. But you remained a hard nut to crack.'

I was taken aback. She was on the verge of revealing a dark secret.

'Oh! How I adored you when we were together in Europe. But you refused even to touch me as if I was not even a woman.'

'Who would like to marry a difficult and bossy dictator like you Phelela? Besides, you are far more successful than I am. I was always under the aura of your success.'

'You're wrong. There were many who proposed to me, but as you said our past is the paradox of our lives. That I sold stolen linen to pay for my school fee does not go out of my system. It's like a bomb that can explode any moment and make me go insane!'

'You could help each other to defuse the ticking time bomb – with tenderness and love – as love has a great healing power.' I tried to ease the tension.

'No Anvita, it's an illusory expectation that something or someone can save you from the insecurity and problems and make you happy. Has your dear husband given you all the security and love you deserved? Do you really live the life you always wanted to, or had dreamt of?'

For a moment all of us were taken aback, thinking and rethinking about our lives, analyzing our own worth in our own eyes.

'Maybe you're right, Miss Phelela. The hero's character in the Indian series of Mills & Boon is different from here. Here, life revolves around another kind of romance – it's not emotional but practical. Here in South Africa, or perhaps in the entire world, love hasn't remained a sensitive emotion that led to a tender sense of self surrender. Today, it has transformed itself into a mathematical calculation. But I believe in the old-fashioned romance expressed with the wholeness of one's being. It's a love that floats in the air like an ethereal white bird. Or shines like a full moon as in our films!' I was transported into memories of old films.

'But your films also define a woman as a doormat – thrown out of the house when widowed like a tattered and stinking rag – because she becomes an economic liability.'

'That's because our society is a slave to money, sex and power. There's no place for love and romance in the battlefield of life.'

'But, sir ... where have all those men disappeared who were powerful and possessive – and loved their women with the strength bordering on worship?'

'What do you think, Anvita, is the definition of a complete man, the ideal man who lives up to the expectation of a superhuman?' Phelela wanted to know.

'I think "He" is the one who's free from the psychological division within – the one who is not discontented – remains calm in various situations in life. He's the one without an ego, without ego hassles, exudes knowledge and transforms the lives of those he comes into contact with.'

'I'm amazed at the way you think,' Phelela touched my shoulder with exquisite tenderness.

'But Anvita, you're talking about a most profound transformation of consciousness of the domestic man – which one can't even imagine in this corrupt world. It's rare Anvita, nobody can be that perfect on this planet!' Mr Subramaniam tried to convince me.

'Don't underestimate yourself, sir! You're a catalyst – helping so many of us to grow and win – that too while maintaining a perfect balance and authenticity. I'm sure, Mr Naso, I, and most of us working for you feel the same. All of us bask in the bliss and glory of your personality.'

The waiter who brought our food lit the candle which was set right in the centre of our table. I folded my hands, 'For me, lighting the evening lamp is a time of prayer and search.'

'A flame is also a splendour and beauty which illuminates life,' Mr Subramaniam added.

3

It was a Friday afternoon. The entire staff was busy reviewing the progress of the structure and addressing other related issues. We were seriously debating the finalization of the wall coverings. Mr Naso got up from his chair abruptly, interrupting the presentation of the colour options.

'Sir, can I be excused? My family is waiting in the car. I've to take my kids to the Lion Park?'

I don't know about the reaction of other staff but I suddenly descended from an illumined action to the realities of the external world.

'What's the Lion Park?' I asked, displaying my ignorance.

'It's a park full of lions. Don't you know Anvita?'

'No, I don't.'

'Here in South Africa, we keep our animals as preciously as you Indians preserve your Taj Mahal or Italy conserves its Vatican.'

'Oh! I have no idea. I've never seen a lion or any other wild animal in my life.'

'Not only the lions but all animals are our legacy. They roamed these lands long before the humans. They are one of our main ways of attracting tourists. Without them, no one would visit Africa,' Mr Naso seemed very proud of the fact.

'You also go with them, Anvita. Don't miss the chance!' Mr Subramaniam suggested.

'I'm sorry sir. I do not have enough space in my car.' Mr Naso's cellphone rang again and he hurriedly left.

'Let us go too, Anvita. It's been a long time. I have also not been to any of these animal parks.'

'Will it be okay for you sir? Or am I asking too much?'

Within half an hour, we reached the Lion Park. It was not too far from Lanacia, our work site. Our chauffeur guided us to a pristine landscape that stretched before me, opening up magnificent views of zebras, grazing herds of African buffaloes trotting back and forth. Even Mr Subramaniam was overwhelmed by the spectacular sight. He laughed and screamed after sighting a bunch of white lions enjoying their siesta under an acacia tree. I was impressed by the magnificent heritage of nature spread out in front of us amidst the swirling dust.

Our chauffeur introduced us to interesting minor details about the habits of the animals. He impressed me with his philosophic expressions. When he said, 'Sir, you know this earth doesn't belong to man. Men belong to this earth. So does the animal. Man did not weave the web of life. God created him with the animal and plants. Man is merely a strand in his web. Whatever he does to the web, he does to himself. That is why here in South Africa we respect animals as our companions.'

I was enjoying every moment of that magical evening – especially the particular perfume that Mr Subramaniam wore. It evoked a vivid imagery and titillated my senses. It was like a floral bouquet that smelled of his success. I thought of Jivesh. The wild earthy smell of his body used to make me restless. I missed him immensely. It had been months since I'd seen him. The workload, money, circumstances and responsibilities were so powerful that they kept us apart.

Suddenly a majestic white lion roared close by and interrupted my thoughts. The lion looked gorgeous in his white fur walking with three small cubs.

'Aren't they beautiful, Anvita?'

'I just can't believe that I'm here. It's an extraordinary sight. I haven't seen so many rare animals before in my entire life, never ever. I feel like a little girl wishing to shout like mad with joy.'

'I'm also delighted to see them again and discover a new kingdom of animals. Oh! How they walk and maintain their attitude!'

I could see a radical change on Mr Subramaniam's face. His formal and serious appearance had dissolved and he behaved like a normal human being. He laughed heartily and looked into my eyes with a melting warmth. He even wrapped me in his arms when I screamed on seeing a lion coming close to our car window.

After a while, we walked inside a guarded area where visitors were allowed to play and touch lion cubs. I was very scared to begin with, but then to reassure me, Mr Subramaniam picked up one of the cubs and held it in his arms. I noticed a black strip on one of the barbed wire fences with a quotation from Aristotle: 'Nature does nothing uselessly – be careful and respond properly because she feels and senses.'

Suddenly, there was a swift but heavy movement at the back. We heard a loud thud. All of us shrieked. One of the huge white lions roared and tore at Mr Subramaniam's coat – scratching his skin. The guards came running to the rescue and led us out of the barbed wire enclosure. We stood there for a while in a state of shock. It was like coming out of the jaws of death. I took Mr Subramaniam into my arms trying to comfort him. It was very seldom that a person of his character buckles down. His heart was thumping hard. It took us some time to recover. Some people helped us to the coffee shop, others got water and coffee for us. The medical attendant came and inspected Mr Subramaniam's arm and back. Luckily, he had escaped with just minor injuries. There was neither a wound nor even bleeding. He was only shocked. He was made to swallow a pill to help him calm down.

Mr Subramaniam did not speak for a while when we were returning. Even I was dazed but still managed to instruct the driver to take us to the hotel.

Suddenly, Mr Subramaniam said, 'I'm very sorry, Anvita. I can't imagine how the incident happened. I'm shocked to the core of my heart. It was almost like encountering death.'

'Thank God you're not hurt. I'm sure it was a very chilling experience. But let's forget it. Please relax!' I caressed his head and shoulders and made him lean against the back of the seat.

It was quite late in the evening when we made it to the hotel. He was feeling better but was very quiet. I asked him, 'Will you have dinner in the dining hall or would you like to order from room service?'

'Let's have dinner together in the dining hall. You must also be hungry. Its been a long day.'

We ordered food and some red wine to minimize the after effects of our unusual encounter.

'Anvita I'm very sorry for all the weakness I displayed. Though I've lots of courage and strength within me, sometimes some images of childhood tend to magnify everything. The leap of the lion was like my mother's attack of epilepsy – which used to drive her into insanity. I almost felt the same.' The blueness of his eyes became deeper when he spoke.

'But Sir, the images do crumble and things diminish with time. They slip through our hands like the grains of sand – never to return again.' His blue eyes became even deeper.

The cool breeze proved a good stress buster and helped us to get over that horrific moment. I patted his hand like a loving partner.

'Sir, please forget what you have suffered as you cannot undo it. Just look at all the blessings you have received. Besides, you have been given a very creative life – enjoy every moment of it!'

'Yes, Anvita. You're right. I also believe in mental discipline as it helps me control my mental powers. But still as a human being, the idea of death shakes your faith and threatens the desire to live.'

'But sir, you have a goal in life that only energizes you and helps overcome the weaker moments.'

Mr Subramanian held my hands. 'From where have you learnt all this? I'm amazed at the level of this conversation. Yesterday even Phelela complimented you. Are you a thinker or a philosopher?'

'Sir, these days I'm also writing a book – a sort of biography of my late Uncle. Through that, I'm learning about the emotional strength of a human being. Writing helps me to explore the inner purity of a soul. During the process, I've learnt to feel the dynamics of human relationships.'

'Who was your uncle? Was he a famous personality of India?'

'No, he was an ordinary conservative middle-class person. He hailed from a small town in Punjab. He had an extramarital relationship but was honest at heart and maintained the dignity of the lady he loved. Today, when I try to analyze their behavior and principles of human unity, the height of spirituality they reached because of the union, it amazes me.'

'Spirituality and extramarital relationship are two contradictory situations of human life, Anvita.'

'I agree, but his attitude of non-possessiveness for the materialistic gains was the essence of his life. His selfless devotion was for the sake of love, it was like a prayer to God. I'm sure that the relationship completed his divided personality. With that, he reached the human dignity – a state of completeness for any human being.'

'You mean this attachment was his actual commitment to the people he loved?'

'Yes. I think so. Because once you are attached, it gives you a feeling of guilt and obligation, obscuring the beauty of other person's emotional self. In a relationship, you must respect the other person's consciousness more than your own selfish motives with an open mind. One learns as one grows within oneself to learn the value of simplicity. And love is the guiding force, not only for living a joyful life but also to attain spirituality. So, sir … you're here on this earth for a special reason. Stop being a prisoner of the past – become the architect of the future instead.'

'You inspire me, Anvita dear!'

When we got up from the dining table, I could see he was not completely stable. He was trembling again. I held his arm and escorted him to his room. When we entered it he looked at me with a strange fondness.

'Anvita, I appreciate the pains you took to look after me, like somebody I belonged to. I like the way you provided an insight for the phenomenon of life. I've a lot to learn from you.'

He took me in his arms and rested his eager lips on mine. He then proceeded to kiss every inch of my face. I didn't know what happened – what accelerated an emotional rush in my heart. The very fibre of my life was transformed by the emotional response of his being. We made love disregarding the ticking time – allowing unlimited expression through our consciousness. I never felt this happy before. The ecstasy of his body – the exotic aroma of his skin was an experiential voyage to an unusual physical pleasure. There were tears in my eyes. He also cried, and said, 'I've never touched a woman in my life, let alone made love. No one inspired me to do so. This is my first time, Anvita. You've ignited an unfathomable desire in my heart and in my body.' He again kissed me hard. We both cried in the silence of the room.

4

It was a different morning. A different bed, a different partner – tender and magical like a newly blossomed flower. The intoxicating sense of Mr Subramaniam's presence overpowered my inner and outer consciousness. I tried to get up from the silken sheets of the bed but my whole being resisted. Something tugged me to stay under the sheets, inside the embrace of those loving arms – all my life. As I stood in front of the mirror and watched myself in the blue shadow of the curtains, my body looked like a peacock feather, slim and amazingly beautiful. I'd never pictured myself like this, never assessed my physical aspect ever like this. Now I wondered why I'd ignored my body – or the importance of my physical beauty.

I looked at Mr Subramaniam. He was fast asleep. His face appeared very serene with a peaceful smile. I looked at the watch. It was already 10:30 a.m. It was time to get ready for office. I got dressed hurriedly, collected my belongings and quietly left. I was careful not to wake him up or make any noise.

The soft aromatic breeze of the external world of reality greeted me. I was transformed into a new human being. The landscaped garden of the hotel stretched in front of me. I felt that the shimmering water of the pond and the cobbled stones of the garden pathway reflected my new mental state. The sound of the rippling water whispered all the unspoken words of last night. It altered my mood and blocked out the unwelcome noise of the people around me. I felt myself metamorphosed – a new person drenched in love with a kind of feeling I'd never experienced before. It was strange – so strange that I wanted to sing. I had never felt like this before.

As I reached the hotel lobby I felt that everyone in that over-crowded place was looking at me. All the eyes were not only focused, but glued on my whole body. Unconsciously I covered my arms with my scarf, though I was wearing a full-sleeved office coat. Hurriedly I hired a cab to reach my apartment. But all the way, I regretted leaving Mr Subramaniam like that without saying a word.

When I reached my small apartment, I felt unusually alone. To divert my attention I fixed a cup of tea for myself and stood near my worktable sipping my tea to delink myself from the memory of the happenings of the evening. I was still drifting between a dream-like space and the harsh reality of the situation. A vague unease was threatening me. I sat under a cold shower to allow my nerves to cool down. But somewhere deep down in my heart I wanted the unnamed pleasure of his caresses and his touch to remain on my body, as my deep consciousness required them to stay on my skin permanently suddenly with my whole being, I wanted to see but also not see his face near my own, hear but not hear his voice within the inner space of my body. It was a nameless essence of those mystic but sensuous moments I spent with him, floating in my veins.

While dressing up or preparing my breakfast, my mind and my feelings were not within my control. The calendar showed it was a working day, but I could not think of going to office, I was still floating, floating in a dream-like sky full of lovely white birds singing merrily a melodious song of love. I don't remember how long I sat like that, in a state of no-perception and no-thought. The doorbell rang. He came in, all dressed up in his office suit, looking as sophisticated as ever. As he stood near the window of my room, a white light surrounded him like an aura of serenity. But to me he looked like a feverish child longing to be taken care of. It was beyond me, not to surrender. I rushed into his arms like a swift breeze. The ecstatic tide ceased ebbed and then it flowed again. The only thing I could hear was the fluttering of angel's wings all around me. He murmured sweetest words of love like the carol of a bird, saying, 'Do not ever leave me Anvita, please, let your radiance illumine the darkness of my life.' It was the last gleam of twilight outside my window when we sat next to each other on my bed, unconscious of time. I don't remember for how long we sat like that without uttering a word. Before leaving the room he kissed me hard on my lips. His intensity was so deep and intoxicating, that a luxurious emotion of the sense of belonging overpowered my whole being. While parting he said, 'Thank you Anvita for this blissful experience, may I tell you that I have never felt anything for any woman in my life. What I feel for you is amazing. You strengthen my intention to live, live a full life.'

'Please don't say … thank you,' utterly fulfilled I had no words to express myself.

'OK, take care of yourself and of these moments Anvita. The time will take care of itself. I am sure that life will not be counted by the number of years, but by each moment that will be fulfilled.'

He left, leaving me alone, in the dark stillness of my room.

5

I did not meet Mr Subramaniam for many days. Mr Mariza, his private secretary informed me some days later that he was in Europe attending some important seminars. It provided me with an opportunity to take an honest look at my life, to decide things, situations and opinion about myself. As life shrinks or expands in proportion to one's strength and abilities. I was aware I had gone very far. But did I have enough courage to walk away from it? Could I dare? The world was brimming with many alluring opportunities and situations, but only my God knows, I was not hungry for that. Whatever happened was an unplanned or unintentional accident. But the fact was that it was a reality. Maybe I will come clean about it all with Jivesh. Being truthful is being honest. My faith in myself was clear, that would determine or indicate my fate.

Yet another month passed by without any news of his coming back. He called me at least once a day, but it was more official than personal. While Jivesh never called, but I was calling him every week. Jivesh's conversation was becoming impersonal and dry, which indicated his deep-seated sense of incompleteness. I wondered about the nature of his job, too, which he never revealed. I suffered emotional pain when I spoke to Jivesh, but it was Mr Subramaniam's voice which flickered in my heart like a perennial flame.

My job was getting more and more engrossing. I spent most of my time at the worksite. It was very fulfilling to see an imagined form of a building taking real shape. It was rising beautifully, or rather majestically, high with a collective identity. When I stood near that half-finished building I wondered if it was not what I had dreamt of yes, it was a manifestation of a dream, which inspired my consciousness when I designed this. It was a fascinating experience, to see the hard work of my countless sleepless nights attaining a concrete form. At a deeper level I knew my design was unique.

But whenever I was alone, I sat in my small room with fragments of the images of the past. I wondered whether my mind and body had achieved a desired goal. My goal was not 'that' what happened in this room, but then why was my heart betraying me, oh why? I will have to store the memory of the recent past somewhere deep in my heart, to move to reality towards my future.

When I was tired of all the heavy burden of my work and the complexity of my psychological problems and conflict, I decided to take a break. I suddenly missed Bano, Ismail's abusive language and the lunches with Kisna and Pereeie. Kevan's medical and personal discussions. Even a wish to meet Pratapji and mom was also weighing heavily on my consciousness, I calculated that it had been almost ten months since I was here in Johannesburg. I hurriedly packed my luggage while Mr Mariza organized a car for me. I even kept my unfinished novel in my briefcase along with the velvet-wrapped packet of letters. I was filled with mixed emotions. Sanju had told me he was in India and Vati Aunty was very unwell. He remained in touch with Arjun and her during almost all those eight to ten months back when he visited me, and I had made him speak to them.

Meanwhile my cell phone rang several times. It was Mr Subramaniam. He asked about the progress of the work, problems and everything official. I heard him eagerly, his voice, whatever he spoke, each and every word the words resonated like the sound of meditative mantra, generating a kind of cosmic energy within me. I never felt as formless, as eternal as I felt at that moment the driver glanced back at me and asked, 'Why are you crying, Miss?'

'Am I?' I was a little startled. I was not conscious of it. But there was a reason for it.

The phone rang again, this time it was Sanju. 'Annu, Vati Aunty passed away last night. She was very unwell. She was in immense pain and suffered quite a lot. May God bless her soul.'

'Oh, Sanju, why everyone has left us, Uncle, Bua and now Vati Aunty. I am so far away; even if I try I can not reach that early to see her face.'

'Don't worry, Annu, after the rituals I will take care of Arjun, I am planning to take him to California with me.'

I cried, 'Oh Sanju, how much I wanted to get my novel published so that she could read it. I so much wanted to glorify the journey of her life, her love that represented a spiritual state of mind, a theme that was free from guilt.'

'I will talk to you after the rituals are over, you take care and look after yourself.'

I grieved in the silence of my car for a while. Again the cell phone rang, it was not Sanju but Mr Subramaniam.

'Anvita, every time I called you I wanted to convey my trust and my feelings to you. My dear, let me honestly admit that I am deeply in love with you. Most of the time when I think of you I feel I am in some kind of a trance, borne aloft in a rhythmical unwavering peace.'

I was overwhelmed by contradictory strains of grief over Vati Aunty's death on one hand and the urgency of Mr Subramaniam's love on the other.

'Why are you crying? Have I said something wrong? I believe you are in Durban, Mr Mariza informed me.'

'Yes, I am on my way.'

'Why are you crying? Tell me is anything wrong?'

'I lost my aunt, she was the only one I had …'

'Want to go to India?'

'No, I don't think so … what shall I do?'

'I will be reaching Durban tomorrow morning, will see you for dinner. Be ready at eight. I will pick you up from your residence.'

It was an order, he switched off the phone without waiting for my response.

6

When I reached Durban, it was pretty late. I found Leelaji and Pratapji indulging in their favourite pastime, watching television. They were almost shocked to see me. 'How are you dear?' Pratapji got up from his chair and hugged me fondly. Leelaji could not do the same as her joints pained. I went down on my knees to kiss her hands. 'Oh Mom! What have you done to yourself? I can see that your health has deteriorated. You have lost so much weight!'

She had tears in her eyes. I also cried. 'I missed you Anvita. The house is so empty without you and Jivesh.' I could feel the tremor in her voice. 'It's been months. And Jivesh has also not turned up from Cape Town. He has not even bothered to send us any money.' She was very blunt about her disappointment. 'But Mom I'd left some money for you for everyday expenses ... anyway, don't worry! I will take care of you till he gets a proper job. Now that I'm back, I will take you to the doctor too.'

'And Jivesh ... is everything fine between you?'

'How can you think of something like that? It's only the circumstances that are keeping us away. After my project is over in a few months, I will come back and take up something here. In fact, let's call Jivesh. You don't know how much I miss him.' I dialled his number. He picked up the phone after about a minute. We spoke. I requested him to come home, meet everyone, including me. 'I'm your wife Jivesh!'

'Life is tough, Anvita. My job does not allow me to even think of taking any leave. But I will try. I also want to be with you, dear!'

His voice echoed – as if resounding through far off mountains – distant and lost. I trembled, as last night's images perturbed me. Will I react the same way to everything as before? Suddenly I thought of Vati Aunty. An ancient mist covered my mind. I longed to remain with her memories. The dinner proved dreary and silent.

When I reached my bedroom, I unlocked my cupboards and took out the velvet-wrapped diary as well as the thick bundle of old pale letters. There were two letters folded together – one was hers and the other was from Jo Jo Uncle. I started reading Jo Jo Uncle's letter first.

'How do I tell you how much I'm indebted to you? With you I live in a very unusual world of total completeness. I did not experience it earlier, though I have a wife and children. I won't say I don't love my wife, I love her. She is a simple, practical and worldly-wise woman. But what I've learnt from you is not to stop at one point, that it's a never-ending journey of learning, learning which leads your senses towards awareness – about the impermanence of all things around you. It reveals the truth that the world is self-centred. Everyone lives for his individualistic ego. I can see extreme egoism even in children, they are so indifferent and cruel.

'But when I'm with you, I'm on a different plane, which sails in the ocean of selfless love. Sometimes, I wonder you don't demand anything, you don't expect any materialistic gifts from me. Is our love an emotional healing for us? Is it therapeutic for you as you could never have sex with Narender, he was sick or maybe …? God knows!

'My dear Vati, can I confess a secret to you? I'd had sex with my wife before I met you, but it was different, a very human action, or role-playing to create children. Every morning when we woke up, we would have two separate identities. She lived in her own world of demands and I lived on my planet so as to fulfill my duties. But now, when I've experienced this strange transformative relationship, I feel your love is blissful. Your love is leading my consciousness towards completion. *Dua ko uthtey nahin haath, tujhey paa leney ke baad.*'

Vati wrote back beautifully.

'I received your gift, Jay, the brass icon of 'Natraj'. I've kept it on my office table where I work everyday. Whenever I'm free, I look at it, wondering why Lord Shiva chose to be a dancer. I received my answer, in Osho's book. I will quote it for you:

> *Why was Shiva a Natraj, the cosmic dancer? Why wasn't he a painter, a poet or a sculptor? When a painter finishes his painting, the painting assumes its own existence. The painter becomes separate from his paintings. It has a life of its own. Similarly, the poet is separate from his poetry and the writer from his novel. But with the dancer the dance and the dancer are the same, they can never be separated. That's why God is a dancer. He dances in His own creation. He is present in the leaves, flowers, rivers, animals and every human being. His dance is all over. He has not created the world, He is the world. The world is God's dance. Just as the dancer's body is the canvas into which the dance pours the colours of feelings and impressions.*

'Jay, my answer was completed when he wrote, "Dance becomes meditation, when the dancer disappears into dance and only the dance remains. This leads to the profound experience of the Advaita. It's a state of consciousness of non-duality. When the dancer dances meditatively, the ego disappears, the dancer disappears. That is what the whole art of meditation is about, the disappearance of the ego, the disappearance of the mind."

'Don't you think we experience the same disappearance in our intimate moments? Don't you feel the non-dual as Osho said, the divine at that time? Aren't these feelings interwoven in our love? Isn't this the essence of our lives?'

I looked up across the window to look up at the sky searching for my Saptarishi. But the constellation eluded my search. There was only one star, maybe it was she, my Vati Aunty. I wondered if she had lived a life of goodness. And how hard she had striven to realize the truth, how earnest was the struggle!

7

When I woke up in the morning, I was filled with mixed emotions. A strange commingling of impatience, weariness and even a faint amusement assailed me. My mind buzzed with Vati Aunty and Jo Jo Uncle's relationship. Their letters were expressions of their private lives, of an unusual relationship, often the stairway to intellectual development. Taking my cup of tea, I sat near the yellow orange of my 'Bird of Paradise' groove. There was a metal and bamboo chime hanging on one of the branches ringing its lovely murmur. It energized me and brought clarity to my perplexed mind. I decided to learn to operate from beyond my own self. Later, I asked for the office car to take Mom and Pratapji for an outing. Besides visiting their doctor, we also went shopping. We bought new winter clothes for them and some articles of daily need. The next stop was the Krishna Consciousness Temple. We prayed in silence. Before leaving, we also partook of the typical Indian lunch at their favourite restaurant, Gokul. Both of them seemed happy.

After dropping them home, I searched for a beauty parlour near home. For the first time, I was aware of myself as a body. I don't know why I was the slave of my mind till now. Suddenly, my body had received an identity, a separate entity of its own. I looked at my chipped nails, crinkled skin and unwaxed arms. When I reached a parlour and talked to the lady in charge, she was shocked. 'Have you never visited a beauty parlour before? Her eyes asked accusingly. She decided to educate me, 'In this individualistic generation, everything is a reflection of your personality. From the shade of your nail polish to the choice of your career, everything points to it.'

I was inspired. I believed in what she was saying. This was again a new learning for me, a learning to gain more confidence. I remembered what Jivesh had once said: 'Your body is the only thing you have.'

While I was busy improving my mind, my intellectual abilities, I'd neglected my external beauty. But to be a perfectionist and according to societal norms, everything was important. One needs to balance the body with the mind. While sitting in the parlour for three hours, I called up Kisna, Bano and Pereeie. We planned to meet. I was very excited. I had to tell Kisna about my novel. When I came out of the parlour after picking up some beauty aids, I felt like a very different human being. I'd metamorphosed into a very modern person like Phelela and other well-groomed people.

Destiny does have a hand in my life. That is why all this is happening. We, two self-centred and estranged people, are coming together – but to what end?

I wore one of my best saris. It was a black silk with very small white and yellow flowers and a broad pallu. I wore some makeup and applied some newly bought perfume. My reflection in the narrow mirror in our toilet looked different from the usual. My eyes highlighted with kohl pencil were not the usual eyes that stared back from the mirror. They looked deeper and larger than before, and searching for something which they had never done before. I was wondering whether my appearance had taken a different identity, or was it the same. My soul walked right beside my body now.

When I came out of my room, I saw a confused expression on Leelaji's face. 'Oh Anvita! You're looking so glamorous. I've never seen you like this. I think the Jo'burg weather has suited you. Isn't it Pratap?' She turned towards Pratapji.

"There is someone waiting for you outside in the car,' he said.

'Yes. Mr Subramaniam, my boss has invited me for dinner. I have to go. But I won't be late still, please don't wait for me. I have the duplicate key.'

'Has he come personally to pick you up?'

'I think so.' I didn't wait for their reaction. I quickly strode out.

As I sat in the car, he looked at me with a critical eye. He smiled and touched my fingers very softly.

'You look great Anvita. This Indian dress suits you very much.'

'Thank you, sir.' He looked at me with a certain expression as I addressed him as 'Sir'.

For the first time, I scrutinized his entire face. It was very attractive – of a very light brown complexion and deep blue eyes. He must have inherited those from his German mother, I surmised. He was tall but not slim. He didn't have the film star looks, but he carried himself with smooth sophistication. He was indeed the head of a prestigious organization, while I was only an ordinary employee. I wondered what he will say tonight. Was I to be his mistress? Or will he throw me out of the job if I wanted to be out of the relationship?

We did not speak to each other till we reached one of the most expensive restaurants in Durban. He had booked a table in his name. The entire place was beautifully done up with flowers and candles.

We sat down on a table that was placed in the corner of the dining area. We sat facing each other. He ordered the finest red wine and just the apt food. I felt an unusual sensation arising in my body. It was like a tidal wave.

'Cheers for whispering a passionate poem. And for creating a beautiful painting within my body, Anvita. And that too, when the vacuum in my life was becoming too much to bear.' He pressed my hand and kissed my fingers. As he did so I could see some tears in his eyes, glistening like stars. 'And listen, I never felt like a child ever before, not even when my mother died. That evening was like a wonderful dream, a sudden revelation of immense beauty that I'd never experienced before. I promise you my dear that your face would remain etched in my heart like the image of a goddess.' He appeared to be incorrigibly romantic.

'Why are you so quiet Anvita? Are you upset about what happened? Do you think I should apologise to you?'

'No. Please don't. Let me admit I will also cherish those moments like a precious jewel all my life. I've also not yet come out of the magical spell of what happened. Even though I'm married. And I love Jivesh. But all my life, your love will flow in my veins like a sacred prayer.'

'Listen Anvita, you're a very precious and artistic creation of God. In future, I will treat you from a distance as an unusual painting. I promise you our relationship will not go beyond its limitations. It won't seek to degrade your character or mission in life. I wanted to tell you all this, that is why I've come here chasing you. I've something to attend tomorrow evening and day after I will be going to Jo'burg.'

I had no words. I didn't even react as I had no time to think. Everything had happened so quickly. We both had to distance ourselves form the event. Who are we? Love was definitely binding both of us, but ....

The entire evening was enchanting, dissolving into an amorphous mysticism. As we reached home Mr Subramaniam got down and opened the car door for me. When I came out, he took me in his arms, kissed me softly on my forehead. 'Good night, dear. See you when I come back.'

'I've a request. Please don't think of me as a hard-hearted goddess but as a human being.'

Suddenly I saw bright headlights coming towards me. A taxi stopped close to us. I pulled myself hastily away from him.

Bobby Singh disembarked from the car.

'Oh! Hello,' we both shouted our greetings together.

'Bobbyji, meet Mr Subramaniam. He's my boss. And Bobby Singh is Jivesh's cousin.'

They shook hands.

'Oh! It's you who they will felicitate tomorrow? I didn't know you two have a connection.' He wanted to give a psychological dimension to the entire event.

'Anyway congratulations!'

'Thank you!' Bobby Singh said with a crooked smile. I knew what it meant.

As we were about to enter the house, I saw Pratapji opening the main door even before I could find the keys.

'Hasn't Jivesh come with you Bobby?' He asked.

'No, he hasn't. Was he supposed to? Anyway we will discuss it tomorrow morning, it's late and I'm very tired!'

'Would you like some coffee or tea?' I asked.

'Yes. Some tea, if you could ...'

I brought some tea for both of them. I was not in a mood for arguments. And I could not talk about my romantic escapade. I just smiled and moved to complete the chore. I knew where the relationship was heading and that was enough. I knew within myself that the random comments could not stop me from pursuing my career.

I reached my room humming a beautiful old song. I folded my sari and opened the velvet bundle of letters and romance. I found one of the letters ending with these lines:

'There is a vast jungle called the heart. Endless are its mazes on all sides. Here I've lost my way.'

8

The residence of the Consul General of India was an impressive colonial structure, surrounded by lush green lawns laden with colourful flowers. We were greeted at the entrance by a very well-clad usher, who tallied the guest list with our cards. There were many people inside by the time we entered. We were finally introduced to the Consul General and his wife. They congratulated Bobby Singh. There were Indian dignitaries, black politicians along with white real-estate developers and sugar mill owners in the gathering. Everyone was very well dressed and they were talking to each other with an ease of being among equals. I saw Mr Subramaniam entering and being greeted by other people. He caught my eye and came towards us to congratulate Bobby Singh and Pratapji. We shook hands with mixed feelings and a fragmented consciousness. I could make out that Pratapji's reaction towards him was not entirely respectful. I wondered what he thought of our relationship, or was he thinking of what was in store? Though my self-esteem and faith were temporarily shaken, the strength of my spirit made me calm. I drifted away from my people, driven by an unconscious fear. I felt I had no control over myself anymore.

The function was organized in one of the huge lawns that was covered by shamianas. Every table had the names of person to be seated there. I felt I sat in an isolated island as I sat between Pratapji and Bobbyji amidst their palpable feelings.

The ceremony began with speeches by various distinguished dignitaries followed by a warm welcome by the Consul General. He introduced Bobby Singh, extolling his personality and sacrifices – his life and achievements – interspersing it with his own interpretations.

Bobby Singh's life was fascinating and frustrating too. When his turn came, he talked about his own career as a firebrand apartheid political leader. As a teenage activist from Shastri College, he'd joined the student movement in a campaign to dislodge the strait-jacketed Afrikaner hegemony. His passion for black politics and hatred of apartheid led to spending eight years and three months behind bars – in Mandela Block in Robben Island. He continued his political education there. Many of the 4,000 prisoners learnt to write and read from him. In between the heated political debates with imprisoned ANC leaders like Nelson Mandela, Walter Sisulu and Ahmed Kathreda, Bobbyji completed his BA degree. When he left Robbin Islands, he looked at the sunny sky, took a deep breath and let the fresh air from the Indian Ocean flow in through his nostrils. For the first time, as a free citizen of South Africa, he picked up his Spanish guitar and boxes full of books and reached home to meet his ailing father. His mother had died earlier during his imprisonment. His academic career had been badly affected. But he never gave up. He was allowed to travel abroad and he studied clinical psychology at Boston University. He returned to Africa as a consultant psychiatrist and soon became the president of the Psychology Society of South Africa. Bobby Singh is an intellectual of note and a political veteran and spent a lot of time in 'healing the nation of the trauma and pain of nationhood.'

People began talking during a pause. Someone commented, 'The people who are truly powerful are the ones who operate from commitment. And the powerless always operate from complaints.'

'Another dimension is to operate selflessly. When we do something thus, we find unknown forces strengthen our hands mysteriously.'

'Can you guess his age? He looks so fit and has such an unusual glow on his face.'

'One of the reasons is that he never married.'

Bobby Singh rose up to acknowledge all those who applauded. With a singular grace; he walked up to the stage where he was ceremoniously handed over the award. He made it clear that whatever he had achieved in his life, was the due to the times he lived in. He had merely joined in as everybody was charged up with patriotic feelings to fight for their self-respect and dignity. In the end, he quoted Franz Kafka: 'Beyond a certain point, there is no return. This point has to be reached. A faith in oneself is the essence of my life. It has been my driving force – it's the instinct that has helped me reach wherever I am today.'

He was given a warm standing ovation and everybody raised their wine glasses to him.

Meanwhile, the programme compere on the stage introduced the 'Power of One – an Indo-South African Cultural Programme' by 'Sewell-Since' dance theatre. The group was considered to be a truly multi-cultural, multi-linguistic dance theater. The programme began with the chanting of Vedantic mantras by a young boy who wore white kurta-pajama. Two young girls dressed like typical Indian film stars followed, dancing to the popular film music of *Umrao Jaan* – replete with adayegi, or mannerisms, fused with localism. Then, a black woman appeared on the stage. She led a band of four white girls very gracefully. They played a South African song symbolizing happiness and harmony. It was followed by many other performances in which young girls and boys of all colours mixed freely and danced.

It symbolized perfectly Nelson Mandela's dream of a 'Rainbow Nation' that was finally becoming a reality. It seemed to be a very innovative, creative and authentic solution for racism in a contemporary, witty and an informal setting. The attempt was to dare people to travel in their imagination to destinations once thought impossible. It stirred the mind to conceive a borderless world based on a mixed culture and Indian vision. It received a rapturous ovation from all guests, blacks, whites and coloured.

After an evening of receiving honour and accolades, the family was in a good mood. We discussed the fabulous reception and the cultural programme over cups of coffee and laughter. But I could discern a cloud of questions in his eyes, whenever Bobby Singh looked at me. What it was, I wondered. Was it my relationship with Mr Subramaniam, or something else? After Pratapji and mom retired to the room, he held my hand and said, 'Anvita, I want to talk to you. Can you sit for a while?'

'Why not?' My heart thumped wildly but I had to face him.

'You have to come to Cape Town with me!'

'Why?'

'To meet Jivesh.'

'Is something wrong? Is he all right?'

'No, Anvita. He's not well. He suffers from myriad complexes. He developed them when he couldn't find a job in spite of being so qualified. He is working in my clinic as an ordinary clerk.'

'I knew there was something awfully wrong with him when he began to avoid meeting me and the family. I've not been able to meet him for the past seven months.

'I thought it was my duty to inform you of all this.'

'Thank you, Bobbyji!'

Emptiness stared at me wherever I turned. With those terse sentences, all my happiness had evaporated within a few seconds.

He is running away from his family. He is ignoring his duties towards me. How strange are pulls and pressures of lucre? It had destroyed the entire dreamscape that we had built for our lives. I was still ambitious about my future.

'Remember, Anvita, nothing is permanent in this life, neither good nor bad. We will tackle this too. But you have to be brave and pull him out of it.'

'Yes. I will … I will come to Cape Town – after a few weeks though my work will suffer.' I stated simply.

He looked at me meaningfully and left the room. A complete silence echoing with meanings ensued.

That night I became restless in my bed. Mixed memories of love and lust haunted me like ugly ghosts. I found an unused 'foot cream' in one of the bedside drawers. I threw it in the dustbin. A very old incident of childhood came gushing in. I clearly remembered when I was just ten, or maybe eleven, that Sanju had brought me a cheap plastic doll from a fair he'd visited with his friends. The doll wore a shimmering sari and shiny jewellery. She had beautiful, flowing, long hair like mine. It was a rare gift, the first given to me by any relative. My birthday was never celebrated – as my date of birth remained a faded writing on my birth certificate. It was in Gurmukhi. It held meaning only for me and Bua.

I loved my doll. She became my only friend. I used to talk to her in my moments of loneliness and pain. One day, I'd gone to school, Nony came up to my room looking for something which she thought I'd stolen. She saw my doll sitting gracefully on my bed. She could neither digest the cleanliness of the erstwhile store room, nor the doll being my precious possession. She tore my books, scattered my clothes and cut my doll's hair. Then she broke it into tiny pieces. As if that was not enough, she went on to tell Bua and Jo Jo Uncle, 'Dekha, I used to tell you that she is a thief, pakki chor. She steals money from my cupboard to buy things for herself!'

I looked at Sanju. He was pale. His face was drained out and he was trembling with fear. I kept quiet as I could not reveal how it came to me. I was beaten up by Nony nonetheless for stealing something that I never did. I turned to Bua and Jo Jo Uncle but they stood as mute spectators. I got beaten even more. But I didn't cry. I remained quiet. However, the humiliation had left me numb. And helplessness, utter helplessness at being punished for something I had not done.

Similar numbness was overpowering me at this moment. I was overwhelmed with all kinds of fears. My future, my security was in jeopardy. I wondered why I took it for granted that my fate will change. And that my escape to a foreign country would help me escape from all my psychological fears and insecurities.

I'd never depended on any divine force, drugs or rituals for instant relief from pain. Right from the beginning, I'd relied on my will power and even today I believed that I'd solve our problems.

Are we, Jivesh and I, turning into traders or looters, I wondered? I cannot stop working against any inadequacy and therefore I have to find a solution to the situation.

9

While entering the apartment, I went blank. I didn't know if I'd be able to maintain my composure when I came face to face with Jivesh. My mind was replaying numerous memories, of our love, how much we loved each other, how he'd filled the empty void in my life. All the emotional comfort, social position – the very prestige he'd provided me. I wondered if I'd be able to survive without this dependence, the attachment to him.

I was sure Jivesh was in a similar emotional turmoil, apart from his financial problems. It was the toughest moment in my life. I always believed in my own self. Like a karmayogi, I believed that one could do anything, reach any goal, if only we worked hard enough. But now destiny stood opposed to my capability and competence. I didn't know if there were knots and tangles designed especially for my failure. It was the worst moment in our lives.

He stood near the door with a vacant, silent look on his face. He looked silent in his misery, cheerless and morose. Unable to control myself, I flung my arms around him, trying to hug him. I somehow believed that whatever the circumstances, catastrophic to say the least, love would help us tide over our fears – and even help reestablish our faith and understanding.

But he turned his face away and released himself from my embrace. I could sense the struggle and fear writ large on his face. Even his body twisted into some kind of deformation.

He trembled and lost his balance somewhat. I helped him to the bed and sat next to him, trying to assess the seriousness of the situation.

'What have you done to yourself, Jivesh? Why didn't you tell me? I'm your life partner. I'm here to share your problems. You know very well that finances are not an issue any more. You know that I've established myself in my career. We can live comfortably with whatever we have. Why are you suffering so much … why?'

He looked at me with empty eyes.

'Oh Anvita, it was my fault. I've ruined my life. I never imagined that my lust for sexual pleasure would lead me to this.'

He cried like a madman. I wanted to hug him. But Bobby Singh stood there instructing me to stay away from his body.

Still I couldn't help trying. 'No Anvita! Stay away from me. You know this disease is infectious!' With great difficulty, he'd confessed. I was shocked to the core, broken, caught in the vortex of despair, I could sense he was slipping away from my hold forever. The beautiful tender dream we both shared about our future, to have children – a family of our own – was shattered and I was not at fault. Deep down, I could sense the onrushing danger; I could feel the beginning of something very ominous happening. That too, when I was doing so well in my career. It was as if I was caught in a whirlpool of poisonous smoke – as if a devilish creature was taking its awful revenge. I don't know what happened next. Everything turned hazy and like a fast moving wheel, everything whirled around me.

When I woke up, I was in a hospital ward – alone gazing at the blank white wall.

Suddenly, Bobby Singh appeared.

'Hi! Anvita! How are you? Feeling ok?'

'I'm fine. But where's Jivesh?'

'You're in my clinic, Anvita. You fainted and didn't revive for a while. So I brought you here. Just take it easy. I think when you fell and injured your right arm. I've called the doctor. He will examine you soon. And don't worry. I'm trying to treat Jivesh too.'

Unwilling to prolong an unnecessary and futile conversation about Jivesh – whom I still deeply respected, I kept quiet. I closed my eyes. But it was difficult to understand Jivesh's sexual drive. What is that a prostitute offers that a wife cannot? Why did he break our intimate norms and bonds? Bobby Singh had told me that Jivesh had gone on planned sex tours. That's how he's got infected. I found myself sulking in the darkness of a defeat, trying to tell myself that he would be cured, somehow. I lit a small flame of faith and hope flickered in my heart. I wondered how secret this flame is, yet the world depends on it.

The weather had turned warm and clammy. I'd spent the last few days in the loneliness of Bobby Singh's house. I confided my plight to Mr Subramaniam, asking him to allow me to take a few days off from my work. He was in London but spoke to me every day – showing his concern. I used to spend the mornings in my room. I opened all the windows, smelling the fragrant flowers which bloomed outside in the garden. But my nausea and giddiness made me restless. My left arm was in a cast but I still had to undergo all the checks required for being Jivesh's wife, even though I'd informed the doctors that I was away from him for nearly seven months. But the bitter reality was my human reality, it was happening to me now. During my check ups, I used to chant the Gayatri Mantra subconsciously. I couldn't find a better anchor in that situation. It took me a few days. For the first time in South Africa, I felt that time doesn't run or even walk, it crawls. Though the doctors told me that HIV/AIDS was no longer a death sentence, I was wild with anxiety. I threw up many times.

There was an article in one of the newspapers, the headline was 'AIDS Infection Rate Less than Originally Thought'. The article indicted the number of people 'infected by AIDS, explained the study and the difference between the lives of an AIDS patient and one not infected by the virus. It ended with 'HIV-Positive equals AIDS equals death in a few years'. I wondered, was it a myth or was it a reality?

When Bobby Singh came home with my reports, I was trembling. I was unable to control my anxiety. His words calmed down a little as he informed, 'You're lucky. You've tested negative. Doctors have cleared you of any disease. Maybe your job or your workload saved you. You had to stay away from Jivesh for so long. But …'

All those words worked like magic, transforming my agony into a cool, joyous reassurance.

'But … what? Bobbyji …but what?! Please, tell me now or the suspense will kill me!'

'Ok … Anvita, since you ask … you are in a morally unanswerable situation – your medical report says that you're pregnant.'

'What?' I fell into a strangled silence. Just a while ago I had felt that a flickering ray of hope had flooded my world. But suddenly it'd ended, and in such horrific darkness.

I sat there motionless, carefully pretending to ignore my own reality. It was elaborate shame, which I would have to prepare for. I felt I had completely fallen down in Bobby Singh's eyes. I'd destroyed his trust in me. But he gracefully left me alone – leaving me to deal with this unexpected disaster by myself.

10

I could not sleep that night. I was caught up in the paradox of my life. The combined pain, suffering and betrayal were hemming me in, imprisoning my thoughts. I could not get away from myself. I was entrapped in a similar anxiety six years after Bua's suicide. It was mind-numbing to stand at the same crossroads again. My mind was a blank. I couldn't think properly. What will become of my life? Its entire meaning was changing so fast.

An old incident suddenly flashed in my mind. I remembered the time when I was in school. One of Bhagwanti's relatives once came to our hometown after a gap of a few years. She was a young girl who used to work in Ludhiana. She looked shattered, a lifeless skeleton, sick and disoriented. At that time, I was not aware of the existence of any infectious diseases like AIDS. But I remembered she was treated very badly. All the neighbours abused and threw stones at her. Finally, she had died of humiliation, illness and lack of treatment outside the city, after living in complete isolation.

I had been shaken deeply. I'd gone through so much in my life but had never experienced a greater low. I wondered how Pratapji and Leelaji will take it. How would I ever explain my pregnancy? But I knew with complete certainty that I would not terminate the life growing within me, at any cost. I would never follow Bobbyji's advice. I intuitively knew how Mr Subramaniam would react. Even if there was no sharing of my life with anyone, I would deliver my child as it would be my only possession that I could truly call my own flesh and blood. The child would be someone like I never had in my entire life. My recent successes and the sense of achievement were giving me strength to live a life on my own. I visited the doctor again and got all my checkups done to find out whether my child was safe. When they learnt that the father was someone other than Jivesh, they gave me a clean chit. The doctor also prescribed some medicines for my pregnancy. With a sigh of relief, I visited Jivesh. I tried to convince him to come clean about the fact to his parents, but he was reluctant. He could not envision where my life was going. He could find nothing to say to alleviate my pain. As always, he was uncertain, indecisive about the serious facts in life. The only thing he could definitely promise was that when he was fit enough, we'd all meet together to plan the future. Before leaving, I thought it was necessary for him to know that I was pregnant, as I wanted to build my relationship on honesty. I accepted completely that I'd got carried away.

The expression on his face changed. He became furious and nasty. 'I knew Anvita … why you're doing so well. Why do you get so much recognition and why money keeps pouring in … and now you've proved it. You're carrying a child and you don't even know who the father is … how many people have you slept with?' He slapped me hard across my face. I was shocked, shaken and not physically strong enough to take it. But I maintained my composure.

'Jivesh, do you remember the number of women you have slept with?' I pushed him back towards the bed. I wanted to slap him back, but didn't.

'Jivesh, I don't have to tell you how much I loved you. I came all the way to South Africa because of my love for you. That is why I accepted and owned up to my indiscretion. Maybe that's my only fault. If only you can forgive me …!' I tried to be as sympathetic as I could as he was breathing hard. We both cried for a while at our destiny. When we parted, he said goodbye to me. We were together looking across the window of his room where the sun-drenched sea now signalled turmoil. I walked out watching the boundless horizons.

There was a huge chemist shop outside the hospital. I stopped there to buy medicines. Suddenly, I saw a very familiar face close by. She looked haggard and was wearing a rather dirty-looking, smelly dress. She was in a hurry to buy a foot cream – in addition to the things she'd already shopped for. I felt horribly uncomfortable when she looked at me. 'Hi Anvita, I'm Julia, you don't recognize me?'

I silently wondered how the wheels of the universe don't move without any complications.

11

While I was travelling back to Durban, I felt my whole world collapse around me. The pivot round which my life revolved had suddenly been plucked and taken away from my life without compunction. I felt so let down by Jivesh's behaviour and illness. I wondered why it had to happen to me. I did not know if he had realized what a mess he had made of his life, but I had become a victim without any fault of my own. Only the revelation of my pregnancy filled me with immense joy in this deep sorrow. It will be another unusual experience of my life. But I was sure my child would be a great catalyst in transforming my life. Yes, my child would help me come out of my delusion and shame and save me from the storm of blame, as also shield me from Jivesh's shame without any ego involvement!

I was not sure how I'd reveal Jivesh's illness to the family. How would I explain my own pregnancy? I stood on eggshells where all relationships were about to lose their meaning. My being was rocked with broken dreams and expectations. I'd trusted the relationship of marriage. I'd staked my entire future on this faith. But the reality was so different from my ideals and mental concepts. It had come to haunt me like an ugly ghost. The whole incident was driving me into a sea of fogged inchoateness, creating a strange hollow in my being where nothing seemed real any more. Yet, the pain and the tragedy were very real.

I reached home wrapped in mental anguish. I could sense the tension in the house. Leelaji began crying loudly when I sat next to her. Pratapji told me in a hoarse voice that they know about Jivesh's illness and about my pregnancy too. Bobby Singh had informed them. I was relieved that they knew the truth. I thanked Bobby Singh silently for telling them as it was – for not sensationalizing my alleged relationship with anyone. I did not want any names to come up. There was a strange silence in the air. I knew they were all disappointed in me as I had fallen from the ideal they had placed me at. I was very far from being the image of a typical Indian wife who lived according to set rules designed for her by the family. I could not explain to anyone, including myself, that an incident had driven me beyond reason – through my love. It happened without any reason or intention. It was like a blessing of God or like the flowering of a tree – this efflorescence of love – between physicality and spirit. I wanted to allow it to transmute into flesh, into my baby.

I had to stay in Durban for two weeks as my left arm was in a cast and I needed help. Laura offered to help but Pratapji and Leelaji's behaviour towards me was indifferent; still they could not ask me to leave the house as, for the last ten months, I had been supporting them financially. I started attending the office, trying to manage my Jo'burg affairs from here. One day Bano caught hold of me.

'Hey Anvita, come let's go for a cozy lunch, enough of the seriousness of the work. Won't you like to meet others? I hope you know Kisna and Pereeie are married and she is about to deliver their baby.'

'Oh really, when did it happen? Why I was not invited?'

'It was a quiet court marriage as she was five months pregnant. You know they were living together after that horrible incident.'

'That's good news. They both needed each other'. We walked to a nearby restaurant, I also needed to talk to Bano as she always contributed in my life in some way or the other to tranquilize my feelings.

When we settled down on a corner table near the window after ordering our food, I told her about Jivesh's illness. I am sure she was shocked as she remained quiet for some time.

'Well Anvita, we all knew in our heart of hearts that there was something drastically wrong. Since Jivesh lost his job and has gone away to Cape Town, he is not in touch with any of us. It's been so long maybe seven or eight months, he does not answer the phone calls or e-mails though he was so close to all of us.'

'He doesn't even call me, but I remain constantly in touch with him, suggesting him to take up something in Jo'burg where we could live together as you know, now for me money is not a problem, I have a respectable place to stay in too, but he has not even visited me once. Tell me how to pardon the feelings of being let down and of betrayal and the stigma at the back of his disease.'

We could not talk for a while. Then I only broke the unbearable silence. 'Bano, did I go wrong somewhere? As a professional or as a wife?'

'No Anvita, you were always very serious about life. That is how you adjusted gracefully in Jivesh's household and consciously took up your profession as an architect, everyone is aware of how you worked hard in spite of all the hurdles. Now it shows – how you have carved a niche for yourself. On the contrary, I am a light-hearted person, I learned so much from you to remain committed and to remain focused.'

'Bano, my past taught me to believe in my own self and in my own abilities to work hard as that is the only way to reach one's goal. For me my profession is my God, and here everyone in the office was helpful. You, Mr Naso and of course Mr Subramaniam was there to set my goals.'

'Yes, here everyone admires you, even our friends Kisna, Pereeie, Kevan and Ismail, they all talk about your positive approach towards life. How you managed your in-laws in the middle-class household and the very demanding work with calmness and grace.'

'It all happened because of love, I genuinely loved Jivesh, that's why I installed all my faith in him. We were happy in spite of all the ups and downs.'

'May I tell you Anvita, Jivesh was always a playboy, but when he married you, we all thought he will mend his ways as you were intelligent also and I am sure he loved your physical beauty.'

'Yes Bano, he is a very passionate lover,' I admitted.

'Then, try to analyze Anvita why, when you proved yourself as an architect, a person not just a body but also with brains, he sulked. He started travelling as much as he could, to stay away from you during that period of your achievements, and indulged in self-destructive attractions.'

'But I was always there, Bano, when he wanted me to be, in spite of my workload or physical tiredness, as a dutiful wife, understand that all of us have basic emotional needs. I valued my relationship. But sometimes circumstances play an unusual role. I must tell you Bano, I am pregnant.'

'What, how did you manage this? And isn't it risky?'

'It's not Jivesh's child.'

'Then, I can guess, it's him, Mr Subramaniam, isn't it?'

'How could you guess?' I was shocked.

'Everyone could see the glint of love in your eyes when you spoke to him.'

'Let me correct you, it was not love it was admiration. I always looked at him with respect as I look at Saptarishi stars, someone very unusually intellectual with perfect manners.'

'What you are saying sounds so rational Anvita, but sometimes one acts more on impulse than on reason.'

'Yes, Bano, somehow I don't feel guilty about my pregnancy; rather the unusual prospect of holding my child in my arms fills me with pleasure.'

She came closer to me and held my hands in hers with loving tenderness, 'Tell me Anvita, how sir feels about it.'

'Bano, I haven't told him as it was kind of an accident; he is above any physical love which can be considered scandalous. Believe me we have no relationship. I think women have no place in his busy life. You have been working in his office for a long time, you know him more than I do.'

'You can't say that, it was a known fact that this famous Phelela Casu chased him wherever he went. Everyone was sure of their affair. But since you have joined office he has become your ardent admirer. Don't forget you are young and beautiful, though you are careless about your looks but let me tell you that you are looking more and more gorgeous after the confidence you have gained during the past few months or may be a year.'

'Bano, you have always helped me with a proper choice of clothes and hair do.'

'Yes, it has made a remarkable difference in you appearance and personality.'

'Thank you for that.'

'Now how will you handle this complex situation of yours, Anvita?'

'Only time will tell.'

Time cannot erase the effects of time, it flows at its own pace. It took a few days to arrive at a decision to shift to Jo'burg, at least till the project was complete.

I packed my bags along with my unfinished novel. I also tried to organize finances for Pratapji and Leelaji. The day I was leaving with my luggage, all of us cried. I touched Pratapji's feet but he pulled away to his own honour-bound world. Mom hugged me but there was no emotional outburst. We parted without any promise of return, or any contact.

An office car took me away from the security of the well-knit family to the loneliness of a small one-bedroom flat next to Mr Naso's residence. Though my mind was in turmoil, I longed for the songs of the blackbird at dusk and the bright orange colours of the Bird of Paradise at dawn. But life goes on even without these. The problems remain but you do not feel them as other layers of the being take over.

12

It was one of the busiest afternoons. The nightmare was about to begin, though none of us had an inkling. The shocking news of the murder of Mr Naso's thirteen-year-old daughter made us tremble. Mrs Naso was driving her back from school with her younger daughter, when it happened. She had left the girls in the car to pick up some medicines and other items when little Emily was hit by a stray bullet. The hysterical mother took her to the hospital. It was too late, she'd already died by then. All of us panicked and stopped our work. Condolences and opinions about the growing incidents of crime against children in South Africa flowed from everywhere, like gurgling water, but refusing to fill the void.

Next morning, the news was all over the newspapers. The anguish of parents whose children were maimed or killed by criminals flowed everywhere.

It was unbearable to watch Mr Naso and his wife. They were totally shattered. Emily's younger sister Mily was so shocked that she sat crumpled in a corner like a lifeless doll. I stayed with them the whole day. I made tea for the visitors and organized something to eat for the family. The cremation was heartbreaking. After the ceremony, children from the Trinity House Preparatory School marched on the streets holding placards reading, 'Our Silence Speaks of the Country'; 'Keep me safe – I'm scared'; 'We are the future of the country – if we survive'. '*Ushmi Wam*?' or 'Where are our leaders?' During an interview, one of the teenaged girls said that the march was aimed at showing the government, 'How serious this business of crime is. It encourages us to see so many people standing together and speaking for our sake as we need to see a bright future.'

The entire march was televised all over the country. One of the parents said, 'The government is not going to convince our children to be loyal to our country with merely an oath. They have to make it a safe country that the children would themselves want to protect. That's where loyalty begins.'

One of the boys commented on the march: 'It is our way of telling the government how we feel and what we are going through. We have to show our anger.'

Though I'd never been concerned about children in my life, it was now different as a new life was swelling in my belly. I was not prepared for the depression that accompanies pregnancy. In sleep, I constantly moved between phases of dreamlessness and suffocating loneliness. That night, my maid had also gone on a holiday.

The cover story of *The Times* (February 18, 2007) carried photographs of the four mothers who had pleaded to President Thabo Mbeki the next morning. One mother revealed that robbers had paralyzed her eighteen-year-old daughter. Her letter was insightful. 'Dear Mr President, I'm not moaning. No, Sir! I'm crying for help! How do I tell my child that she will never be able to walk again when she wants to be told something different? Please Mr President, help us to raise our children to be free from fear in our own homes and our own vehicles. Please Mr President, use the power vested in you to make our country safe and restore some faith in you!'

Crime was becoming a great concern. Parents invest their hopes and dreams in their children, planning and envisioning a great future for them, but when the children's lives are taken away, their lives shatter. At the church service, Mr Naso revealed that his daughter always dreamt of becoming a fashion designer in New York. We all broke down after seeing Mrs Naso's grief. The trauma had also left a scar on Emily's younger sister. I was sure she would need a therapist or counseling to come out of the grief. To witness such an incident, to see it covered on the television, to be relentlessly shown the coverage about innocents becoming victims of criminal violence and the subsequent lack of justice disturbed me. I was terribly shaken.

My professional commitments were keeping me so busy that I had neglected myself. I began to deny that I had to show myself to a gynaecologist. Ignoring the cruel reality I focused on the blossoming life and finally paid a visit to the doctor. A sense of belonging swept over me – making me float into an ocean of joy. I felt like the ancient mariner searching for new, unexplored lands. I felt true, unfettered freedom from miseries all around me when the doctor convinced me that my baby was healthy and doing fine.

13

Shortly after the tragedy, I received an e-mail from Sanju:

Dear Annu,

You must be wondering why after so many days I am writing to you. Actually I am on a holiday, and in spite of my insistence, Arjun does not want to leave India; instead he wants me to stay here with him, and take up something till he finishes his studies. I had to agree as I am very impressed with his fine manners and politeness, which are unusual for me as all my life I faced Nony's provincial rough mindset. Arjun and I decided to explore different cities here, so we visited Agra, Jaipur, Varanasi, as a journey expands human consciousness along with its geographical aspects. Varanasi was a great spiritual experience. To visit the old temples and to watch celestial Gods where one realizes that our small human affairs are unbelievably petty … it was a different awareness.

But after knowing about your personal dilemma I am shocked to the core of my heart. May I tell you that I was not very surprised with what has happened to Jivesh, as he was into something when we were in the U.S. But where was the time to tell you? I must admit I was happy to see you settled in your married life, after the traumatic days of your childhood, though I admired your earlier self, which was mature even at that tender age. I suggest you come to Delhi, if you can pull yourself out of your professional commitments. I feel it will be comfortable to have your baby here, as there is a lot of help available, plus here nobody is aware of Jivesh's horrible ailment which can become a stigma for you and your child's future.

I must say Annu, you are amazing. Even in such drastic circumstances, pain and loneliness, with all the confusion you are spending your time writing a novel based on Papa and Vati Aunty's letters. I am sure they must be worth great emotional weight. Or maybe in your present circumstances writing your novel helps you with introspection.

It is after midnight, 3 a.m. I cannot sleep as my heart is filled with your pain. I am trying to chant mantras … for you and for myself. Though we both believe that faith in oneself and one's abilities to do hard work is the way to reach God, mantras also give a lot of mental strength.

Sanju

14

It was an exquisite dining area created in the extended verandah that opened in the well-manicured garden. The place was serene as it was cut-off from the loud traffic screeching outside the high walls of the hotel. The fragrance of fresh flowers wafted in to gently stir the senses of the people enjoying the evening. The beauty of the carefully manicured plants pleased me. The sacred, soothing nature of a garden never failed to transform me. I always found solace in being close to nature. I was thanking my stars that I was visiting all the places meant for the rich and the famous. Inwardly, I thanked Mr Subramaniam's generosity that opened the most magnificent and graceful world to me. Along with that, he also provided a new meaning to my life.

When he entered the hall, my whole being – no, my whole consciousness down to the cells in my body became aware of him. He wore the same perfume – intoxicating me – making his magnetism more overpowering than what it was that night when I had conceived.

There were two other people with him. I could hear him say, 'I've just attended the Chamber of Commerce and Industry meeting. They discussed the new budget.'

'Yes, I know. In fact, the budget does not deviate noticeably from the Medium Term Budget Policy announced last year and shows a determination to adhere to a steady economic path. The spending priorities focus on measures to combat crimes and poverty, investment in education and skills development and infrastructural development,' said the other person. They exchanged their views for a while, before he noticed me. I was quietly staring at the lily pond.

'Hi! Anvita. How are you? Sorry, I'm late. My meeting got prolonged. And you know what? They've passed building plans worth Rand 80.4 billion last year, up 6 per cent from last years. That's what the South African statistics data showed today. All the main building categories contributed positively to the rise with additions and alterations at 1.2 per cent. Plans passed for other residential buildings were down 3.1 per cent.'

I looked into his eyes and I began to drown helplessly into them. Consciously, I pulled myself and brought myself down to the two-dimensional professional world. I watched all his mental moves and moved on to the problems I had to discuss with him. The atrium design and the adjoining area of the building where the huge picture window was to be created needed some clarifications. One moment flowed into another. Food was ordered. He spoke of his trip along with his meeting at Chamber of Commerce where he was offered a new project in a city called 'Gauteng'. I observed his discipline, energy, power and optimism as if he believed he was there to achieve some divine purpose of the universe, to unfold something magnificent. How very important he was for the country!

Two black singers with violins sang Neil Diamond's Love on the Rocks for us.

Love on the rocks
Ain't no surprise
Pour me a drink
And I will tell you some lies
Got something to lose
So you just sing the blues
All the times

Mr Subramaniam took out some Rands from his pocket and gave it to them. They flashed their magnificent smiles. 'Bless you, lovely lady!' They said to me.

The air stood still between us after they went away. Suddenly he said, 'How are you coping with "Love on the Rocks", Anvita? I've come to know about Jivesh.' He looked straight into my eyes. I found it very difficult to face those eyes as their radiant gaze was drowning me in a sea of illusions. With great difficulty, I shook myself into the real world.

'Jivesh's cousin, the one you met, Bobby Singh, has taken charge of looking after him. He has a professional setup in Cape Town. Besides, he feels that Jivesh will be cured of his illness. Maybe, I will shift back to Durban after that and take up projects there. Anyway, it will take us a few months to complete this journey of challenges.' I was reluctantly nurturing a hope, for something pleasant to turn up. Not knowing what to say, we sat quiet for sometime.

'Okay!' he said in his usual cheerful tone. 'I nearly forgot Anvita, the reason for calling you to this dinner. I have good news for you. Can you guess what?!'

My heart started sinking. Everything stirred like a spinning wheel – or was it roulette? I wondered what he was going to tell me.

'Anvita, during the board meeting of the company, the directors collectively discussed your professional qualities. They all agreed to give you an important position with the designation of Chief Architect in our organization. They were all impressed by your talent and the dedication towards work. So congratulations, dear!'

'What …' It was such an unexpected ray of light in the gloom of my life that I became confused. I got up from my chair.

'Do you think I'm capable of shouldering such a responsibility?'

'Of course, I am sure. Do you think you lack anything? You're capable of doing anything. Everyone agreed on one thing, that your designs exude some kind of tranquility that is so needed in the modern world. The way you combine high ceilings with the water bodies in the interiors of the buildings make those look so pure and tranquil. It speaks volumes about your brilliance. Besides, your plans are sensitive to social and environmental issues.

I trembled with unexpected joy.

'Sir, I work with a passion. My passion stands free from any material desire or aim. My creation is a kind of dream fulfillment – or you can say – a realization of my dream. My passion is to see my building taking shape and to stand majestically in front of the world with grace and sophistication.'

He came closer and held me in his arms. We stood there for a while close to each other. At the very moment he kissed me on my forehead, a very soft kick in my belly brought me back to reality. I wondered whether he felt it. There were no words exchanged on that topic. But did it really matter? Could he feel the existence of his own being within the flesh of my body? I grabbed his fingers tightly, bringing them to the stirring skin of my body to realize our oneness. It was love – the deepest love one can ever experience in one's life. Within his tight embrace, I felt myself immersed in a sea of immense beauty and joy.

The two black singers sang a mix of retro romantic melodies and songs that spoke of unrequited love. Heady Congolese beats climaxed the evening and made the notes of violin break out in sparkling melody.

15

When I heard the health minister on television speaking on HIV patients, I was instantly concerned. He said, 'We will soon move to make the Bill an Act to deter the discrimination against HIV patients in workplaces, educational institutions and medical treatment centres. It is worrisome when medical doctors turn away HIV patients or the corporations shun people who are HIV positive. Another worrying factor is schools refusing admission to HIV positive children.

'The government has set up 147 treatment centres and expects to treat 300,000 patients free of cost in the next three years. After treatment, they can live in a family, like they have always done.'

I could see a distant light at the end of the tunnel. I could feel it was trying to illuminate my life, however dimly. It was like an answer to my deepest worries, a sort of resolution of my predicament.

But simultaneously, there was shocking news in the morning newspaper. At a time when the government was thinking of sweeping health reforms, the discontented parents of HIV children, fifty two of whom had died, were demanding justice. It was discovered that an unnamed foreign drug company had used six foreign medics as guinea pigs for medical trials of an anti-HIV drug. Investigations revealed that even the careless nursing staff was also to be blamed. Blood samples taken from HIV children showed that more than half had been infected with other diseases. It became obvious that they were routinely reusing unsterilised needles to save money. All the six medics were put on trial while the medical company made an appeal for a magnanimous pardon.

Finally, I called Bobby Singh and asked, 'What do you think I should do?'

'Well, let me inform you Anvita that Jivesh's condition has become worse. The more he deteriorates the more negative he becomes. It expresses itself quite recognizably as in many forms – jealousy, withdrawal, and unspoken resentment. He suffers more from complexes and failures than from the disease. I'm trying hard to help him through counselling to counterbalance his mental and emotional pattern.'

'Bobbyji, do I have a chance? Any hope?'

'None. Stop living in illusion.'

I watched the setting sun from my window. I could see that the world was only a formation of shadows. Everything around me sank into a deep valley of darkness. I stood in an empty valley of nothingness where all thoughts had ceased.

I was on the verge of finishing my novel. As I wrote more about Vati Aunty's relationship with Jo Jo Uncle, it became more of a collage of lyrical experiences that sounded too close to my inner turmoil. In one of the letters Vati Aunty wrote:

> *Jay, nowadays I feel transformed, for me everything has become very meaningful. A small coloured stone shines in the sun to guide me with a ray of hope. When I look at the grass every morning, the dewdrops create small rainbows around me and add colour to my life. It's all your reflection, limitless and pure. You have given me a meaning of life in the form of Arjun. He has heightened my sense of being alive. Whenever I look at his face, I see an embodiment of the oneness we felt together.*

In the end, she quoted Nagarjuna's lines. 'Even offering 300 bowls a day does not match the spiritual merit gained with one moment of love.'

As I finished my novel, I felt much fulfilled, with a deep sense of achievement.

I was very excited about the novel. I called up Kisna as I sometimes did. Keeping in touch with Kisna, Bano, and Ismail had in fact ensured emotional support. It was my most rewarding human connection here in this part of the world.

'Kisna, it's me, Anvita! Can you believe it? I have finished my novel.'

'Oh really? That's very good news!'

'Can you help me publish it?'

'Why not? I can speak to my publisher. Send me the script.'

'I will. How are Pereeie and the baby?'

'They are fine. How about you? Jivesh visited his parents last month. We're very shocked to see his condition.'

'Yes. He also asked me to come over. Though I was keen to meet him, the doctor did not allow me to.'

Silence interspersed the conversation.

I spoke to Pereeie, Bano and Ismail too as I felt a sense of incompleteness without them.

16

He called very rarely. He travelled so much that we could not meet for days. Often we could manage to meet only during crowded official meetings. He would touch my shoulders with a caressing hug – but only discreetly. I took it as a carefully calculated compromise with the situation, even though the loneliness was tearing me apart. I was also very confused and nervous about my impending motherhood, uncertain whether it would prove to be the right decision in the circumstances.

I was thrilled when Mr Subramaniam called. I could not believe my ears when he said, 'Anvita, our mall has been selected for a very prestigious national award. You know what they have written in the report? That "it has perfectly balanced old-world charm with modern infrastructure and facilities. It is a mega mall with immense potential and absolutely stunning design."'

While he was saying all this, I closed my eyes to contemplate the source, the dream I had when I first visited the site. The gold-framed picture of a hexagonal building with Gothic columns was my inspiration – the guideline for my creation. His voice vibrated with excitement as he said, 'Our company could succeed so much because of your imaginative power and hard work.'

'I'm only a blade of grass, sir!'

'No, Anvita you are a blade of grass no more, you've become a tree that is spreading into the South African skies.' His voice reverberated in my whole body.

'You're praising me unnecessarily, sir! I could have not done it without your support and encouragement. Thank you, anyway. I will renew my motivation to take on more challenges on my journey of progress.'

'Yes, very soon we will start a new project in Gauteng, get ready for that. I will also reach Jo'burg after a few days. Mr Naso will inform you about the meeting. Are you keeping in good health?'

'Yes.'

'Do take care.' Was it a case of initiative or guilt? I wasn't sure whether he remembered I was pregnant. But his voice echoed within me and with it rose a wave of pain. Pain, flaring questions as well as depression about the future – especially as a single mother – engulfed me. I could not think of anything – but the pain cramped my body.

When I held my baby in my arms, I felt as if a new light had descended on me – as if a new door had opened. I could feel a divine happiness everywhere, all around me and outside. How beautiful he was! I was amazed like all new mothers – trying to be too concerned about the responsibilities motherhood had brought along with it. I touched his forehead – counted his little fingers and toes many times – marvelling about the craftsmanship of god. To hold him was such an overwhelming experience. I could not bear to be without him anymore. I had butterflies in my stomach when the nurse took him away from me.

'Congratulations, what a lovely baby boy!' the doctor said with a smile.

'Thank you, doctor. I'm so happy – as if I've grasped the farthest star!'

'Have you chosen a name for him?'

'Oh no! Let me think.'

I looked at the sky. It was utterly empty of clouds, only the 'Saptarishi', which was my anchor of faith, was awake.

'I think I will call him Rishi.'

'So should I write it on his birth certificate? I was waiting for you to recover as there is nobody with you.'

'Yes. You can. I feel this name is very fluid and poetic.' I said bravely, as I had nobody who could suggest anything else, or even fuss around me. I was alone at that moment of immense happiness in a lonely room of the hospital.

'And father's name?'

'Please leave it blank, let it be – I'm a single mother.'

The next day the newspapers published the news of the award-winning mall along with Mr Subramaniam's photograph. The government not only praised his work and dedication but also his simplicity in creativity. He was seen to be rising fast on the corporate ladder to gain the topmost position as a real-estate tycoon. Whereas, I was only an ordinary architect – as well a single mother now – living alone without any emotional support.

There were many genuine questions arising out of my experiential source. I would have to focus on bettering my relationship with myself. I was learning to forgive myself, for my situation. I started feeling more aware of myself with every passing day and found myself reflecting on the proverb: 'Living life is not as simple as crossing a field.'

17

Mr and Mrs Naso visited me with flowers and a small chocolate cake. I was glad to see Bano was with them. She brightened the entire room with her radiant appearance.

'Hi, Anvita. Congratulations for the baby. I could not stop myself. So I came here to meet you. Where is your baby?'

'Thank you so much. How lovely to have all of you. Please sit. I will tell the nanny to bring the baby.'

When everyone was settled, Shanti brought the baby wrapped in a blue blanket. Bano took him in her arms. 'Oh how lovely he is! His complexion is exactly like yours, Anvita. What have you named him?'

'Rishi.'

'And how do you feel after the baby?'

'I feel as if I have achieved a kind of divine fulfillment in my evolution.'

Mrs Naso also came closer to look at the baby. 'He will grow up to become a handsome boy, Anvita. Strange, he has very unusual eyes, isn't it Bano?'

'Yeah. Even I was wondering!'

Mr Naso's cellphone rang. After the call, he said, 'Anvita, it was from the office. Sir wants to meet us for a very important matter. Will you be able to come?'

'I don't think so, Mr Naso. I have not recovered fully yet. The baby is not even a month old.'

'Ohh … Ja! I forgot to tell Mr Subramaniam that you have been blessed with a baby.'

He dialed Mr Subramaniam's number, spoke to him and them passed on the phone to me. His deep, husky voice struck my ears. I only half understood what he was saying, 'Thank you sir, both of us are fine,' I just managed to say.

He mumbled, 'I will see you as soon as I reach Jo'burg. Look after yourself.'

'Thank you, sir.'

'Do you know that Mr Subramaniam is insistent on taking up the new project in Gauteng?' Mr Naso told me.

'He's a workaholic and crazy!' Mrs Naso commented.

'Where is this Gauteng? I have never heard of it.' Bano was more than curious.

'The city is still getting itself up by the bootstraps. It's still absolutely underdeveloped. The minority rights are being redefined as the rights of the minorities to receive equal treatment. There are ethnic clashes and disputes everyday as most of the residents are either tribals, Afrikaners or Zulus. It's like riding a storm. Rest assured, we will face lawlessness and protests once we step there. I'm very scared, Anvita. After losing my daughter, I have lost faith in life.' Mr Naso looked very pale.

'Besides, there are other construction companies eager to take up the work. They are also trying hard. With the amount of incompetence and complexities present in the government, we are not sure whether we will get the contract.' Mr Naso sounded not very confident.

'Don't forget our company is headed by a South African Indian.' I was proud of the fact.

'We were too white during apartheid and not black enough after the movement,' remarked Bano.

'But Mr Subramaniam is very confident that our company will get the contract. He's become even more sure after we received the national award. Also, he enjoys challenges.'

'He can do that because he has no family – but we cant, darling.' Mrs Naso was speaking through her tears.

'Mr Naso and Ismail have told me that there are many unlicensed traders active in the area. They cannot be depended upon. Anything can happen. Let us try to discourage Mr Subramaniam.'

'He's planning to visit next week. I will go with him, Bano, to assess the situation,' Mr Naso assured us.

Mr and Mrs Naso left us alone. The baby started crying. I called the nanny.

Bano asked what had been perturbing our minds. 'What have you decided, Anvita? Live here or come back to Durban? Your in-laws must be pressurizing you to come back. They must be thrilled about the baby.'

'I don't know. I have not spoken to them. The only person I spoke to is Bobby Singh. He told me Jivesh is almost in his last stages – the infection has reached his brain. And even if we leave aside the horrible disease – his behaviour, my faith in him – Bano, tell me is there any dimension left in our relationship that has remained unsullied? Loss of prestige is more unbearable than death. Material well-being was never the central objective of my existence. I came here for love, love that was an inaccessible part of my life. It's almost a paralyzing experience to discover the loss of faith and love faded, lost and gone.'

'But the baby?' Bano had a question in her eyes.

'Bano I can only say that he is a gift of God, to save me from all the disappointments in life. He is like a spiritual unfolding of my being. I feel fulfilled.'

'I don't understand your philosophy, Anvita. But I know that you are mad. Grab that man, marry him – enjoy the position and the money. He will not refuse a person like you.'

'Any person who touches my soul becomes my kin forever. But I don't think he realizes it. He's not a worldly man. I will not demand anything worldly from him. I didn't even tell him about Rishi's birth. Our dharma does not teach us to exploit anyone. Rather, it teaches us to be content in whatever we have. I will live contentedly with this beautiful gift. I will live for my cosmic dharma that is above any sensory pleasures.'

'I don't think it's a realistic assessment of your life situation, Anvita. Living, I feel, is an art of relationships. Look at it without any prejudice, or preconceived notions. From what I know of you, you have a gift for discovering the relevance of life situations.'

The baby started crying. Bano looked at me. She was ready to go back to Durban as the car was waiting. 'But come to Durban – whenever you can. All friends want to meet you. Even I want to spend more time with you, "dil abhi bhara nahin".'

'I will try, before leaving for India. When my book is ready, I will speak to Kisna and inform you. At that time I will even visit Durban.'

'For how long are you going to India?'

'I don't know!'

It was late in the evening. Yet the sky was still awash with the luminous orange hue of the setting sun. There was no wind. I could see that my potted plants were very still in my tiny balcony. A single Bird of Paradise had bloomed in one of the pots. It stood erect as if in a meditational repose. In all this stillness, I could feel the beating of my heart – it thumped wildly.

When he entered, my small room was filled with the aroma of his perfume. It was enhanced by the fresh flowers he carried for us. He hugged me gently before sitting down opposite me. He appeared very dignified, like someone beyond approach, like the formidable sea. What was I? A mere droplet who could not even think of approaching the ocean? Like a passing thought, I was insignificant in his life, a life that was acclaimed in the social and political worlds. He lived in a world of his own – a world that was filled with different contexts.

'Will you care for some tea?' Shanti had entered with tea and snacks as we'd planned.

'Oh, yes!' He picked up a plate.

'You also take something. You look so pale.' I'm sure he did not even remember the baby.

'Yes.' I also picked up a plate. He got busy eating. We waited. I had to start the conversation.

'How was your trip?'

'Oh it was fine. I'm on the verge of finalizing our new project in Gauteng. I am planning to go there with Mr Naso. Will you come too?'

'Sir, I can't, as I have not fully recovered yet.'

'Oh yeah. I forgot. Congratulations! Where is the baby?'

'I will bring him. But first you have some tea.' Shanti poured tea for both of us.

'But sir, Mr Naso was telling me that Gauteng is not the right place to work, it's not very secure as it is inhabited by minorities who believe in ethnic nationalism. How will you deal with the impoverished masses?'

'I'm aware of it. But we have to upgrade those informal settlements. It's our duty to do that. Besides, the government is now focusing on all issues that will assure the human rights of the minorities. Remember, they will be provided with a better lifestyle.'

'I agree. But even others can do it. Why take a risk?'

'Let me visit the place. Then we will decide. But you must become a part of that project.' He looked at me with his deep blue eyes. They had a mysterious magnetism, an indefinable biological gravity. What was it, I wondered. Was it love, compassion, insight or intelligence, I wanted to know.

'Actually, I'm planning to go to India.' I wanted to free myself from the illusions of my own making.

'But you will come back – you have to!'

He kept looking at me for quite a while – not knowing what to say. Those moments became my fulfillment. 'You have carved a niche for yourself in this country. You've a future here. Gauteng will be a challenging job – to prove yourself. It's a huge project. I'm sure you will like it as you're not afraid of challenges.'

'But sir, my baby is very small and at the moment he is my first priority.'

'Oh yes! Look at me! I totally forgot, please bring him!'

When I placed the baby in his arms, it was like a river meeting its shore. At that moment, a vibrant orb of emotions rose on his face – like an enormous wave of water. He hugged the baby fondly. I was amazed and awestruck to see the similarity between the two.

There was a kind of mist of embarrassment on his face as he said, 'What a lovely child. He has beautiful eyes.'

I'm sure he was reminded of that insignificant moment not so long ago in his life and about the paradox of the its implication. But truth always maintains an identity due to its permanence.

'I believe life is a mosaic of diverse migrations. On this planet, I stole him from God.'

As he tried desperately to control his giveaway body language, he stared at me with eyes like rain clouds, without a sense of otherness that was undefined. I gently lifted the baby from his trembling hands and held him to my heart.

'I want your help, sir!'

'What?!' He was clueless.

'I want you to help me with his passport.' I brought the papers from my study table and handed it over to him.

He looked into the papers.

'What name have you given him?'

'Rishi – the one who is unreachable – one who worships god – or possesses a pure soul.'

He took the papers. His cellphone rang. He got up, came close to me and handed me an envelope.

'This is the award our company won – and the cheque is for you and Rishi. Please don't refuse.'

He took out his camera and took some photographs of Rishi and me. I too clicked some pictures of him with Rishi.

There was a deep silence again which spoke volumes. He put his hand on Rishi's head saying, 'God bless you my dear! Go to India … but please come back as our organization needs you. I will have the visas made, along with his passport. Somebody from the office will bring it. Else, you let me know.' Again his eyes changed expression. They had a practical and professional hue again. All the colour of desire had evaporated – while I still longed for it. But something inside told me that 'He knows!'

18

As my car stopped near the main entrance, I couldn't believe my eyes. Was this the same place where I'd lived just a few months ago? The wooden gate had many cracks and the sprawling ancient tree that usually bore tiny yellow orange flowers had withered. It was leafless and dry. Its branches had become like the bare arms of an old woman. All its grace that once seemed almost divine had disappeared. The grass of the small front lawn near the verandah was dry and bushy. Nobody had watered it for a long time. The once green bushes had turned dry and yellow. My favourite Bird of Paradise groove had turned into a garbage dump.

The living room was empty. Leelaji and Pratapji were not sitting on their usual chairs – nor indulging in their favourite pastime – watching television. The furniture had become dirty and ragged. The wire and coir had begun peeping out from the torn upholstery.

As I walked up, I could see that the walls had become coated with dust. All the black and white portraits, as well as Sanju's paintings looked faded and dull. I became conscious of my expensive and clean dress as I entered the room. I was also seized by the nervous tension and grew breathless.

I asked Shanti to wait in the living room with Rishi. Upon entering my bedroom, I saw Leelaji sitting on the chair that I used to sit on while working on my projects. Pratapji and Bobby Singh were sitting on the small sofa upon which Jivesh and I sat every evening to chat. I saw Jivesh lying on the bed – one of his eyes was closed while with the other, he stared at me anxiously. My heart began to pound again … we were meeting like strangers.

Bobby acted like a bridge and told me about Jivesh's condition. Veering away from the symptoms and other technicalities, the whispered conversation turned towards Jivesh's destiny, where he'd landed himself – a point of no return where his life had no opportunity to move forward. Leelaji and Pratapji continued to be immersed in a ghostly silence in the colourless light of the emptiness of the room.

Finally, I was compelled to break the silence. I went near Jivesh and sat on the same bed that was witness to our once beautiful relationship. I looked at his face. It was dark with a shadow of immense pain and gloom. When I touched him, he opened his eyes. He fixed his astonished eyes on my face. His large beautiful eyes had sunk into their sockets. His face had become like a cracked mirror. How mercilessly life changes!

'Hi! Anvita!'

'Yes, Jivesh. I've come.'

I held his hand in mine. His fingers trembled in their self-inflicted inadequacy. I could feel I could not carry on much longer emotionally. I was fighting my tears.

'I'm glad you came. I wanted to meet you before dying.' His voice was very faint. I could not hear him properly.

'You're not going anywhere. Jivesh, you cannot leave me like this. You're the only person I loved in my entire life. I came all the way to this island of love holding your hand.'

His grip tightened around my fingers. 'I know, Anvita. I also loved you. It's me who is to be blamed. I'm sorry for that.'

We both cried in silence.

'Don't worry Jivesh. You'll be alright. And we will live the way we lived earlier.'

'I wish we could. But I know Anvita. I know the end is very near. This dreadful disease has damaged every cell of my body. Though Bobby tried his best, but …!' I could see he could no longer converse.

Suddenly Rishi cried. His loud scream broke the spell.

'Oh! You have brought the baby here?'

Bobby seemed perplexed. His face was contorted in agony. But I calmly went down to fetch Rishi. My cellphone rang.

It was Kisna. 'Hey Anvita, where are you? There is some good news for you. Your book is ready. Where should I deliver it?'

'Oh really?! That's great. Listen. I'm in Durban with Jivesh. Can you come here with the book?'

He paused. And then he asked, 'How is Jivesh?'

'Not so good, I'm afraid.'

'Ok. I will be there with Pereeie.'

'Please.'

I carried Rishi in my arms and brought him near Jivesh.

'Here Jivesh. See, this is Rishi. I wanted you to meet him. You're the only two people I love in my entire life. Bless him Jivesh so that I'm free from all the guilt.'

Jivesh touched Rishi's hand softly but no words came out from his mouth.

Bobby Singh was horrified. He almost pushed me out of the room. 'Anvita go downstairs. Keep the baby away. Are you not scared of infecting him?'

'Don't worry! Nothing will happen. True love is our greatest protection. Nothing will happen. I had to meet Jivesh, Leelaji, Pratapji and you before leaving for India.'

We all came down to the hushed stillness of the living room.

'Why are you going Anvita? You're so successful. The other day, I read in the newspaper about the international award won by your company.' Pratapji wanted to know.

'Everything is meaningless without love. Jivesh's illness has killed something inside me. I believed in dreams – not in the flow of money. Yes, I agree success was also part of my dreams. But again it has no relevance if I have nobody to share it with.'

'The world is an illusion, Anvita. And it's changing everyday. One should learn to live with it, Bobby tried to reason.'

Kisna entered with Pereeie. He was holding a large packet of my books. I was so excited to see the first copy of my novel. It had my name emblazoned on it along with the title, *The Echoes of Silence*. It was a moment full of memories and nostalgia.

'May I say that, Uncle, her novel is like a delicious meal which you will love to finish at one go. The storyline is spontaneous and original. And the best part is that her story reveals spiritual substance along with a courageous extramarital relationship!' Kisna's eyes sparkled as he spoke.

'Oh! Is it the protagonist's or author's actual confession along with a plea for forgiveness?' Bobby Singh looked at me meaningfully.

'No. It's about my uncle and his unusual relationship. In my book, the dead are more alive, more immortal than you or me.' I wanted to clarify before I left.

'Why did you choose to give it this title?' Pratapji wanted to know.

'That is to highlight the unique unspoken quality of the story. The soft whisper is a mysterious thing. It hides more substance than a sentence of spoken words. In my book, the whisper wears a spiritual armor too and speaks much. Because I feel the unspoken speaks volumes in its unfathomed silence. We only need to listen in the gap between the words.'

Bobby Singh had ordered some food from 'Jaipur Palace'. Laura started setting the table. I held Rishi in my arms and said, 'Well, Kisna while I wrote the novel, I never thought I had to justify anything. I was doing it willingly, spontaneously, instantaneously. There was a part of me that wanted to write. Write about people who lived an unusual and audacious life.'

'But your – spontaneous, unconscious mistake has resulted in something much unexpected.' Bobby Singh commented looking at Rishi's unusual eyes.

'I've certainly grown with this – this motherhood, a desire that every woman longs for in her life.'

'But you should not keep the baby in this house – it's dangerously infected.'

'I wanted him to meet Jivesh. It was my desire that they should meet. Every heart has its own reasons, Bobbyji.'

'I will take your baby along with the maid out with me, Anvita, if you allow me,' Pereeie offered.

'That will be very kind of you. Though I wanted to check in to the nearby hotel I'm not sure whether Shanti and the baby could stay alone without me.'

'Don't worry. I will look after him,' Kisna took Rishi in his arms.

All of them left after lunch with Rishi. Kisna and Pereeie kept to their place and only peeped from afar. I took the book to Jivesh – trying to involve him in some kind of conversation. But he was slipping into a strange vacuum. I held his hand. It was trembling. His eyes had gone blank. There was no response to my queries.

Within a few hours, the doctors came. They gave him some injections. But nothing could revive him. His body lay lifeless, but nobody could take him away from me. He was alive in my heart as a tender flower of love. I knew that whatever happened, I would cherish his memory within my heart, all my life. I became numb. Leelaji and Pratapji kept repeating, 'He only waited to meet you Anvita!'

I wondered why death always snatched away everyone I loved, first my parents, Jo Jo Uncle, Bua and now Jivesh. Death always took them away my life. The pages of my book fluttered open to a quotation:

When death comes and whispers to me,
The days are ended
Let me say to him
'I've lived in love
And not through mere time
He will ask,
Will thy songs remain?'
I shall say, 'I know not,
But this I know,
That often when I sang
I found my eternity.'

I could see the bald Swami of 'Connect-Ticket' had entered along with some other members of the group. They recited mantras from the Gita. Then Jivesh's body was taken away in an ambulance to an electric crematorium somewhere in the city. I stayed back with Leelaji. She was delirious with grief. I had no energy to think of anything. I saw a bleak vast emptiness around me. A mysterious indecision and condemnation blanketed my faith. I could find no words. The loss was so great. It had made me a stranger in the house that I'd entered as a bride. I had no idea how to respond to the situation I was trapped in. How would I face the subtle change in the attitude of my in-laws towards me in this culture-conscious family?

19

I lost count of the time as the unseen and unheard wheel of Time moved on its axis. There was numbness in my body – in my veins. It was becoming very difficult to dissociate from the memories of Jivesh – even when my self-evident reality was so different. I was merging and dropping into some kind of strange silence. I was capable of only answering Sanju's calls or Rishi's demands. They were my lifelines, saving me from sinking into depression.

The priests performed rituals around the sacred fire chanting mantras. I did what I was supposed to do. I looked up at the sky. There were no birds. Even my Saptarishis had disappeared. I could not go away, I had to sit and perform my duties as a widow.

During those four days of utter void, Bano helped me with worldly affairs – to fulfill my responsibilities as a daughter-in-law. Pereeie helped me with Rishi. I transferred most of my money into Leelaji's account and handed over the passbook to her. Then I closed my bank account and handed over the bank passbook to her. I collected my mother's jewellery from the bank locker before leaving Durban. Leelaji gave me a few gifts, along with a wooden rocking horse on which Jivesh used to play when he was a little boy. But Pratapji was stiff and maintained a formal distance. On the day I was leaving, he asked me, 'Why are you leaving for India … that too after achieving so much success?'

I could almost sense the mocking deprecation, criticism and intolerance in his voice.

'At the moment, I'm just not able to think of anything as passing away of Jivesh has shattered me completely. It has shattered my very being. I need time to get out of the personal misery.'

'Is it a path of reality or that of escape?' I knew what he was hinting at.

'I don't know.'

'But you have no one in India.'

'I've nobody even here.'

I was trying to grapple with his dry behaviour. But Leelaji came to my rescue.

'I'm your Mom, Anvita. I want you and Rishi to stay with us. As you are the only one we have.'

'Yes, mom. Whenever you need me, I will be at your side. I will always cherish and remember the inexhaustible treasure of love you bestowed on me. I spent the best time of my life here in this house.'

We were all standing under the scanty shade of the ancient tree which stood witness to the long history of the misery of the family. We parted with heavy hearts as the essence of all the relationships dissolved into a strange emptiness.

For the flight to Jo'burg, Bano was with me like my spiritual armor. She had been a pillar of strength, helping me maintain my equilibrium.

'I know Anvita, what is hurting you most – the person responsible for Rishi has not come forward to be with you at this time. He has not even come forward to accept Rishi.'

'I'm sure he's on his triumphant tour of Europe and engrossed in his economic philosophy. Besides he's not a worldly man Bano.'

'Have you tried to tell him?'

'No I didn't. I don't think I will ever do that. I feel I'm not supposed to say anything or claim anything. Bano, I believe God, the overseer of this universe in the highest heaven can only solve my problem. I don't want to display my lack of faith and gratitude towards Him.'

'I think you're mad, Anvita. In this age you live with some decrepit ancient idealism – it's crazy.'

'No, Bano life is difficult. But it's a wonder without end.'

20

While on my way to Jo'burg, I saw many SMSs on my cellphone. They had accumulated in the past few days Then I came across one that said, 'Listen and silent r 2 wrds wth d same alfabets n are very imp 4 frndship coz only a frnd cn lisn to u wen u are silent.'

It was him. I wondered how he knew that I'm silent – numb and frozen within myself. I wondered about his heart sutra. Can he translate desire into meaningful sentences, separating it from the realities of the external world? A world that was made of inadequate realities? How much did I know him? I only knew him through the major landmarks he had created all over the country. Was it enough to judge him, I wondered.

When I reached Jo'burg, I found a large envelope waiting in my mailbox. It contained an album of enlarged photographs of Rishi. Mr Subramaniam had clicked them for the passport when he visited us. There was a letter too from his secretary Mr Mariza saying, 'I came to deliver your passports and tickets, but since the house was locked, I did not leave them. They are important documents and I could not take the risk. This is to inform you that your flight from Jo'burg to Delhi is on this Sunday afternoon at 3 p.m. Please call me when you receive this message.'

I called him. 'Yes, Mr Mariza. I'm back. You can deliver my passport and tickets. It is Saturday today and I've to leave tomorrow.'

'I'm in Gauteng today. But don't worry, I will deliver every possible paper tomorrow morning. In the meantime, please finish the packing. I will personally see you off at the airport.'

On Sunday, after an early breakfast, I held Rishi in my arms and asked Shanti to lock the house. Mr Mariza helped with the luggage. As I came out of the apartment, I saw Mr Subramaniam waiting in the car. He got off the car and stood facing me, tall and graceful as ever. I looked at his face when he said, 'Sorry Anvita, I couldn't reach you in Durban though I tried my best. I heard about Jivesh. I wanted to be with you and the family but just couldn't make it. I am sure it is a tremendous loss for the family. He was a bright young man.'

There was unspeakable pain in my heart. It flowed through my eyes. He came closer and with warm gentleness, put his arms around me to console. He hugged me softly to soothe my sorrow. He even took Rishi in his arms when I began crying.

Shanti and Mr Mariza sat in one car with the luggage along with the now-packed rocking horse that I wanted to carry to India. When I got into his car, Rishi was already in his arms. He tried to caress him with unaccustomed warmth. Rishi smiled back at him. For a long time, he looked at Rishi. Then he snapped back and told me about his favourite topic – the Gauteng project. I retracted my emotions, accepting that it was impossible to bring this successful entrepreneur down to the world of practicality. His mind, his feelings, his way of life was only work-oriented. His brain was constantly planning and outlining different schemes. I did not get actively involved even in listening to the details of the latest project.

Suddenly, my cellphone rang. It was Sanju, enquiring about my flight details. I realized that all the tickets and passports were with Mr Mariza.

When we reached the airport, Mr Mariza had already checked in the luggage – except the rocking horse. As he handed me the boarding pass and passports, I almost shouted at him, 'But Mr Mariza, I'd have paid extra baggage charges for this. I really wanted to carry the rocking horse for Rishi as it is Jivesh's gift for him.'

Mr Subramaniam's face changed colour. He said 'Mr Mariza, keep this in my car. We will courier it to India – if need be. You can leave with the nurse.'

'Ok, Sir.'

I tipped both of them, Shanti and Mr Mariza. Shanti took Rishi from his arms and made him comfortable on the stroller before bidding me goodbye lovingly. I kept the tickets and passports along with an envelope that he had handed me.

We were running short of time. The boarding was announced. Suddenly, Mr Subramaniam held my hand and took me in his arms. 'Listen … Anvita! I saw Rishi's photographs. I was taken aback at the resemblance with my childhood photographs, especially his eyes. They are deep blue quite like mine. I don't know how your family and others reacted to it, but I'm sure his eyes reveal the secret. Why didn't you tell me that Rishi is my son – my flesh and blood? Oh! I'm sure he is the outcome of that one and the only heavenly moment of love and fulfillment in my life.'

They were announcing the last and final call for boarding the plane.

'Do you have to go, Anvita?'

'Yes. I think I need a break to recover from whatever has happened to me in the past few years.'

'Ok. Go. But please come back. Don't let Rishi grow without a father – like you and I did.'

'I will think about it.'

'You're really strange Anvita … you never demanded anything – but you should have at least informed me about this.'

The ground stewardess came and stood near me. The last and final call was announced. I'd to leave, ironically at the exact moment I would have made my final decision about the future. He kissed Rishi hurriedly and then me.

'Please call me as soon as you reach there. I will be waiting to hear from you.'

As I turned, a huge glass door slid shut, acting as a barrier between us. The noise around me was unbearable, but I remained lonely. An echo of silence enwrapped my heart. I just could not react.

As we entered the security check, I saw Rishi's boarding pass. His name was mentioned as Rishi M. Subramaniam. Hurriedly, I scrutinized his passport and I could make out that the gap that I'd left earlier had been filled up. Now there indeed was a father's name: Mani Subramaniam. Holding the passport in my hand, I looked back. He was there quite far, very far, but I could make out he was looking at me with his deep blue eyes.

We were separated in silence. I could feel it. The silence was of mutual respect and confidence. In that silence, I was not allowed to impinge. It was a kind of an affirmation of a relationship. In that silence, we parted as we really were – he as him – I as myself. He stood staring at me – he was as graceful as ever but the blue eyes were brimming with many abstract questions.

When I sat in the plane, I looked at the blue horizon from my window. The glorious sun in the western sky was about to set.

GLOSSARY

Afrikaans	One of the two official languages of the Republic of South Africa (the other being English); is similar to Dutch but many German, French and English words have been adopted.
Afrikaners	Afrikaans-speaking South Africans; they are almost all descended from the Dutch, Huguenot and German colonists who first settled in South Africa; this group makes up most of the farm populations.
Apartheid	Derived from the Dutch words apart (meaning separate) and heid (meaning hood-grouping). In South Africa it means the segregation of the inhabitants of European descent from the non-European.
Bantus	Dark skinned native Africans who moved southward into South Africa from the equator; most of them belonged to the Zulu tribe.
Boers	Dutch settlers; Boer means farmer.
Coloureds	One who has some European blood but is not of "pure" European origin; most Coloureds live in and around Cape Town and are called Cape Coloured.
Hottentots	Members of South African race formerly occupying region near the Cape before the coming of the Westerners.

Kaffirs	Member of a South African race of Bantu family. In Arabic a Caffre (Kaffir) means a heathen or non-believer. It is a derogatory terms.
Rand	Currency of South Africa; One Rand = Indian Rupees Ten (approximately).
Uitlanders	Means outlanders; denoting those English men who poured into the Boer Republics of Orange Free State and the Transvaal when diamond was discovered at Kimberley in 1869.
Voortrekkers	Boers, who after 1836 moved to the north and east in the Great Trek and eventually established the two republics, the Orange Free State and the Transvaal.
Zulu	One of the most uniform Bantu language spoken in South Africa; one who speaks the Zulu language.

Xhosa Language

Needa	Please
Needa	Excuse me
Enkasi Kakublu	Thank you
Unjani	How are you
Ndisapila	I am very well
Ngubani Isna Lakho	What's your name
Yimalini	How much is this
Hamba Kable	Good bye
Molo	Good morning
Ja Ja	Yes yes

REFERENCES

Books

Indians in Post-Apartheid South Africa by Anand Singh (2005)

Let my People Go (The Autobiography of Albert Luthali) Nobel Prize winner (2006)

Lotus People (Winner 2001 Sanlam Literary Award) by Aziz Hassim (2002)

Ismail Meer, A Fortunate Man by Fatima Meer (2002)

Plain Tales from the Raj edited by Charles Allen (1975)

Here's Mudd in your Eye by Jack Mudd (Bush Lales) (1960-2002)

What's Love Got to do with It? And other stories (Winner of Oliver Schreiner Prize-2003) by Deena Padayachee

Journals & Magazines

The Economist (Sept. 13, 2008)

'Satyagraha, In Pursuit of Truth' (Nov. 2006, Sept. 2006, April 2006, Dec. 2006)

'*Lounge*' (Newspaper) Aug. 11, 2007 Essay – 'Friend and Countrymen'

'Sawubona' South African Airways (March 2007)

'The Bodasings' 125 years Commemorative Brochure (3 July 1999)

'Indian Annual 2000' (140th Anniversary of the coming of Indian Settlers to S. Africa)

'Valliamma Munuswami Mudliar' Child Martyr (1998-1914)

The General Retires and other stories – Nguyen Huy Thiep Oxford University Press – 1992.

The Star Monday, 19 March 2007.

'*Post*' (Newspaper) The voice and hear of the Community (March 21-25, 2007)

Travel + Leisure Experiencing South Africa (April 2007)

'Time of the Writer' International Writer Festival (Seminar) (19-24 March 2007)

Elizabeth Sneddon Theatre, University of Kwazulu, Natal.

By the same author

Novels
Sing Me No Songs
Travelling with the Sun Beam
Sheltering Shadows
The Widows of Vrindavan

Short Stories
My Lover's Name and Other Stories

Poetry
Only Stars Shine

Autobiography
As I Am

Travelogues
Cultures
Discovering Latin America